I0817831

The Long Way

MICHAEL CORBIN RAY
& THERESE VANNIER

The Long Way

BAAA! PRESS

for Mom and Dad
and
for Dad and Mom

Published by Baaa! Press
http://www.baaapress.com

All of the characters in this book are fictitious,
and any resemblance to actual persons,
living or dead, is purely coincidental.

ISBN 978-1-940776-05-7

CONTENTS

The Long Way

Chapter One

The Second Ugliest Girl

Leung Chi-Yen had only ever learned one useful lesson from her mother, but for twelve treacherous years it had served her well.

"Chi-Yen," her mother had whispered long ago, "beautiful Chi-Yen. To live a happy life, you must strive to always be the second ugliest girl in the house."

Chi-Yen had never forgotten those words, even though she remembered little else of the woman who spoke them. Some days while running errands through the humid, sticky streets of Canton, she would detour to the water's edge to look out past the crowded merchant barges, past the junks and the sampans nudging their way through river traffic, to the ornate flower boats anchored and tied together offshore. If she were lucky enough to catch a glimpse of the ladies on board—lovely sirens calling out for customers, enticing the men their way—she would wonder: Is that her? Is that?

For Chi-Yen had been sold as a slave at the age of four, and her memories of the time before were few. She had a new mother now—Old Mother—and a hard life in one of

Old Mother's several boarding houses. In truth these houses offered little in the way of board and somewhat more of entertainment for rough men whose idea of fun exceeded that permitted by law. Sailors and soldiers, farmers and government officials, businessmen, smugglers, pirates, and gangsters—they all came as customers to Old Mother's doors.

These were men best avoided, and so as Chi-Yen swept and scrubbed the steps, as she washed and hung the laundry, as she cut the vegetables and ran to market and back in her bare feet, she always kept her head low and always, always endeavored to remain the second ugliest girl in the house.

The trouble with being beautiful was that you drew too much attention to yourself. The girls who spent time before the mirror—the ones who painted their faces, who shaped their eyebrows, who combed their hair and perfumed their bodies—these were the girls who attracted the notice first of Old Mother and then of Old Mother's clientele.

Any young girl deemed pretty enough to bring a profit to the coffers would first have her feet forcefully bound. This early form of cosmetic surgery involved breaking the toes and arches, then folding them under and wrapping them with tight cloth. The procedure ensured that the feet would never grow into the ungainly, callused working pads of a peasant woman. The girls were trained to dance on these delicate, lotus-like stubs—although walking was difficult enough—and to sing and play musical instruments and to flirt and engage in witty conversations designed to separate a man from his money.

But Chi-Yen preferred to run, and she liked her feet the way they were. She liked them ugly. Chi-Yen was fast for a girl, and for that at least Old Mother did notice her, as on the morning our story begins:

"Worthless slave. Look at this mess!"

Old Mother dragged the tip of her index finger across the

surface of a carved teak desk that Chi-Yen had just finished polishing for the third time in a week. She held the spotless finger up as an example of indolence for her other twelve girls, Chi-Yen's sisters in bondage, who watched with relief that it was Chi-Yen in trouble again, and not them.

"Useless bigfoot half-breed! I curse the day I paid good silver for the lazy daughter of a whore too ugly for any man to love. Go! Buy two roosters and deliver them to the barbarian house."

Old mother threw several coins at Chi-Yen, and Chi-Yen dropped to her knees to pick them up from the floor.

"Quick-quick! Hurry! Complete this task and if you are lucky I will beat you only half as hard when you return. Run fast on your filthy giant's feet!"

"Thank you, Old Mother. Thank you," Chi-Yen said, bowing low as she backed out the door, then turning to run as fast as she could, which really was quite fast.

Old Mother's number one house was located within the walled Old City, conveniently near the treasury and the bunkhouses of visiting Imperial Guard troops, who spent freely and provided a measure of protection for Old Mother's less legitimate business interests. When Chi-Yen ran, her first goal was to put as much distance as possible between herself and these soldiers, whose tongues were as sharp as their swords.

"Blue-eyed devil," they cursed her as she hurried past. "Spawn of a poxed father! Traitor to the Empire, have you no shame? Return to face us and feel the full force of our arms!" But the stones they hurled fell harmlessly far behind Chi-Yen as she extended the distance between herself and her tormenters.

It was the same every day. These soldiers, their morale at its lowest and their futures uncertain following years of humiliating defeats under the punishing guns of invading British warships, now sought easy victories wherever they could find them. Threatening a twelve-year-old orphan girl was most often the best they could do.

Chi-Yen continued her run down the main street known as the Avenue of Benevolence and Love, slowing when necessary to thread her way among crowded market stalls. Her right hand clutched the coins as beggar children accosted her from all sides. The filthy black rags they wore barely covered their bodies, but they came at her with the confidence of citizens who owned the street, the city, the nation—who knew that Chi-Yen was a plague on their land, that she was the cause of all their troubles and their poverty. They grabbed at her clothing and her hair and tried to pry her fingers open, but her momentum carried her through their cluster until she slipped free and left them scrambling in her wake.

"Dead ghost girl!" they called her. "Go die with your ocean mother!"

Chi-Yen dodged to her right to avoid a crowd noisily bartering for sacks of rice. She leaped over a stream of raw sewage coursing the center of the street, dodging to avoid a collision with a sedan chair traveling at high speed in the opposite direction. The chair—an enclosed shoulder carriage with golden silk curtains hiding its occupant—was supported by two long wooden poles, which were carried in turn by uniformed servants front and back, their shirts drenched in humidity and sweat. The passenger likely was a local mandarin, an important city official. The odds were good that he was headed to Old Mother's house, perhaps on official business to collect a bribe or to confiscate and destroy her opium inventory—or perhaps to purchase time and a mat upon which to smoke the drug himself.

As the sedan chair cleared her view, Chi-Yen passed on her right the Temple of the Six Banyan Trees with its tall Flowery Pagoda rising high above the city. The temple grounds were older than a hundred Chi-Yens, but during her own troubled age they had seen nothing but neglect, with absentee caretakers letting the gardens run wild to devour statuary and reach their tendrils deep into buildings, fracturing walls and collapsing ceilings. The epiphytic banyan trees that had given the temple its peaceful new name more than seven hundred years earlier were now the seeds of its slow-motion destruction, having planted themselves in building crevices and sprouted through windows and even from the high rooftop of the monumental pagoda itself.

This was China in the two-hundred-twelfth year of the Qing Dynasty—by the lunar calendar a year of the dragon—or, as the uncivilized barbarians called it, the year 1856 A.D.; this is what had become of the empire.

The fall of nations was nothing new. They rose up and collapsed with the cycles of the ages. Romans followed Greeks followed Egyptians. Aztecs and Incas dropped to conquistadors and disease. China herself had witnessed the ebb and flow of the dynasties Zhou, Han, Jin, Tang, Liao, and Ming, among others. And now in the time of the Qing, ships had begun arriving from across distant seas, their holds packed with chest upon chest of sticky brown opium and their decks bristling with powerful cannons, and the Chinese people had soon enough given over their riches of tea and silver in exchange for the drug's intoxicating vapors.

One in five men now neglected his duties in favor of fleeting, addictive dreams. Government officials grew fat with bribes. Farmers forgot to collect their harvest. Soldiers loaded their opium pipes to relieve fears before battle, and as a result were slaughtered by rebel forces. Even the monks, supposed spiritual leaders of the people, gave themselves up to clouded hallucinations.

Chi-Yen saw the evidence around her every day: in the decay of the Six Banyan Trees and the stone-built suburbs of the city's southwestern Manchu quarter; in the abandoned echoes at the Temple of Emperors; in the filth piled against the walls outside the Temple of the God of War; and in that pathetic, lazy monk from Seven Dragons who spent his days half-conscious on a mat in Old Mother's common room as she swept the floors around him.

But all that meant nothing to Chi-Yen. All that mattered—all that could matter at that moment, on that day, to a slave of Old Mother—was to trade the coins for roosters and to deliver the birds to Old Mother's second house, a low-rent brothel dedicated to servicing those same British and American invaders who had coaxed her country to the edge of ruin.

Within the rules forced upon her, though, Chi-Yen over the years had developed some room to maneuver. And so she ran past the first poultry merchant, the one favored by Old Mother, and then again past the next farther down the avenue, and she passed through the West Gate outside the walls of the Old City. She crossed the bridge over the first stinking canal, turgid with effluent, and through the Fourth and Fifth Wards into the quieter western suburbs, and here at last she began to slow.

Here she knew old man Fong had roosters to sell—on a good day almost the size of the finer birds in the better markets—and without much effort he could be bargained into including one or two of the fresh pork buns cooked by his wife in a bamboo steamer behind their home.

Chi-Yen arrived to find Fong squatting on the stoop before the entrance to the small mud-brick dwelling. He smoked tobacco through a long, thin, and well-worn reed pipe. He drew the smoke into his lungs and ignored her approach, taking all the pleasure he could from his meager supply of the noxious weed. He smoked until the fire went out, then removed the pipe from his mouth and peered into the tarred nickel silver bowl at its end. He tapped the pipe with the palm of his hand, frowned, and set it aside.

"Dirty half breed," he said, finally turning his attention to Chi-Yen. "Here again to take advantage of a feeble old man?"

"I need two roosters," she replied. "At a fair price."

"Fair price? Fair price? You pay half what my birds are worth. Good birds, too."

"Good birds? If I wanted good birds I would buy in the city. I buy from you because your birds are low quality, and the drunken barbarians don't know the difference."

Fong grumbled and spat at the mention of the foreign devils, but he smiled at Chi-Yen's insolence. He was sixty years old but could have been a hundred judging from the hard lines on his face, the leathery bald head beneath his black silk skullcap, and the thin wisp of a white beard dangling from his chin.

"You speak of the barbarians as if you know their minds," he said. "Almost as if you know the name of your own father. But we both know your father is a hundred syphilitic English sailors. Your mother knew every smuggling pirate in the southern seas." He spat again for emphasis. "My birds are good."

"Should I tell your wife that my mother knew you also, old Fong? And your birds have lice."

Still tucked into his squatting position, Fong stomped his right foot and gave the impression of being a frog about to launch. "All birds have lice!" he shouted.

All this was the usual prelude to the real negotiation—the price for the roosters—which in the end came out as it always did, with Chi-Yen exchanging her coins for two dead birds and a pair of dumplings, which she wrapped in a white folded cloth that she pulled from her pocket.

"If your Old Mother finds out you are cheating her, she will have your head, young Leung Chi-Yen," Fong warned. "Or worse than that."

Chi-Yen knew he was right, but she also knew that Old Mother would have her head one way or another. There was no escaping it. She had done well so far to avoid the worst of the punishments. The occasional beatings were a small price to pay, and something that Chi-Yen sometimes even actively sought out. After all, a good strike to the face resulting in a swollen black eye or a split lip could go a long way toward disguising the natural beauty that more and more threatened to reveal itself to the world.

Her real mother's words continued to haunt her: "To live a happy life, you must strive to always be the second ugliest girl in the house."

Second ugliest. That was the catch, and it was something Chi-Yen was reminded of every time she approached the wards surrounding the factories of the wealthy foreign visitors. These factories rose up high and immaculate with straight white walls and pillared porticos, with spiked iron fences surrounding manicured riverfront gardens and paths—which Chi-Yen would never, ever be allowed to visit—and the flags of distant nations flying proudly, impudently, for all to see.

Standing in stark contrast to these rich barbarian monuments was the mass of China piled all around: the shops and homes of the native Chinese stacked side by side and one upon another, the wooden shanties of the workers and the servants and the merchants who serviced the foreign traders. The streets here ran thick with sludge and sometimes blood. The reek of sweat and urine and dung—human and animal—overpowered. Steam rose and flies and mosquitos buzzed and every man carried a bamboo fan that he used to clear the air and wave wildly about as he made his point in arguments with other wildly gesticulating men.

And then there was Old Mother's second house. Not at all secluded from the surrounding chaos, it distinguished itself from its neighbors only by the frequency with which foreign-born sailors approached its doors. English and American, mostly, they arrived sober and cautious, but flush with fresh pay, only to stumble out dead broke an hour or a day later, sick on cheap wine, more than a little in love, and vowing to return as soon as they could scrape together a few more coins.

Chi-Yen stood across the street from the house, working up the courage to enter. She held the dead birds in her left hand, dangling them by their feet, and she checked her pocket to make sure she still carried the warm pork buns. She watched as a foreign sailor made himself sick in the gutter while his two friends laughed and prodded his stomach with the tips of their black boots.

"Choke it up, Finnegan," said one of the upright men to his fallen companion. "Cap'n sees you like this the night before we sail, you'll be six months in this godforsaken pit waitin' for a ship."

American, then. Chi-Yen recognized the accent—or rather, she recognized it as not being among the often incomprehensible dialects spoken by crews of the English-flagged vessels.

From a young age, first with her own mother and then while moving from one to another of Old Mother's various houses, Chi-Yen had been surrounded as often by foreign speakers as by those of her own native Cantonese. But unlike the women and girls around her, she seemed to have a remarkable ease with languages. While she never had cause to speak them herself—in fact she kept the breadth of her knowledge a secret—she knew enough to understand most English, a good deal of Portuguese, a smattering of Russian, and of course the simplified pidgin used by the Chinese servant class to communicate with their foreign masters.

The Americans bent to take their sick companion by the arms and raise him to his feet, but this inspired a burst of violence from the unsteady man. He swung a fist at his helpers, boxing one hard in the ear, and for his trouble received a knee to the face. He dropped back to the ground, a gush of blood from his now broken nose spilling into the slick of his vomit in the street. He mumbled something through thick lips dangling a web of pink saliva.

"You reap what you sow, Mick," said the one who had spoken first, the seeming leader of the trio.

The man with the cuffed ear spat into the gutter near his friend—now his enemy—and added: "These heathen bastards'll slit his throat for a penny soon as the sun hits the horizon. I vote we let 'em."

Chi-Yen found nothing unusual in this scene. She had witnessed it countless times before, with different men each time. Sometimes they were angry, sometimes somber, sometimes laughing. Sometimes they helped one another and others they stumbled fighting from Old Mother's doors and didn't stop, for all she knew, until long after they had returned to their ships and set sail on a course that, with any luck, would send them straight to the bottom of the ocean.

It wasn't the men who gave her pause, though, but her knowledge of what was happening now behind closed doors—the women, the girls, her friends who would be taking this brief moment between customers to relax, to breathe sighs of relief, to wash the stains from their robes and their bodies. They would be shaking out the bedding to remove all traces of the dirty, hairy barbarians. The younger girls, the newer girls, might sometimes cry, but that never lasted long. If any were injured they would treat the wounds, washing cuts and applying poultices to bruised flesh. And all the while Mei-Xing, Old Mother's assistant and manager of this brothel for barbarians—a woman half Old Mother's age and yet half as forgiving—would be counting the profits and measuring the remaining stocks of wine, demanding efficiency from the kitchen staff and beating them with a switch if her mood were foul, as was often the case.

Chi-Yen stepped into the street and kept her gaze down, avoiding any chance of eye contact as she rounded the men and made her way into a narrow side alley and toward a servants' entrance. She refused to look at them, but she felt their eyes on her as she heard the words that chilled her very bones, that stood the downy hairs on her neck and almost caused her to drop her roosters into the alley muck.

"Next time," the man on his knees managed to choke through the bile in his throat, "I'm comin' back for that one."

The second ugliest. The strategy had worked so far in Old Mother's primary house. Chi-Yen had so far managed to keep herself in that ignored zone between pretty and ugly—between the girls who had been promoted to the service of wealthy Chinese men, and those so useless that they had been cast off as playthings for the less discriminating—and more violently vulgar—foreign boatmen. But now she had been noticed.

Chi-Yen hurried into the house and shut the door, leaning against it both to separate herself from the street and to rest and regain the breath that had vanished from her lungs. The short, dark hallway stood empty. No one inside had noticed her arrival. She heard chopping from the back porch kitchen and movement overhead from the girls upstairs. There was none of the telltale laughter and moaning to indicate customers on the premises, which was not surprising given the early hour.

Straight ahead, the door to Mei-Xing's small room under the stairs stood closed. With luck Chi-Yen could complete her duties and return to the Old City without having to face the mistress of the house.

She delivered the birds to the kitchen, where the old cook hung them to age from a hook near the open window. Chi-

Yen could have left then through the same side door she entered without repercussions. There would be no harm in avoiding Mei-Xing and returning home immediately to her true mistress, Old Mother. But she knew she would not be missed right away if she tarried a while longer, and there were reasons to stay—reasons that made the risk worthwhile. Many of the girls upstairs, after all, were friends. They had lived with Chi-Yen before being moved to this steaming riverside slum.

She crept past Mei-Xing's closed door and stepped as quietly as possible up the wooden stairs, avoiding the steps that had been loosened to squeak out warnings to residents of the house. Still they heard her, and by the time she reached the landing they had all gathered together, soft as mice, to usher her into a private room where they spoke in delighted whispers, peppering her with questions about news from within the city walls. How was Old Mother? Any new slaves in the house? Were the soldiers prepared for the coming war?

Chi-Yen answered all their questions until it was time for one of her own: "Xiao-Niao?"

The girls grew silent and cast down their eyes. Xiao-Niao was the most recent to join their staff. Three months earlier she had been sent straight from Old Mother's first house, where she had long been a mentor and guardian to the younger Chi-Yen. But her stay in this new place had not gone well. An Englishman with the unlikely name of Basil Malvenue—unpronounceable to the Chinese tongue—had taken a liking to Xiao-Niao and become a repeat customer. He was a bitter, cruel man who bragged of a dispensation from the Queen herself. But because he paid well, greedy Mei-Xing had turned a blind eye to his cruel appetites and quick temper.

During the man's third visit to her room, Xiao-Niao had made her first and only attempt to escape. So he beat her and kicked her as she lay on the floor begging for mercy, her screams and cries echoing throughout the house. When Mei-Xing could ignore it no longer, she approached the room and the man threw three times his usual fee at her. He called for dinner and ate while sitting on Xiao-Niao's bed, watching the flies as they crawled across her broken face. It wasn't until he left the next morning that Mei-Xing allowed the girls to lift Xiao-Niao and clean her wounds, to dress her and brew a tea that would help her sleep.

Now three weeks into her convalescence, Xiao-Niao smiled when her young friend Chi-Yen entered the room. Although it seemed like a painful effort, the smile went a long way toward lessening the horror of the scars she would always bear. In fact it was Chi-Yen who had the harder time speaking, who seemed to be in the most pain. Tears welled in her eyes as she studied the yellow and purple bruises on Xiao-Niao's face and arms and the bandages wrapped around her chest to hold cracked ribs in place.

"Chi-Yen, Chi-Yen," said Xiao-Niao. "Do not cry for me."

"How can I not cry? Look what they have done to you."

"Yes, look. What dirty barbarian will want me now?" And Xiao-Niao smiled again, knowing that Chi-Yen of all people would understand. "What do you think? Will I be the second ugliest girl? Perhaps Old Mother will take me back and let me work in her kitchen."

Chi-Yen removed the dumplings from her pocket, unwrapped them, and fed them to her friend. She had planned to save one for herself, but with the truth of these circumstances—and the implications for her own future—Chi-Yen had lost her appetite. Old Fong's warning, the drunken sailor, the increasing hostility of the soldiers and the city's beggars—it all added up to one bad future. Chi-Yen's world was closing in around her, herding her, pushing her toward a miserable destiny. She had been a fool to think she could escape it.

And then there was Mei-Xing, watching her from the

doorway, appraising her worth as if seeing her for the first time. In her hands she held the two feeble excuses for roosters that Chi-Yen had delivered to the kitchen.

As her fierce mistress looked from the dumplings to the birds, Chi-Yen's unhappy fate revealed itself at last.

The man from the street stepped forward from the hallway behind Mei-Xing, leering, a crust of blood in his mustache, the reek of fresh vomit rising from his damp shirt. He wavered unsteadily and leaned a hand against the wall to keep himself from keeling over. He pointed a scabby finger at Chi-Yen.

"She be the one what I want," he said.

Chapter Two

The Barbarian Threat

Chi-Yen ran. She ran harder and faster than she had ever run before. She ran past the proud foreign factories and their red-coated English guards. She ran past rubble-strewn city walls, recently kissed and scarred by foreign cannons angered over distant diplomatic slights. She ran past the River Gate and the docks and the ferry landings and the blockade of warships offshore, past the parade grounds, past shrines and temples, past rice paddies and farmers' shacks. She ran without looking back as the noise and smoke of the city receded behind her, as peasants in their fields paused to watch this strange blaze of a girl compelled by unknown fears and tears.

She did not hesitate, did not pause, did not slow as the road steepened before her, as her feet grew heavy with mud, as a warm afternoon rain began and her lungs burned and a runner's pain stabbed her side.

When at last she collapsed to the ground, her hands and knees hitting hard and scraping flesh, in her mind she continued on through the wet green hills and then down to the riverside shore, to where she dove in and washed herself free of the mud and blood of China, where she shed her clothing and her skin and her life and swam with the current and then the tide, down the delta past converging rivers and out to the southern seas, where stroke after effortless stroke took her … where?

She clutched her side as she coughed and heaved into the wet soil inches from her nose. The rain coursed through her dark unbound hair, draping it across her forehead and cheeks to where the tips floated in puddled runoff from the fields. She stared at the torn heels of her palms, at first not feeling or acknowledging them as her own. Then she forced the sting as she held them up to the sky and watched the falling water dilute the blood and grit and run it down her wrists to her elbows.

She be the one what I want.

The words still echoed in her ears. The image of the man who spoke them lingered, leering, refusing to leave her mind. Up close, in Xiao-Niao's room, he had been even more vulgar than in the street. The smell of the ocean crossing hung from his clothes and his body, seeping from his pores—unwashed brine and grease, the commingled sweat of a hundred seamen, the mixture of sickly sweet rum and the rotting decay of blackened teeth on his breath.

He had pointed at Chi-Yen, had reached out for her with his hard, thick fingers. She froze at the sight of the man moving across the room toward her. She stood petrified, unable to flee.

"She be the one," he said, his speech slurred. Then he took two steps and collapsed to the floor at her feet, unconscious at last with the alcohol pickling his brain.

Mei-Xing ordered her girls to carry the man out the back door and deliver him to a trusted sedan chair, which could dispose of drunken foreigners in a most convenient and perhaps mutually beneficial manner. Then she slapped Chi-Yen hard across the face.

"Thieving rat. You think you can steal from me? You think you can steal from Old Mother?"

Chi-Yen knew better than to defend herself. She hung her head and looked to the floor, readying herself for whatever punishment Mei-Xing might choose to dole out.

"These birds are worthless, eh? You take from my mouth to put extra food in your own." She shook the dead roosters in front of Chi-Yen's face. "You will be lucky if you ever eat again, ungrateful beggar."

"Mistress, please," Xiao-Niao dared to say from her sick bed. "Young Chi-Yen only meant to help me. She is—"

But Mei-Xing silenced Xiao-Niao with a look that spoke volumes about the beating she would deliver upon her later that day.

"I apologize, Mistress," Chi-Yen said. "Please do not punish Xiao-Niao. Punish me instead. Beat me for all that I have done and all I will ever do."

Chi-Yen dropped to the floor and bowed low, kowtowing in the submissive posture that put her body at the mercy of any switch or brick that Mei-Xing might find within reach. But instead, the woman nodded her satisfaction.

"Stand up," she said. "Wash yourself. No more mud. No more dirt. No more lies. Comb your hair. Then visit me in my office. Quick-quick."

Mei-Xing left the room without looking back, knowing that Chi-Yen would do as she was told. The other girls took Chi-Yen by the hands, comforting her with their company, all of them knowing what this meant, each of them having been through it themselves.

They called for a bucket of heated water from the kitchen, then undressed Chi-Yen and scrubbed her body with a warm, wet cloth. They moistened her hair, toweled it dry, combed out the tangles, and tied it back with a simple ribbon, not braiding it but pulling it clear of Chi-Yen's face and eyes, knowing that Mei-Xing would demand this, that she wanted an unobstructed view of the merchandise. Nobody spoke as they lifted Chi-Yen's arms and put her into an ill-fitting cotton robe, which they knotted at her waist.

"Very pretty now," the girls said. "Go to her. Do not make her angry."

Mei-Xing's office was sparsely decorated. A carved wooden chair sat behind a small desk where Mei-Xing balanced the business accounts. Two additional chairs faced the desk—the one on the left reserved for honored visitors—but Chi-Yen was not asked to sit in either. Two illuminated scrolls hung side by side on the far wall, and on an altar beneath them an offering of sweet incense burned, filling the windowless room with sticky clouds of sandalwood and clove.

Chi-Yen stood waiting for Mei-Xing to acknowledge her. At last the woman laid down her quill and set aside the letter she was writing. Chi-Yen could see the elegant strokes crowding the page, but from a distance, and with the characters upside-down on dingy parchment, she could not decipher their meaning.

"This is a message for Old Mother," Mei-Xing said. "You will deliver it for me."

This was not a request—not even a demand—but simply a statement of fact. There was no question that Chi-Yen would do her duty.

"For too many years you have been a drag on both our houses," Mei-Xing continued. "That is about to change. From now on you will earn your keep. I am asking for Old Mother's blessing in this matter, and Old Mother will give it. We have spoken of this business before. Now is the time to act."

Chi-Yen said nothing. It was not her place to speak.

Mei-Xing stood from her chair and moved around the desk

to approach the girl. She wore a loose tunic of shimmering blue silk with golden embroidery decorating the wide sleeves and matching trousers. Her long black hair was pulled and wrapped tight, studded and held in place by an array of decorated pins. The severity of the hairstyle served to widen her face and tighten its lines, disguising her age but also narrowing her cold, dark eyes and pulling straight her painted lips, which curved into a cruel hint of a smile. She raised one arm and pointed a finger at Chi-Yen, flashing her long, shielded nails—a badge of honor signifying that, whatever her past, Mei-Xing now had others to do the hard labor for her.

"Remove the robe," she said, and Chi-Yen did so, allowing it to fall to the floor and revealing her naked body trembling beneath it.

Mei-Xing stepped closer, walking around Chi-Yen to view her from all sides. With each step her hips swayed with an exaggerated grace, a natural result of having had her own feet bound at a very young age. She grunted once—neither approval nor disapproval—and then she announced Chi-Yen's future:

"That sailor in the gutter," she said, "he will not be your first. He has not the silver for that. For your first time—and for as many times as we can pretend it is your first time—you will lie with real men who have real money. Possibly even Chinese men, if fortune is with you. But I will tell you now, Old Mother will not want you in her first house. You will live and work here."

It was all Chi-Yen could do to remain standing in place. To collapse to the floor would have been easier, or to sprint for the door, or even to grow wings and fly—but she remained where she stood, absorbing the words and the gaze of her harsh new mistress.

Mei-Xing reached out and with her knuckles—her delicate nails making it difficult to do with her fingertips—she pinched Chi-Yen hard at the waist. Chi-Yen absorbed the pain without making a sound.

"Not a drop of fat on you," Mei-Xing continued. "Only straight muscle. No breasts, no hips, no fur. Some men like that. They will want to pretend you are a young boy."

She looked toward the floor, frowned, and shook her head in disgust.

"You might as well be a boy with those hideous feet—your bones have already set. It is good for us that the barbarians have no appreciation for beauty. They will not notice how truly ugly you are."

As she spoke she opened Chi-Yen's mouth to examine her teeth. She pulled back the lips to reveal the gums and pressed the pad of her thumb against them. Then she lifted Chi-Yen's tongue to look beneath it on both sides and—evidently approving of whatever she did or did not find—she backed away from the girl.

"Healthy enough," she said. "Some of our customers might even want you as their special favorite, since you are already half barbarian yourself."

With that Mei-Xing clapped her hands twice and the door to her office opened. Two of her girls had been waiting outside, and now they entered to escort Chi-Yen from the room. Mei-Xing folded her letter to Old Mother and dripped hot wax onto the seam. She stamped the wax with her private seal then handed the letter to the first of the girls.

"See that she does not leave without this. And arrange for Doctor Woo to visit tomorrow at noon. I want to be sure this miserable cow is free of pox and can still be mistaken for a virgin."

Helped back into her dirty old clothes and sent through the servants' entrance to the side alley, Chi-Yen saw this neighborhood teeming with foreigners and beggars and criminals from a new perspective—not only as a strange place to dread and fear, but also now as her new home. All her instincts in that moment screamed one simple word:

Run.

And so she did, until she could run no more.

The late afternoon showers began to lighten as she knelt on the muddy path. Then they stopped as easily as they had arrived, with the clouds parting to blue skies and steam rising all around her where the sun's rays met wet ground. She wiped her wounded hands as well as she could against her shirt, and as she did so she felt the letter tucked away inside the folds.

Without pausing to consider the consequences, Chi-Yen pulled the letter free and broke the seal. The ink smeared and blurred beneath her wet fingertips as she unfolded the page. Despite her lack of formal education, she had managed to develop a limited grasp of written Chinese—a system derived from pictographs that had evolved over many years into thousands of characters, each with a different meaning—and she could make out just enough through the smudges on the paper and the gaps in her own knowledge to confirm her fears.

As Mei-Xing had explained, the letter stated that the time had come to transfer Chi-Yen to the second house, where she would begin her life as a prostitute to the foreign invaders. No training would be necessary in the finer aspects of this most elegant profession, as Chi-Yen's beauty, intelligence, and potential for refinement were far below the expectations of Old Mother's distinguished Chinese gentlemen customers. If Old Mother would kindly confirm the terms as previously discussed, Mei-Xing would begin accepting bids for the initial transactions from her more prominent barbarian regulars.

The letter, as far as Chi-Yen could tell, went on to discuss recent political and military difficulties with the English. Both the quantity and quality of Mei-Xing's clientele had suffered due to this conflict, but Mei-Xing assured Old Mother that the situation would be resolved amicably in the coming days. When the foreigners realized the overwhelming superiority of China's armies, they would resume their activities under terms both more agreeable and more profitable to local interests.

Chi-Yen crushed the letter in her hands, then she opened it back up and tore it into a hundred pieces. For the first time in years she allowed herself the luxury of self-pity. She cried aloud as she pushed the shredded paper deep into the earth. But she stifled her sobs as a family of poor farmers approached her along the road, headed home from their daily labors.

A father, son, mother, and daughters still muddy from the fields walked barefoot one behind another. They were normal people living a normal life, so unlike her own. Their hands were callused, their skin dark from sun-soaked days despite the wide conical bamboo hats they wore as protection. Their pants and shirts were faded to gray from years of wear.

They stepped wide around Chi-Yen. The father and son stared at her as they passed, but the mother spat and looked away. The daughters kept their eyes low to the road, well aware of their own precarious positions. They knew the dangers of being a girl in this age and place. A simple twist of fate—one not yet avoided—might easily land them in a world much like Chi-Yen's, or worse.

Proof of the casual and often hostile regard with which the birth of a daughter was received lay only a field or two to the north at a stone tower hidden a short distance past the city's ancestral graves.

The tower was not much to look at. Six flat sides supported a carved tile roof that peaked at less than the height of one man upon another's shoulders. There were three high open windows but no door, because this was a structure that no man wished to enter, or even to acknowledge. For while it was only natural to glorify ancestors and preserve the posterity through the auspicious selection of grave sites and offerings, the death of an infant was best forgotten—the sooner the better.

Following the unfortunate parting of a young child, there was no need for great expense or ceremony; rather, a plain straw mat was tied around the body and the bundle was carried to this lonely place, where it was passed through any of the tower windows and dropped into a great pit below.

The rumor, whispered among young and old alike, was that this pit contained the remains of far more daughters than sons, and that the girls were often still alive at the time of deposit.

Chi-Yen felt an odd mix of envy and pity as she watched the family disappear around a distant bend in the road—envy because they would spend this night together in a home, loving one another and protecting one another from danger as she imagined families must do; and pity because, in spite of it all, unlike these gaunt strangers from the country, she had never yet gone to bed hungry. In that, at least, Old Mother took care of her girls.

Chi-Yen owed Old Mother her life. And as bleak as her prospects were, the alternative was worse.

She began her long walk back to the city.

Scrubbed clean only hours ago, she had already reverted to her accustomed disguise of ragged filth. Her simple pants and shirt were torn and blood-stained, wet with both sweat and rain. Her hair hung tangled and matted with mud, and her face as well was streaked black with fertile soil. But her blue eyes shone through it all perhaps clearer than before—bright jewels from a far-off land, strangers to this ancient Middle Kingdom of China—and with each step her head rose higher as she determined to meet her fate with every ounce of strength.

Within half an hour she passed south of the compound of

the Blind Men's Residence just outside the Old City. But as she neared the main East Gate she stopped short, startled by a detachment of Imperial soldiers standing armed and alert in battle formation, not lazing about in the shadows of the stone wall as was their usual habit.

Peasants returning to the city with shouldered buckets of water or tools dirty from a day in the fields were being halted and searched, their belongings thrown to the ground as they faced shouted questions and commands.

"What are your names?"

"What is your business here?"

"Form a line against the wall."

Chi-Yen had no idea what commotion had brought about this show of force, but it was too late to avoid. A soldier armed with a long pike herded her into a group of two dozen nervous farmers. Before she could even consider escape—breaking free and running inland, perhaps, past the Home of Aged Women toward one of the smaller northern gates—the group was forced to move.

At first they stepped a slow march, but the prodding weapons of the soldiers turned it quickly to a jog. They headed through the eastern suburbs back down to the congested Pearl River.

The colors of the day were fading to evening as the sun lit the bamboo sails of ships anchored along the far bank at Honan Island. On the near side, the burnt ribs of a destroyed fleet of war junks rose up from the shallows like bones of giant sea beasts, while the hulls of smaller fishing boats and sampans suckled the muddy river bottom, waiting for the tide to turn and set them free.

A group of fishermen tending to damaged nets turned to watch the miserable mass of conscripts until several soldiers broke off to round up these men as well. Soon they were joined by more groups their own size and larger until they numbered in the hundreds, and the soldiers began to lead them in chants that focused their energy and eased the panic of the mob:

"Death to barbarian invaders!"

"Fire to foreign factories!"

"Sink the devils' ships!"

Flaming torches began to appear in the hands of angry citizens, at first just a few and then more and more, passed from person to person. The mob became a self-propelling force with Chi-Yen caught in its middle as the soldiers either faded away or removed their uniforms. High above on the city wall, though, grim-faced bannermen displayed their military might. Their crossbows, swords, and spears bristled the parapets, daring any to approach their position.

In the river itself, upon the decks of the battle junks, the sleeping giant of China's navy was rousing itself as well, with sailors priming guns in anticipation, prepping the shot and the stinkpots and the flaming arrows and fireboats.

A roar went up from the crowd ahead just as Chi-Yen passed the River Gate for the second time that day. She could smell the smoke already—not simply the torches around her, or the usual joss paper offerings and cook fires, but something much bigger.

She quickened her pace to keep time with the pushing and shoving as she passed the smaller Oil and Bamboo Gates, ignoring them both. She did not glance at the motionless ferries mid-river, nor at the small island fortress occupied by a worried English navy. Chi-Yen ran with the rest now until she saw it with her own eyes: the foreign factories were ablaze.

The buildings of the English, the Americans, the Dutch, the French, the Swedish, and others caught in the mix—all of them side by side in a pretty row—belched smoke and fire into the darkening sky. Behind them, in the private gated gardens, foreign merchants and soldiers had gathered to attempt a bucket brigade, but the muddy low tide made it impossible to gather sufficient water from the river.

At the front of these compounds, busy Thirteen Factories Street had been ceded to the Chinese mob. Thousands now rejoiced in their victory. They chanted slogans authorized by Canton's provincial governor, denouncing barbarian aggressions and insults. They exulted in their might and laughed that their triumph had come so easily after all the troubles these foreigners had caused. They waved their torches and tossed them over the walls, into the windows, feeding the flames of history.

To Chi-Yen, though, this had nothing to do with history. To Chi-Yen this was something else. This was her doom.

If she had held any hope on this day for her own future, it had been hope that this conflict between the nations would not be settled any time soon, that hostilities would continue to frighten the foreigners from the streets—that Mei-Xing had been wrong when she predicted a sweeping Chinese victory, with the barbarians seeking consolation for their losses in the warm embrace of the poor girls at Old Mother's second brothel. But Mei-Xing had been correct, for the foreigners had been soundly defeated on this night, and not by soldiers but by poorly armed peasants.

Chi-Yen stood in the center of the street, watching the spectacle of smoke and fire, coughing with the old men as the night breezes turned. She felt the light and the heat and the camaraderie from the mob who in this moment of joy counted even an orphaned half-breed girl as one of their own, as a slave un-slaved.

But the girl knew better, and so did the hostile eyes that watched her through the crowd.

A painful twist and tug on her right ear brought Chi-Yen to her knees. A hard slap to her cheek followed, and this time

Chi-Yen felt the sting as the woman allowed her sharp nails to slice into her face.

"No more running for you," Mei-Xing declared. "Tomorrow we hobble your feet."

Chapter Three

An Uneasy Peace

Chi-Yen spent the remainder of that night confined to the upper quarters of the second house along with the rest of Mei-Xing's girls.

She heard the faint, distant chants and shouts of the mob, and several times a crack and rumbling crash rang out as the foreign structures gave way, collapsing inward and showering the streets with sparks and embers.

Chi-Yen could see none of this from the isolated room, but news traveled fast through the city, from servant to merchant, merchant to beggar, beggar to gangster, gangster to mandarin to soldier to street urchin. Whispered words soon found their way through silk curtains and paper screens to the girls upstairs:

—*A glorious victory for the people of China.*

—*Three hundred barbarian soldiers cower in factory gardens.*

—*Brave fighters for the empire rain fire upon foreign vessels.*

Morning, though, brought the echoing boom of cannon as English ships at last returned fire with round shot, bombarding city walls already weakened by earlier assaults. That—

combined with a discharge of Royal Marine rifles—dispersed the Chinese crowd, which had anyway grown tired and bored with watching the smoldering ruins.

In the rare quiet that ensued, the girls slipped into brief unsettled dreams. But Chi-Yen was soon enough startled awake by the unexpected pounding of hard fists at the front door downstairs.

She crept to the top of the steps to peer toward the foyer, where Mei-Xing's delicate feet tapped across the tiles. A spray of light and shadow filled the floor as the door opened, and several red-coated soldiers pushed their way inside, their harsh foreign voices barking commands. Mei-Xing teetered back, almost losing her balance but catching herself against the bannister.

From her hiding place above, Chi-Yen could see Mei-Xing in full now along with the uniformed English marine who pinioned her against a wall, holding her wrists as he issued orders to his fellow soldiers. The man was stiff beneath his tight wool tailcoat and awkward shako cap—an outfit out of place even at the start of winter in subtropical Canton—but his discomfort did not in the least decrease his fierce dedication to the mission. Mei-Xing, in contrast, seemed but a wisp of a woman, clothed only in a thin night robe and towered over by the Englishman, even discounting his extra ten inches of feathered hat.

There were six men in total. While the first held Mei-Xing at bay, two remained outside to guard that flank as the other three searched room to room. They tossed Mei-Xing's office and brought the cook forward from the kitchen, then they ran up the staircase with their bayonetted guns at the ready. They remained exceedingly polite—as good gentlemen soldiers must—as they pushed Chi-Yen and a dozen panicked girls down the stairs, shouting "move, move, move," all the while.

"Clear up top, Lieutenant," said one of the men, who all but Chi-Yen recognized as a regular—if unremarkable—customer of the house.

"Take the whores outside," replied the lieutenant, adjusting his grip on Mei-Xing as he turned toward his men, not so much to review their work as to escape the gaze of his prisoner, whose still, unblinking eyes were causing him to doubt his own upper hand. "Mister Cosgrove, gather the kindling."

Chi-Yen and the others were then ushered out to the street as two of the soldiers began piling furniture and fabrics into the center of the room, breaking Mei-Xing's chairs with a hatchet and emptying the papers from her desk drawers onto the mess.

The scene was repeating itself up and down the avenue, with alert marines raising their weapons at every door as Chinese men, women, and children in various states of dress and undress were pulled from their shops and homes, shouting all the while at these white devils.

Chi-Yen heard a scream from the house. She turned just in time to witness Mei-Xing flying through the doorway, propelled by the blows of the angry lieutenant.

"Damned heathen cow," he swore, kicking her hard in the gut as she lay where she fell, rolling her into the gutter, and then kicking her again.

Slowly and with difficulty Mei-Xing rose to her hands and knees. She looked back at the man, locking eyes with him again as if daring him forward. Her lips were a mess of blood, but through the red she showed the same thin smile that she had offered Chi-Yen the day before. She spat into the dirt, and from her mouth came more blood and a chunk of flesh.

Chi-Yen leaned forward for a better look, realizing with horror that this strange meat was the lower half of an ear. She looked up to the lieutenant in the doorway. The man held one hand tight to the side of his head. Blood pulsed from his wound past his fingertips and into the sleeve of his coat.

"Mister Cosgrove," he said, "burn this house of sin to the ground."

Chi-Yen helped Mei-Xing to her feet. Along with one of the other girls, she supported the woman for every slow step of the long walk back to Old Mother's only remaining house.

By the time they arrived, word of the morning's events had preceded them. The English had plastered the outer city walls with proclamations of their intent to regretfully burn the waterfront suburbs. It was a preventive measure, they claimed, to protect their ships from the stinkpots and flaming arrows of unruly marauders. Multiple columns of heavy black smoke rose as a testament to their success, and many hundreds of Chinese now wandered the streets in search of new lodgings. Combined with the haze from the factory fires, the city that morning was a dark, sooty place.

The girls from Old Mother's number one house welcomed the girls from number two into their sleeping quarters, and Old Mother called for a doctor to attend to Mei-Xing's injuries. Several old men already deep into their opium stupors watched through glazed eyes as the population of the house doubled.

"How do I feed so many slaves?" Old Mother asked as the new arrivals passed her by. "No money, no customers for you. Ai! Worthless girls."

She began to calculate aloud the cost of keeping these workers from the second house against the cost of purchasing and training new ones once the conflict ended.

"I should cast you all into the streets," she said. "Without foreign customers, you do nothing but drain my purse."

Chi-Yen imagined herself disappearing into the wall behind her, out of sight of Old Mother's wrath, but it was too late for that.

"Chi-Yen!" Old Mother called out. Chi-Yen stepped forward and allowed the woman to grasp her by the chin, turning her head to the side to examine the parallel cuts along her cheek. "You are a disgrace."

"I apologize, Old Mother."

"You run. You fight. You stay out while there is work to be done."

"I am a worthless slave."

"You dishonor me. You dishonor my house."

"Please forgive me, Old Mother." Chi-Yen dropped to the floor, prostrating herself in submission as was her habit. "I am stupid and weak. You are kind and generous and I fail you yet again."

Mei-Xing, who had been by all appearances unconscious on a nearby divan, smiled through her pain. "For once the dirty thief speaks the truth," she said.

A word from Mei-Xing would give Old Mother all the excuse she needed to first beat Chi-Yen severely and then sell her to the lowest bidder. Chi-Yen expected the worst. But the distant clanging of a war gong sounded before Mei-Xing could continue. Old Mother hushed the injured woman and commanded her to sleep as she stepped outside the house to view the street.

A large procession was making its way from the west along the Avenue of Benevolence and Love, with colorful banners and the upraised pikes of marching soldiers marking its pace. An excited crowd darted around the parade, each onlooker negotiating for a better view.

Chi-Yen and a number of the first house girls joined Old Mother on the stoop. An Imperial Guard soldier from the bunkhouses across the way, noticing this gathering of attractive women, moved eagerly toward them.

"Old Mother! Old Mother!" he called. "Have you seen the proclamation from Governor Yeh?"

The soldier handed a placard to the mistress of the house then explained—for the benefit of the rest of the girls, and with the authority of a man privileged with insider information—that the foreign devils had fled to their ships, pulled anchor, and departed the waters of Canton.

"The burning of the waterfront suburbs this morning," he said, "was the desperate final act of a frightened English army cowering before the might of China."

The placard he had given to Old Mother was an official announcement that the presence of Englishmen on Chinese soil would no longer be tolerated, and that the government was willing to pay handsome rewards for any foreign spies still loitering near the city.

At this point the gong rang out again, overpowering the man's words as the crowd began to pass them by. Chi-Yen and the girls, who had been so captivated by the soldier's story that they had stopped watching the procession until it was now upon them, looked up and saw the reason for the crowd's heightened excitement.

The uniformed soldiers marched in four columns of ten men each, their fine blue silk uniforms signifying the high esteem in which this guard of honor was held by local officials. The first two rows, eight fighters in all, marched with bows at the ready in order to ensure a clear path forward. In the two outer columns the men were more relaxed, waving the banners that encouraged the people to be of good cheer, for victory was at hand. But it was the middle columns, the soldiers in positions three through nine, who captivated the crowds and left the people unsure whether to cheer or stand in stunned silence.

These were the pikemen, whose ten-foot-long spear-tipped poles had proven useful time and again in battles throughout the history of this great land. Today, however, the pikes were capped not with bronzed barbs but with heads—fourteen human heads staring frozen stares, eyes wide open with the shock of their final witness; mouths clenched tight or agape, their last words locked and lost in an instant; necks cleanly cut by single blows of a sharp blade, the severed spinal columns protruding as shocking discs of white alongside the fly-swarmed coagulation of flesh.

How long ago? Not long. The blood on the wooden shafts had not yet dried. A few still dripped onto the shoulders and hands of the grim-faced bearers below.

"These men are barbarian invaders killed in the fields of battle," shouted an enthusiastic bannerman. "This is what happens when you take arms against the Emperor of China!"

But for one, at least, Chi-Yen knew better. She recognized the man, not much bluer than he had been just the morning before—the rotting teeth, the broken nose, the mustache still caked with blood, his eyes red not from the strain of battle but from the excesses of the cheap wine cask in Old Mother's second house. Finnegan, his friends had called him.

She be the one what I want.

Had those been his final words? Had they dragged him to the executioner still unconscious from drink? And then an unexpected possibility: Had Mei-Xing shared in the reward for his capture? How great had that reward been, and had Old Mother received her rightful take?

As the procession moved on toward the East Gate—headed out for the villages of the countryside—jubilant stragglers from the crowd shifted their focus.

"Victory calls for celebration!"

"And celebration calls for Old Mother!"

Soon the house was filled with raucous customers. Old Mother set aside the quiet calm of her regular opium smokers in order to satisfy the more carnal needs of this new majority, and even Mei-Xing's second tier girls were called into service. Mei-Xing herself was moved to the back of the house to make room for business.

For the rest of the day and deep into night, Chi-Yen ran bowls of rice from the kitchen to the tables, filled drink cups before they became empty, wiped spills from the floor, and helped carry sick men into the street. As early customers ran out of money or stamina, new ones arrived, propelled by the laughter and screams of too many young girls having too much fun. Soldiers left their barracks without authorization, merchants shut their shops, and husbands left their wives—all in the service of Empire.

Chi-Yen had no complaints about the hard work, especially since all the revelry kept Old Mother away from Mei-Xing. Doctor Woo came and went, warning that Mei-Xing's condition was grave but that she would recover with proper rest and medicine.

By daybreak the party had ended, and Old Mother went straight to her private quarters to rest. Chi-Yen alone was left to clear the mess, stacking dishes for wash and sweeping out the floors, cleaning and hanging the lamps and the mats and the bedding. She worked quietly, gingerly, so as not to disturb the few guests who remained sleeping or passed out where they had fallen. One man arrived to retrieve his brother, happy to have arrived before the brother's wife. Another man's wife arrived to find he had left hours earlier, and likely now slept in the wrong bed. And then there came a young boy in the golden robes of a monk, moving so softly through the doorway that Chi-Yen did not hear his footsteps.

"I am Tam Sin-Feng," he said, "here in search of my master, Liu Kun, a great warrior sworn to the Temple of the Seven Dragons—"

Chi-Yen did not pause in her work, did not even look up from her scrubbing. "Yes, yes," she said. "Under the table."

Chi-Yen knew Tam Sin-Feng, or at least she had spoken

with him several times a week for the past three years. He was her own age or a bit younger—a slight, polite boy whose speech never varied and who always arrived for one reason and one reason only: to retrieve his wayward master. Chi-Yen had given up on engaging Sin-Feng in conversation, though, having long ago discovered that no amount of talking or teasing could sway him from his task.

"Be careful," she said. "He drank much last night."

Sin-Feng squatted beside the table and tapped the man's shoulder. "Master Liu Kun? The Abbot desires your presence."

Liu Kun groaned and rolled away from his servant. Like the boy, he wore his hair in the strict Manchu style with the top of his head shaved and the rest braided into a long queue at his back. Although he could not have been older than thirty, his face bore the creases and bags of too many indulgent days and nights swept up in the bottle and the pipe. He was a good sized man, quite possibly a great warrior as young Sin-Feng claimed him to be, but his muscles had softened with years of neglect, and now lying under the table he resembled nothing so much as a fat old dog—albeit a dog in the fine silk robes of an honorable order.

"Away with you, flea," the man muttered. "Leave me to die in peace."

But Sin-Feng was persistent and experienced in these matters. "Master Liu Kun," he said, "I have the ingredients to cook your breakfast. Return with me to the temple, please."

"Do I look like a man who can eat food?"

"Master Liu Kun, I told the Abbot you were training for battle in the northern hills."

"Yes, I am training. I will be training for the next eight hours." He clenched his fists to his ears, desperate to block out the boy's pestering voice.

"Master Liu Kun, have you prepared my lessons? I desire to be a great warrior, as you are, one day."

"Here is your lesson: Never mix Chinese wine and foreign rum. Old Mother, what have you done to me?" The monk reached out for his crumpled cap, which lay discarded on the ground nearby, and he threw it over his shoulder at the boy—missing him by several feet.

"Master Liu Kun, I overheard a discussion at the Abbot's council. If you continue to miss the morning bells, the Abbot will withhold your meager allowance."

Liu Kun sat up so quickly that he rammed his head hard into the bottom of the heavy table, rattling cups and saucers yet to be cleaned. He fell back to the floor then hurried again to his feet and stood before Sin-Feng as if the concussion were but a minor annoyance.

"What did they say?" he demanded to know.

"Your salary is in danger. The Abbot has heard whispers of how you spend your days and nights."

Whether true or not, the words had the desired effect. Sin-Feng once again succeeded in coaxing his master from the wickedness of Old Mother's place, protecting him as always from the man's own baser instincts.

Meanwhile, all around the city, men and women were feeling similar foggy regrets for their recent binges. The foreigners had been expelled—for how long none could say—but with them went the trade that so many had come to rely upon. There would be no more silver for tea, no more factory jobs, no more pay for serving English or American masters. The rice harvest had been poor that year, and rebels and robbers roamed the countryside stealing food and treasure.

Despite these troubles, however, Old Mother prospered. The cravings of her customers were greater than they had ever been, although the men came now with more surly attitudes and were mean with their money. They complained of the high cost and poor quality of the opium but—as Old Mother reminded them—they were the very ones who had closed

China's ports to the superior product imported from India by the foreign merchants. She scolded them and told them to find their smoke elsewhere if they could, and in the end they grumbled and paid.

In this manner the days turned to weeks turned to months. For Chi-Yen the time passed most uneventfully. She turned thirteen years old and grew a bit taller. She washed many dishes and swept many floors. On two occasions she helped the boy Sin-Feng to wake his master by dumping a bucket of cold, dirty wash water onto the monk's head.

Her greatest difficulties came, as expected, from Mei-Xing, who had slowly recovered from her physical injuries—walking now with the support of a cane—but not from the damage to her pride.

If Old Mother was unhappy with boarding all of Mei-Xing's girls, she was even less happy with taking in Mei-Xing, whose failure to protect the second house from the foreign soldiers rankled the old woman more each time she thought about it—and she thought about it often. And as often as Old Mother mocked and criticized Mei-Xing, Mei-Xing lashed out twice as hard at Chi-Yen.

Whenever Old Mother left the house on business, leaving Mei-Xing in charge, the other girls were commanded to rest in their duties while Chi-Yen was singled out for extra work and punishment. If Xiao-Niao or any other girl had forgotten a task, Chi-Yen was dragged by the hair and forced to complete it. As Chi-Yen knelt over some mess—a bowl of rice knocked to the ground, spilled wine, or a drunken man's vomit—Mei-Xing would approach the girl from behind and push her head down, rubbing her nose into the floor as she would a poorly trained dog. Or she would slap Chi-Yen with a reed, leaving painful, stinging red welts across her back. But it was only after Mei-Xing began to beat the bottom of her feet with her cane—leaving Chi-Yen for a time unable to walk, let alone run—that the girl at last dared to confront her tormentor.

She waited one day for Old Mother to leave the house—on a visit to the treasury to collect a sizable outstanding debt from a high-ranking civil servant—and then Chi-Yen crept into Old Mother's office, where she found Mei-Xing asleep with her head on the desk. Chi-Yen cleared her throat, hesitant despite her resolve, still frightened by what she was about to do.

"How dare you!" Mei-Xing exclaimed, startled awake by the intrusion.

"Forgive me, mistress," said Chi-Yen.

"I shall not," Mei-Xing said. She stood and limped around the desk, searching out the cane that she would use to teach this impudent girl another lesson in manners. "I shall beat you until you learn to respect your superiors."

"Forgive me, mistress, but you shall not."

Mei-Xing froze in her steps—this open resistance was something new—and her hesitation fortified Chi-Yen's courage.

"You shall not beat me again."

"How dare you defy me!"

"I have no wish to defy an honorable servant of Old Mother," Chi-Yen said. "But you are not an honorable servant."

Mei-Xing slammed her cane hard enough onto the desk that Chi-Yen winced, knowing the damage that blow would have done to living flesh. But she knew also—because the blow had been directed only at a table—that she had Mei-Xing's attention, and that she had a chance.

"An honorable servant," Chi-Yen continued, "would first have consulted with Old Mother before collecting a reward on a loyal customer's head. And an honorable servant would then have shared that reward with her mistress."

Beneath the layer of white makeup on Mei-Xing's face,

her skin turned even whiter, and Chi-Yen knew that her guess had been correct. Mei-Xing managed to contain her rage—and her fear—and she replied in a slow, threatening voice: "Such a reward would be enough to easily arrange the death and disappearance of an insignificant servant girl, with enough left over to celebrate for a year."

"An insignificant servant girl," Chi-Yen replied, "could as easily destroy the reputation of her mistress, but would not wish to celebrate such an action."

And so Chi-Yen and Mei-Xing came to an understanding, with Mei-Xing reluctantly treating Chi-Yen as an equal to the other servants, and with Chi-Yen keeping the secret of Mei-Xing's betrayal.

For the rest of that year, for as long as Old Mother ruled the house, there was nothing to fear—until on the twenty-ninth day of December, 1857, when English soldiers at last returned in force and swarmed the city's eastern walls. On the fifth day of January, as these red-coated invaders marched side by victorious side through narrow streets in the wake of retreating Chinese guards, a stray ball from a P53 Enfield rifle-musket sailed up the Avenue of Benevolence and Love and through the open door of Old Mother's first house.

Old Mother fell dead in an instant, not even grasping at the new red rose spreading across the silken robes above her breast.

Chapter Four

The Fall of Seven Dragons

"I am Tam Sin-Feng. I come in search of my master, the great warrior Liu Kun."

Chi-Yen's back ached and tears stung her eyes as she sat in the center of the room, scrubbing sticky wet blood from the floor. Mei-Xing had wasted no time, beating the girl even before Old Mother's body had been removed. She had dragged Chi-Yen into the street and called out to the passing marines in her best English:

"Soldiers! Have cow child cheap. I sell, you buy. See? Pretty, pretty half-English, very young virgin."

The barbarian soldiers marched past in disciplined rows, intent on their retreating enemy. But several turned their heads to leer at the merchandise, anticipating post-victory celebrations.

Throughout the city was subdued chaos. Because the Chinese military defenses had been expected to hold indefinitely, only a few families had abandoned their homes in advance of the invading army. But the defenses had not held. The English had captured their first fort within hours of beginning their bombardment, and by morning were signaling their ships from atop the city walls. Now the people of Canton were hiding what remained of their valuables while putting a brave face to their loss. In the Manchu quarter of the city—still controlled by forces loyal to Governor Yeh—four hundred traitors were rumored to have been executed since the start of the attack.

In Old Mother's house, the girls were overcome with grief at the death of their benefactor. Old Mother had been a harsh but fair mistress; Mei-Xing promised nothing but cruelty. To set an example for the other girls, she striped Chi-Yen's back with her switch as Xiao-Niao and the cook lifted Old Mother's body from the floor, laid it out on a table, and covered it in a sheet. After offering to sell Chi-Yen at a discount to the very soldiers who had murdered Old Mother, Mei-Xing had slapped the girl in the face and demanded that she wash away the pooled blood.

Amidst all that, the boy Sin-Feng had returned and now pestered Chi-Yen from the doorway: "I am Tam Sin-Feng. Where is my master, the great warrior Liu Kun?"

"Who cares?" Chi-Yen replied. She made a half-hearted effort to wipe away her tears before looking up at the boy. A smear of Old Mother's blood stained her cheek. "If your master were such a great warrior, he would be in the streets fighting the war."

Sin-Feng stared at the blood on her hands. "Along with your house," he said, "our Dragon Temple has come under attack. Many monks lie dead in the street. My master Liu Kun is needed at once."

"Your master dreams with an opium pipe in his hands. He is of no use to you or anyone else."

A crack across Chi-Yen's back told her she had spoken too much or not enough or out of turn—it didn't matter which. It was Mei-Xing with her switch again, and as Chi-Yen tensed from the sharp pain the woman stepped round and gave her another blow, this time to the face, leaving a sharp line from ear to lip. Tiny beads of blood rose up and threatened to drop, an angled row of ruby tears clinging to the thin red welt.

"Never speak ill of a paying customer!" Mei-Xing shouted. "You are a worthless slave, not fit to scrub pig feces from a shoe."

Mei-Xing kicked at Chi-Yen, who remained kneeling on the floor. The woman's small, padded foot was nothing compared to the sting from the switch.

"I apologize, mistress," Chi-Yen said, lowering herself again to her work.

"Get up! Get up! Help the boy with his garbage. Make yourself useful for the first time in your life."

And so on Mei-Xing's orders, Chi-Yen and Sin-Feng fashioned a stretcher from two poles and a canvas sheet. It was evening by the time they rolled the sleeping monk out of his bed and carried him out the door. Because the monk was still too heavy for two children to carry on their own, Xiao-Niao was ordered to accompany them.

"If I'm lucky you'll both be captured and shot," Mei-Xing said as she pushed them out the door. "But if you survive, return immediately or I'll hunt you down and beat you so that you never run again."

A volley of gunfire and the sharp commands of English officers sounded from up the street—from the direction toward which Sin-Feng pointed the stretcher—but despite the danger Chi-Yen felt enormous relief at leaving Mei-Xing behind. Her face stung and the flesh of her back ached, and the air outside was heavy with burnt powder, but there was nothing now that could make her return. She could leave Old Mother's, leave Mei-Xing, leave the pathetic monk Liu Kun here in the street and start running—east, west, north, south, she didn't care.

"We must hurry," Sin-Feng said. "The Abbot awaits."

He began to trot forward without looking back, his master lying with glazed eyes on the stretcher behind him, with Chi-Yen and Xiao-Niao compelled to take up the rear. They had the street to themselves, although they felt the eyes of the city upon them, the hundreds and thousands of people peering out from behind screens and cracked doorways.

Sin-Feng's footsteps echoed off the building walls, announcing their approach to any who would hear.

"I do not like this," Xiao-Niao whispered to Chi-Yen. "We will be taken and killed or worse."

"What could be worse than Mei-Xing?"

As she spoke the words, though, Chi-Yen knew what was worse, and she knew that Xiao-Niao had survived it—Xiao-Niao, who had been beaten nearly to death by an English gentleman. Still, it had been Mei-Xing who invited the man into the house, and who had done nothing to stop him, and who had accepted money for her trouble.

Sin-Feng turned and led them up a narrow side street just as the sun was setting. The shaded ground darkened before them as their pace slowed with the gradual incline. They stopped to rest their hands, setting the stretcher down. The monk Liu Kun shifted, looked up at the partial moon, and moaned.

"Master, are you awake?" Sin-Feng asked.

"He is not awake," Chi-Yen said. "He will sleep for hours still."

"We can drop him into a canal," Xiao-Niao suggested. "That might wake him."

"He would sink. And he would stink more than he does now." Chi-Yen opened and closed her hands to help restore the circulation. "Let us continue. I no longer hear the guns of the English. Perhaps they have stopped for the night."

But as they moved on it became clear that the fighting

continued. They followed an ever-increasing trail of destruction through a neighborhood of parks and ancient temples. In the darkness around them the buildings and trees stood out against the background as nothing but black silhouettes. They marched over ground littered with broken valuables disgorged from the surrounding structures. Altars, scrolls, and shattered statues blocked the path. A broken Buddha lay before them, its carved head shattered and no longer recognizable. They veered around these obstacles and stepped through a litter of incense sticks and candles. An old man sat by the roadside holding a small pillow to staunch the flow of blood from a blow to his forehead.

"This is not the way for you," he said when he saw the young trio and their burden. "Turn back or face the barbarian tiger."

"We bring help to the monks of the Dragon Temple," Sin-Feng announced. "My master, the great warrior Liu Kun, has been summoned to the defense."

"Three children and an opium addict will be no help to a temple that has already fallen," the injured man said. "China is lost. We have new masters now."

As if in response, a quick series of explosions went off in the distance, followed by loud cheers. Sin-Feng ran toward the noise, still gripping tight to the poles of the stretcher. Chi-Yen and Xiao-Niao hurried to follow, holding up their end.

The Temple of the Seven Dragons was one of the oldest in the city—older, some said, than the city itself. To pass it by on the street, however, was to see nothing special. Its facade had been taken down and rebuilt many times over the course of the building's history, but not within the lifetime of even the oldest living monks. The red and gold paint was faded now. The eaves were cracked. The seven stone dragons outside the entrance were worn and weather beaten.

Sin-Feng and the others stopped a hundred feet short of the temple, hidden in the protective shadows of an empty caretaker's residence. They laid Liu Kun's stretcher to rest and they stood still as statues, still catching their breath from the sprint, as they watched the scene unfold.

A group of twenty foreign soldiers stood in an arc in the street facing the temple, their guns primed, loaded, and ready to aim. Two additional soldiers kneeled outside the heavy temple door, which Sin-Feng knew at this hour, under these conditions, would be locked and barred on the inside.

A better look at the soldiers showed them not to be the typical English marines who were busy fighting the last of the Chinese army, but brown-skinned, black-haired mercenaries who fought without uniforms. Their leader, though, was English through and through, carrying himself as the invincible, rightful owner of all he surveyed.

"Light the fuse," he demanded. "We haven't got all night."

The two soldiers at the door applied a flame to a cord, then ran back to join their fellows and their commander in the street. Moments later another explosion shook the earth, this one twice as large as those heard earlier. As the soldiers removed their hands from their eyes, shaking off the rain of dirt and splinters, there came a creaking noise from the door as it scraped free of its battered hinges and collapsed into the temple. Again the soldiers sent up a resounding huzzah.

As the dust settled, the Englishman ordered half his men inside, leaving the other half to guard the doorway.

"I told you," Chi-Yen whispered to Sin-Feng. "Your master is of no use here. Even if he were not a drunken fool, he could do nothing against twenty guns."

But Sin-Feng was intent on watching the entrance to the temple. There was panicked shouting from the inside—in both Chinese and English—and an old monk in robes similar to Liu Kun's ran out the doorway. A volley of gunfire from the soldiers knocked the man dead into the street. As he fell, the lifeless lump of his body matched several other obscure shapes already lying in the gutter. Chi-Yen could see now that this was not the first fighting to take place here today.

"What do we do now?" she asked.

Sin-Feng was grim faced, and it pained him to say the words. "I am a warrior of the Temple of the Seven Dragons, but I am also a child without proper training. I must wait." Chi-Yen caught his glance toward sleeping Liu Kun, and for the first time she witnessed in the boy's gaze something short of full admiration for the great man.

The soldiers outside had reloaded their weapons by the time their compatriots returned to the street, dragging with them another old monk, this one alive and protesting: "No, no. You are mistaken. We are peaceful men. We do not have what you seek."

The leader of the soldiers stepped forward from the shadows. He was a tall Englishman with dark hair and a dark mustache, but from this distance, despite the flickering torches held by a few of his soldiers, it was difficult to make out much more than that—except that he spoke fluent Chinese.

"My dear Abbot," he said, "let us not pretend. You know what I want. You know what I will do to get it. Save yourself the trouble."

Without warning, the man kicked the helpless monk in the stomach. In their hiding place in the shadows, Sin-Feng tensed as if it took all his effort to keep from charging to the Abbot's futile defense. Xiao-Niao, meanwhile, shivered and shrank back toward the shelter of the building behind her as if she were trying to melt herself into the bricks.

"Are you well, Xiao-Niao? Would you like to return to Old Mother's?"

Xiao-Niao managed an almost inaudible, terrified whisper. "Malvenue," she said. "The man is Malvenue."

The name meant nothing to Sin-Feng, but Chi-Yen knew it immediately. Basil Malvenue was the Englishman who had beaten Xiao-Niao nearly to death at the second house. He had bragged of his mission for the Queen of England, he had broken Xiao-Niao's arm and ribs and knocked out several of her teeth, and now he drew a long knife from his belt and kneeled beside the helpless Abbot of Seven Dragons.

"Are you sure?" Chi-Yen asked.

Xiao-Niao nodded, almost catatonic with fear.

A scream from the Abbot did not help. It was impossible to see what had been done to him, but the repeated short, sharp gasps that followed could only come from deep—even mortal—anguish.

Chi-Yen looked around for something, anything, any idea, but their only hope lay passed out on the stretcher. She crawled to Liu Kun's side and began pulling at his robe.

"Help me undress him," she said, unfastening the monk's belt and then rolling him onto his stomach.

"What are you doing?" Sin-Feng hissed, shocked by this rude girl's disrespect for his master but careful to keep his voice low.

"Do you wish to save your Abbot? Then remove your master's pants."

Sin-Feng refused to help, but he did nothing to stop her. Within half a minute Liu Kun lay naked in the dirty street, oblivious to his change of state, as Chi-Yen stood with the garments bundled in her arms.

"What will you do?" Sin-Feng asked.

"Something very stupid or something very wise," Chi-Yen said. "Ask me again in ten minutes."

She stepped into the street and ran toward the barbarian mercenaries and their guns. She called out in angry, rapid-fire Chinese:

"Where is the Abbot of the Temple of the Seven Dragons? I come with a message from Old Mei-Xing, mistress of the First House of Opium Blossom Girls. The Abbot must answer for damage caused by twelve of his dragon monks hiding tonight in our chambers."

The soldiers pivoted their guns to face this new threat, but relaxed their guard at the sight of the harmless young Chinese girl.

"Where is the Abbot?" Chi-Yen continued. She threw Liu Kun's robes into the street at the feet of the soldiers. "His monks have spent much silver this evening on wine and affections, and now they run naked through our halls. They abuse our girls. The Abbot must visit Old Mei-Xing's house tonight to restrain his loyal servants."

The tall Englishman stepped through the mass of soldiers. As they gave way, Chi-Yen could see four monks lying dead in the street—all of them much older than Liu Kun—and the ancient Abbot nearby, a stain of red spoiling the stomach of his robe. The man Malvenue eyed her intently as if appraising her honesty, and Chi-Yen imagined that his cold eyes reflected the truth of her lies.

"What is your name?" he asked, his Chinese flawless. "I do not recognize you as one of Mei-Xing's girls."

"I am Leung Chi-Yen," she said, "formerly a faithful servant of honorable Old Mother, who died today in the fighting. Mei-Xing is my new mistress."

With his foot he turned over the pile of robes in the street. "This is the garment of one man," he said. "And yet you claim to have twelve naked monks in your house."

"Monks are like geese. Where one goes, the others follow. Proof of one is enough for the Abbot to know the truth of my words."

The Abbot, in fact, had begun to moan at this news.

"What do you say, old man?" Malvenue asked. "Have your dear boys gone off mission? Have they fled with my treasure only to be corrupted by its power on their very first night?"

But the Abbot clenched his jaw and closed his eyes, refusing to speak again. Malvenue turned his attention back to Chi-Yen. He reached out for her and touched her chin, turning her face to the side. He ran his fingertips beneath the fresh wound on her cheek.

"Such a pretty young girl," he said, "with such strange eyes for a Chinese. What a shame to scar this canvas. You must be very angry at those mischievous monks."

"They are men, as all men are. They are not yet aware of their own limitations."

"Then what do you say we teach them?" The opportunity delighted the man. "If I am not mistaken, your mistress Mei-Xing's previous establishment burned to the ground last year. You shall be our guide to this new location, and in return we shall remove these vermin from your home."

Malvenue commanded his mercenaries to set fire to the Temple of the Seven Dragons. They used the robes of Liu Kun and the dead monks as kindling. They left the old Abbot clothed but dying in the street.

Chi-Yen then found herself leading a column of twenty foreign fighters through the ghostly, shuttered city, reversing her earlier path from Old Mother's. She looked straight ahead as she passed the shadowed alcove where she had left her companions, afraid to draw attention to the spot. She imagined she heard a grunt from Liu Kun, a sob from Xiao-Niao, but it could have been a scuff from Malvenue's boot beside her. Either way the man paid the sound no notice, and they continued on. As they marched, though, she felt his gaze fall upon her.

"You were born in a dragon year," he said. "That makes this your thirteenth."

"Are you an expert at guessing the age of young girls?"

"I have some experience in this matter, yes."

"It is a useful skill, I am sure. You should sail home to England and find work in a traveling carnival."

"You have spirit. I like you. How much is Mei-Xing charging for an hour alone these days?"

The sound of footsteps running toward them through the darkness interrupted her reply—a relief, since she had no idea what to say to that.

"Chi-Yen! Chi-Yen!" a voice called out, and then there was Xiao-Niao standing before them, panting to catch her breath. If the girl were frightened by the sight of her tormentor Basil Malvenue, she did not show it. But at the same time she locked her eyes on Chi-Yen's, drawing strength from her friend. She spoke rapidly and all at once, as though a pause might invite collapse and failure.

"I am very happy I found you. Mei-Xing has a new request. The monks have grown tired with drinking and now sleep peacefully in our beds. The Abbot can wait until morning to scold them. But tonight Mei-Xing needs you to fetch Doctor Woo. It is an emergency. Our mistress is ill in the stomach again, and needs the medicine that only Doctor Woo can provide. Only you can be trusted with finding him and returning in time."

Lies. All lies, and Chi-Yen knew it. Xiao-Niao must have doubled around the far streets and then circled back with this desperate plan. But why? Simply to sacrifice herself for her friend? For a sacrifice it surely would be when they arrived at Mei-Xing's to find not a single monk.

"Xiao-Niao," Malvenue said, "my dear Xiao-Niao. What a pleasure to see you again at last."

"Mister Malvenue. I … I have thought of you often," Xiao-Niao said. "I have waited for your return."

"Xiao-Niao," Chi-Yen said, "this is not necessary. I can escort these men to visit Mei-Xing, and still return in time with Doctor Woo. You should not be here."

But Malvenue had lost interest in Chi-Yen, and with one strong arm he pushed her away. She fell into the street. The barbarian soldiers, who had been unable to follow any of the conversation, laughed at this unexpected comedy.

"Come," Malvenue said to Xiao-Niao, taking her by the arm. "Lead me to your quarters."

Chi-Yen sat in the dirt and watched them go. One girl against twenty guns—what could she do?

By the time she returned to Seven Dragons, the flames were rising high from the tiled rooftop and the street was loud with the snap of burning timbers. She saw Liu Kun, still naked in the shadows, and she knelt beside the dying Abbot in the middle of the road. He took her by the hand.

"You are a brave girl," he said. "And resourceful."

"Where is Sin-Feng?"

He shook his head. His remaining strength was better spent addressing more important matters. "I know about Liu Kun. I have always known. Sin-Feng's greatest strength is his loyalty, but he is not yet ready for this world."

Chi-Yen looked around the street, trying to find this boy she barely knew, her last remaining friend. Where had he gone?

"But you," the Abbot continued, "you know the truth of what is, and how to lie in the service of what should be. My own cup runs empty. My honor bleeds from the cracks in this age."

"You speak in riddles, old man. I am not a monk. Where is Sin-Feng?"

"This is more important than the apprentice," the Abbot said, gripping her fingers now with everything he had. "This is more important than you or me. This is more important than China or any dynasty. We protect the earth and the sea and the sky—"

A loud crash came from the temple as part of the roof collapsed, flushing sparks and smoke out the entrance and into the street. The Abbot clenched up at the noise and the heat, which was just as well, Chi-Yen thought, because he seemed to have lost his mind. But he pulled her closer as he coughed and whispered his final, almost inaudible words.

"Do what you must to protect our burden," he said. "Promise me …"

Chi-Yen cradled the Abbot's head in her lap and rocked him to his final sleep. She heard a cough and looked up to find Sin-Feng standing nearby. His yellow robes were coated black with ash and the braided tail of hair at his back was singed. In his arms he held a bundle wrapped in smoldering canvas.

"Is he dead?" he asked.

"Were you inside? Was there anybody else?"

"They fled this afternoon. What did the Abbot tell you?"

"Crazy talk." She shrugged. "But he gave you instructions?"

"Yes. And your friend Xiao-Niao?"

Chi-Yen tried to smile. It was not easy.

Despite the lateness of the hour and the fact that they were now down to two, they found the strength to return Liu Kun to the stretcher and to head south again. Sin-Feng did not bother to find a blanket to cover the naked man. They kept to the shadows at the side of the road and moved as silently as possible, careful not to disturb the already unsettled night.

It wasn't until they reached the main avenue through the city, the Avenue of Benevolence and Love, that they spotted the first body. The man lay face down—or rather chest down, since neither face nor head remained attached. His clothing marked him as one of Malvenue's mercenaries, but his killers had relieved him of his rifle and ammunition.

"Xiao-Niao!" Chi-Yen said, expressing as much admiration as concern, for she now understood her friend's plan.

She dropped the stretcher and ran across the avenue and down a block, passing scattered bodies of both mercenaries and Chinese Imperial Guard. Instead of turning east to

Old Mother's, Xiao-Niao had led the soldiers south into the Manchu Quarter, straight into the last holdout of resistance against the invaders. The battle had been bloody. The mercenaries had been taken by surprise, for their dead outnumbered the Chinese by three to one. Chi-Yen counted at least fifteen barbarians—Malvenue unfortunately not among them—when she stopped at the body of a young girl.

"Brave Xiao-Niao," she whispered.

When she returned to Sin-Feng, she found him seated beside the stretcher, protecting his wrapped bundle in his lap.

"You are no longer safe as an apprentice of Seven Dragons," Chi-Yen said. "You will need to find new clothes."

Sin-Feng nodded.

"I know a place where we can rest tonight, and where we can throw cold water on your master. It might cost you some money."

"I have silver and gold," he said.

"Of course you do. But do not speak of it. Do not even tell Liu Kun."

With that they picked up the naked monk and headed through the unguarded West Gate and out of the Old City for the last time. They crossed the bridge over the canal and passed through the Fourth and Fifth Wards and into the western suburbs. It had been more than a year since Chi-Yen's last visit to this place but the mud-brick house looked the same, if somewhat less welcoming in the middle of the night.

As Sin-Feng waited out front, she climbed the stoop and pounded the front door several times. She heard a groan and a gruff voice calling out from inside. "Who dares shake my house in the middle of my dreams?"

"It is Leung Chi-Yen, formerly a servant of Old Mother, here on a mission of utmost importance."

"I sell no birds before sunrise. Come back in the morning."

But Chi-Yen knocked again twice as long and twice as

loud until the door flew open, revealing Old Fong only half dressed, his white beard kinked to the side with sleep. He spat onto the stoop near Chi-Yen's feet.

"What do you want?" he asked.

"I want my mother."

Chapter Five

The Flower Boat

By sunrise that morning the three fugitives were stowed away in the cabin of one of the hundreds of flower boats cluttering the byways of the Pearl River. These were not seagoing vessels, but permanently moored, brightly painted, elaborately carved wooden houseboats—or rather, houseboats of ill repute. Floating brothels or bordellos, for the most part, they offered dinner, drink, smoke, and somewhat willing women to any man who tied his skiff to the side and slipped a few coins to the owner.

At daylight Chi-Yen peered out through a latticed window at the back of the boat to see that they floated two hundred feet from shore, resting almost in the shadow of an anchored English warship. She could hear the voices of the foreigners who had gathered at its railing to bargain the price of eggs and duck meat from a merchant sampan below.

Onshore, meanwhile, the first of many Chinese laborers arrived bearing heavy chests from the city under guard of English marines. It was rumored that these men were being paid a rate of one dollar per day to help empty the Imperial Treasury of all its silver.

Although she was exhausted from the long night, Chi-Yen could not sleep. She had negotiated a flat fee with Old Fong, who had ferried them here and then left to hire another boat that would arrive under cover of darkness for the next stage of their journey.

As far as Chi-Yen was concerned, it could not happen soon enough.

The reunion with her mother had gone as anticipated—which is to say it had not gone well. The woman, in fact, slept now in a bunk in this very room, sharing the platform with one of her fellow workers, while Sin-Feng and Liu Kun shared the bunk below. The place reeked of fish oil and urine and the worn out bodies of women who bathed infrequently in nothing but a shared bucket of salt water.

The years had not been kind to Chi-Yen's mother. Those who worked the flower boats were often treated as slaves, purchased or kidnapped at a young age and confined on board for the bulk of their lives, forced into prostitution and for their labors paid little more than meager rations of food. When Chi-Yen had been born, her mother had been not much older than Chi-Yen was now. But thirteen years, thousands of customers, and several children later, she was well on her way to resembling Old Fong, only without that man's spirit.

She had recognized Chi-Yen at once—it was all in the eyes. The woman had practically hissed at her first daughter.

"Get out! Get out! Why are you here?"

Chi-Yen had rehearsed so many questions, but the instant she stepped on board the flower boat, she knew all the answers. This was her fate if she stayed in this place. Her life with Old Mother had been a gift from her true mother, an opportunity to negotiate with the world before being thrust into it. But she was no longer the second ugliest girl. It was not until that moment that she made the decision.

"I am here to say goodbye," Chi-Yen said. "I am leaving."

"Good. Go. Never come back."

Her mother had retired to her bunk without another word, and Chi-Yen had helped Sin-Feng and Liu Kun to board the boat.

Old Fong had made arrangements that the three were to remain undisturbed through the day and that no other customers were to be taken on, which was an easy arrangement to make, considering the unsettled matter of the angry foreign warship over their shoulder, which was scaring off most business anyway.

Liu Kun, it turned out, had a much better recollection of the previous night's events than would be expected from a man who had been unconscious throughout the action. At Old Fong's he had opened his eyes at just the moment that Chi-Yen and Sin-Feng readied a bucket of canal water to dump over his head. He had demanded that Sin-Feng hand over the secret wrapped bundle, and especially the satchel of silver and gold. He also ordered that Chi-Yen and Sin-Feng continue to transport him through the city on the stretcher, which he found quite comfortable. But while obedient Sin-Feng seemed willing, Chi-Yen had laughed in the monk's face.

Now within fifteen minutes of settling in on board the flower boat, Liu Kun was again fast asleep. The arduous trek on foot from Old Fong's to the river must have taken a lot out of him. Sin-Feng, who could be excused for closing his eyes following his unceasing labors of the past twenty-four hours, soon joined his master.

Chi-Yen, though, after surveying the river, lowered herself to the customary Chinese squatting position to wait for the day to pass. An hour later the boy rolled from his back to his side and drooled into the wooden slats of the bunk. Half an hour after that, Liu Kun began to snore.

Chi-Yen stood and stepped lightly across the deck. From between the two sleeping dragon men, she teased the canvas-wrapped package that Sin-Feng had removed from the burning temple, and that Liu Kun had taken from Sin-Feng.

It felt solid and heavy as she carried it outside the room and onto the outer deck of the boat. She sat in the shadow of the cabin, out of view of any prying eyes on the English warship or the more distant American and French vessels that had returned to these waters in anticipation of the city's reopening.

Chi-Yen unfolded the rough fabric to reveal only two items: first, a letter, quickly scrawled and folded, not even sealed; and second, a carved stone box, a cube roughly nine inches on each side.

She opened the letter first. It was addressed to Liu Kun and signed by the Abbot of the Temple of the Seven Dragons. The ink had been smeared in the rush to put characters to paper, and again she could not decipher every symbol, but she understood as follows:

Liu Kun, we are discovered. Your brothers have dispersed according to plan. The final piece falls to you. Your apprentice Tam Sin-Feng is loyal; if you make half the effort of which you are capable, he will grow to be a fine Guardian. Teach him well, and teach him to teach his own apprentice well, and one day with good fortune our descendants may again unite the Celestial Kingdom on Earth, as today we have proven ourselves inadequate. You will be welcomed at 618 Dupont Street in the city that the barbarians call San Francisco, in the young Flowery Flag Nation. After that, Liu Kun, the future is yours to create—or to destroy.

Chi-Yen read the letter three times, hoping for some hidden revelation between the lines, but there was nothing. It likely had been written as the soldiers were placing explosives outside the temple doors, but still it was careful not to spill its secrets to any who did not already know.

In contrast to the hurried letter, the box must have taken many years to carve, so intricate was the detail and depth of its workmanship. But it was no less a mystery. It appeared to have been cut from a single block of granite—probably some great, revered rock of ancient history—and the six outer panels told some sort of story in pictures. There were mountains and barren earth, rising forests, ocean waves, men with spears and flaming bows, and woven through it all, wrapping the world in its talons and limbs and tail so that one could not see the entire creature at once, a single ornate dragon. Alone in the top panel, the beast's fringed head stared up as if challenging the holder of the box. When she tilted it at a particular angle, however, Chi-Yen could almost imagine a wink and a smile.

It was the most beautiful thing she had ever seen, although to be honest, she had to admit, her life to this point had been mostly devoid of beautiful things.

She turned the box over and around several times but could find no seams, no hinges, no hidden latches, nothing to indicate an opening. Perhaps it was not a box at all, but a statue, a sculpture, some object of worship to those old-fashioned monks.

Well, not anymore. The monks were gone, all but Liu Kun, and he was more interested in his satchel of coins, which he had tied inside the waistband of his trousers.

Chi-Yen returned the box to the canvas and placed the letter upon it. As she began to rewrap the material, though, she heard a soft pop and a reluctant hiss, as of sand or air escaping a tightly sealed container. She pushed the letter aside and there it was: the opening. A circular hole expanded from the image of the dragon's head, like a pupil dilating within the iris of an eye. As the opening grew, revealing the contents within, Chi-Yen was nothing if not confused. Whoever had built this contraption had gone through a great deal of trouble to protect a mottled brown rock—a remarkably smooth rock, yes, but still a rock.

Or not.

As she reached into the opening and removed the object, she felt a tingling sensation run through her body as she realized that it was actually an egg, five inches long with a gritty shell, cradled in a nest of dirt.

Could it be? The Temple of the Seven Dragons ... monks dying in the street to protect a secret ... an ancient box with a picture of a great serpent carved into its lid ... an egg belonging to no bird she had ever seen.

No. It could not be.

When the egg began to warm in her hand, she attributed the feeling to an excited imagination, or to her lack of sleep. When she felt a kick against her palm, she knew it was nerves. She dropped the egg back into the box and immediately the iris closed—a mechanical reaction, surely, triggered by the weight of the relic.

Flustered, she replaced the letter and canvas, picked up the bundle, and stood. But she froze outside the doorway of the cabin at the sound of voices—not Liu Kun and Sin-Feng, but English voices from the nearby warship—and one English voice in particular.

"I'm telling you, Captain, I need a blockade of this entire river."

"It's not possible, sir. All my men are committed to the city. We've not yet captured Governor Yeh. The treasury will take days to empty. There are still armed Chinese mobs walking the streets."

"This is more important than any of that, damn you. Where is the Admiral?"

"The Admiral has returned to Hong Kong, sir, to prepare the next stage of the campaign. One city does not give us an entire nation."

"One monk gives us a damn sight more than that. I have a dispensation from the Queen herself."

Malvenue. So he had survived the battle with the Imperial Guard. Chi-Yen listened, more grateful than ever for her knowledge of the English language. The news she heard was both good and terrible—good because the ship's military captain was unwilling to grant this civilian's request; but terrible because of the great depth of Malvenue's determination, his hatred, and his knowledge.

He knew her name. He knew Tam Sin-Feng's. He knew Liu Kun's. He had detailed descriptions of his quarry, including their ages, heights, appearance, clothing, even the regional accents they spoke. He suspected they were en route to Hong Kong, although he was not yet sure of their ultimate destination. For their capture he was prepared to offer a reward in silver greater than Chi-Yen could comprehend.

After Malvenue and the captain parted with angry words, Chi-Yen returned the box and letter to its place in the bunk between monk and apprentice. She knew what she had to do. She borrowed several cups of fresh water from the mess, along with a sharp knife and a small mirror, and she wet her hair and slowly, carefully, shaved clean the top of her scalp above the temples in the manner required of all Chinese men and boys. Then she tied what remained of her hair into a tight braid that fell straight down her back. After changing into simple, weather-worn clothing—she had stolen similar garments for Sin-Feng and Liu Kun the night before—there was no longer any question: her old life was over.

That evening at sunset, as arranged, a sampan pulled alongside the flower boat and loaded three passengers—a peasant farmer and his two sons—along with their meager belongings.

It was a matter of little curiosity to the watchman aboard the English ship, as similar scenes repeated thousands of times a day in these waters surrounding the Chinese city of Canton. Had he peered closer, however, or had the light been better to reveal the strange blue eyes of the second boy—so unusual for a Chinaman—it might have triggered recollections of the overheard argument between his captain and that arrogant merchant. He might have recalled the offer of a reward. Instead, as the sampan sailed away, he kept his attention on the floating brothel below him and the women gathered on its deck, one of whom, the watchman would have sworn, struggled to hold back her tears.

The voyage to Hong Kong was uneventful. The monk Liu Kun, as was his custom, slept for most of the trip. Sin-Feng and Chi-Yen spoke only occasionally, and in hushed voices, careful not to reveal their secrets to the family steering their voyage. Strangers, in times such as these, could rarely be trusted.

Earlier that afternoon on the flower boat, Chi-Yen had told Liu Kun and Sin-Feng of the danger that they faced. She had repeated Malvenue's demands and revealed the reward on Liu Kun's head. She warned that the authorities would be searching for them in Hong Kong, and explained that her new disguise as a boy would help the three of them travel unnoticed.

At this Liu Kun had protested vehemently.

"Who are you?" he exclaimed, spitting onto the cabin floor. "A brothel bastard expects to accompany a great warrior of Seven Dragons?"

"The great warrior would be wise to speak softly," Chi-Yen whispered, "for the Englishman Malvenue understands our

Chinese tongue and remains within shouting distance on board that warship."

"I am Liu Kun! I fear no man! I take no advice from the worthless daughter of a worn whore!"

Chi-Yen had not pressed her argument; the monk's belligerence was sure to get them all captured if she angered him further.

Upon arriving in Hong Kong, where the Praya was thick with foreign sailors and red-coated English marines, Liu Kun had commanded Sin-Feng to seek out the next ship bound for America while he, the great warrior Liu Kun, attended to important business in the city.

"If you smoke opium with all that gold in your purse," Chi-Yen warned, "you will wake up with no gold at all."

"I am Liu Kun! No man dares rob me!"

"Perhaps a woman, then. Or a girl. Mei-Xing stole from you every week at Old Mother's."

Liu Kun scowled and seemed almost ready to strike with his fist, which Chi-Yen would have welcomed, as a black eye along with the scab across her cheek would have completed her disguise. But the monk restrained himself.

"You speak entirely too much," he said. "Sin-Feng!"

The boy stepped forward to his master's side.

"Use this money to buy two tickets to America. Not three, two. And take this burden from my hands. I do not wish to be weighed down while I conduct my business."

Liu Kun gave a portion of his gold to the boy, along with the canvas bundle, then turned for the city. The docks and streets were crowded with people, and for a moment Chi-Yen considered following the man. He would never know. But she figured the odds were even that they would never see him again, and that would be a bit of good fortune.

"If he does not return in three days," she said, "we should travel to America without him."

"I would never abandon my master," Sin-Feng replied. "Let us give him five."

It turned out, though, that the next available ship carrying passengers to America was not leaving for another two weeks. That was enough time, Chi-Yen thought, for Liu Kun to ruin everything.

They found the ticket broker for the ship, the American clipper *Round World*, and attempted to bargain three for the price of two. Chi-Yen managed to cut the broker's commission by half, but the base cost of the fare was set by the ship's captain, and was non-negotiable. Liu Kun had estimated well, so that when Sin-Feng handed over the gold for two tickets, there was little left over on which to survive for the next two weeks.

As for Chi-Yen's own passage, the broker suggested contacting a District Association, where men familiar with a boy's trustworthiness and capabilities might loan him money for the journey, although the boy would be required to work for them for quite some time afterword in America to pay off the debt.

The only positive note from that bit of advice was that the broker revealed no suspicion that Chi-Yen might be a girl.

With the passage for two secured, they explored Hong Kong's muddy Queen's Road and its bustling central market. The young city was a strange mix of factories, European mansions, Chinese shops, and ramshackle beggar's shanties. Thirty years ago there had been nothing here, just flat beach leading to steep hills and granite mountains lush with vegetation but mostly unsuitable for agriculture or habitation. Now Victoria Harbor and the docks and naval yard served thousands of ships every year, including the English who had taken the island as their base in China, the foreign ships of other nations who welcomed that security, and the endless stream of Chinese who profited from foreign trade.

Chi-Yen and Sin-Feng purchased cooked rice and fish from an open stall, and while they ate she learned from the vendor the most likely places in town for a new arrival to purchase and smoke opium. When they tracked the monk down that afternoon, though, they found themselves late on the scene. Standing beside Liu Kun's rented bunk, where he lay with eyes glassy and uncomprehending of events unfolding around him, were two armed English policemen and—once again, unrelenting, impossible to shake—their pursuer Malvenue.

Chi-Yen barely had the chance to grab Sin-Feng from the doorway and pull him back into the street, so eager had the boy been to rescue his master.

"What he wants is in your hands," she warned. "Do you wish to give it to him so easily?"

Sin-Feng did not.

"Do you have a plan?"

Again, Sin-Feng did not.

"I am the only one of us that the Englishman knows by sight," Chi-Yen said. "If you enter the building, I must wait outside. I can hold the box if you wish."

Sin-Feng held the package more tightly in his arms. "Only an initiate of the Order of the Seven Dragons may—"

Chi-Yen pressed her hand hard across Sin-Feng's mouth. "Do not speak," she said. "Only listen."

They stood outside the opium den, a structure that was rundown and decrepit from the day it was built. Mismatched siding on the outer walls—patched together from scrap wood of various sources, some of it painted and some of it not—provided a partial windbreak that would not survive the next typhoon. The roof was much the same and there was no door, so that it was easy to hear the voices inside.

Malvenue spoke in Chinese to the owner of the shop, whose own English was limited to a bit of pidgin, owing to the fact that his business catered to locals rather than foreigners, and even his opium was supplied by Chinese middlemen.

"They would have arrived this morning," Malvenue said. "A man, a boy, and a girl with blue eyes. They would be looking for lodging for at least two weeks."

"No lodging here," said the shopkeeper. "Opium dreams only, then out the door."

"And which of these gentlemen are new to your fine establishment?"

"Information costs. You pay?"

There was a pause followed by the click of coins being counted out.

"What do we do?" Sin-Feng whispered.

"Be ready to run if we have to."

But when the shopkeeper spoke again his words were surprisingly welcome. "Liu Kun, you say? A man called himself by that name this morning. He purchased a pipe and flashed a great deal of gold. He was looking for passage up the coast to the Yellow River."

"He came to you for a ship?"

"He came to me for a pipe, but he talked a great deal more than he should for someone with that much gold in his purse."

Malvenue continued to question the man, but even after counting out additional coins he learned little more—and nothing truthful—about Liu Kun's whereabouts, his belongings, or his companions. After a few threats from the policemen regarding the dubious legality of an opium den in this location, in this condition, the shopkeeper paid them part of the bribe he had just earned from Malvenue, and the matter was settled.

By the time the three men exited the establishment, Chi-Yen and Sin-Feng were well hidden on the far side of the building. When the street cleared they returned to the front entrance to find Liu Kun still dreaming and the shopkeeper expecting them.

"You," he said to Sin-Feng, "are to stay here and protect your master. You have two weeks, paid in advance."

Then he turned to Chi-Yen and scowled.

"You are to leave at once and never return. Go back to your mother. Go anywhere. Nobody cares. Only stop trying to rob the great dragon warrior. Burden him no more with your greed and your lies."

Chapter Six

Fifty-Eight Days

Of course Chi-Yen could not be gotten rid of so easily. For one thing, to return to Canton would be to succumb to the life that had destroyed her mother and her friend Xiao-Niao and so many others before them—that was not an option. But another, increasingly important reason was the box and the rock or egg or whatever it was that nested inside. Ever since she had returned it to its hiding place in the bunk on the flower boat, she had been unable to stop thinking about it. And in her mind, in her imagination, that brief, odd feeling when she touched the egg—for yes, she was sure now that it was an egg—had grown to something substantial and strange.

She had felt the heat; she had felt the movement. Something was alive in there, and bad people wanted it badly, and the monk Liu Kun was no fit guardian.

She recalled the Abbot's dying words to her: *You know the truth of what is, and how to lie in the service of what should be. Do what you must to protect our burden.*

Chi-Yen owed the Abbot nothing, but he had at least believed in her. And that egg … she could not get that egg out of her mind.

So she did what any young, multilingual, half-Chinese girl disguised as a boy needing passage from Hong Kong to San Francisco would do. She tracked down the ticket broker for the ship and—watching from a distance, for she did not wish to draw attention to herself—she marked then followed as many potential passengers as she could. To each she offered her services, refining her sales pitch and bargaining her rates until she had a group of thirty men willing to join her for daily lessons in basic English.

By the time the ship sailed, she had earned enough money not only for a ticket but also to provision herself with extra food, bedding, a blanket, and heavier clothing for colder weather. All of this she tied into a package that she hung from the end of a bamboo pole, which she carried over her shoulder to a skiff that ferried her across the harbor to the waiting clipper.

From a distance it was a beautiful ship, a fine example of the barbarian technology that had not only allowed the foreigners to master the Asian nations, but given them the incentive to do so. Two-hundred-twenty feet at the keel, with an additional sixteen feet on deck, the *Round World* was sleek and steeply angled, free of ornament, and masted for maximum sail. At her fastest she was said to have made the trans-Pacific passage in just thirty-three days, but that had been ten years earlier and since then, as Chi-Yen would soon learn, her well-earned reputation as a hard-luck ship had come at great cost.

After climbing aboard the clipper, Chi-Yen was given no opportunity to explore. She was taken through to the dark, dank hold below decks. There had been only seven others aboard her skiff, but there were plenty more skiffs on the harbor and by the time she reached the hold there were hundreds of men crammed into place, with more still on the way.

She was fortunate, though, in that her students had saved her a generous space.

"John! John!" they shouted, for that was the English name she had given herself, recommending that they all do the same to ease their way among Americans in the New World. "Here you! Here you!"

She settled among them and set about teaching them to pronounce the name of the ship, *Round World* proving to be a tongue-twister.

More and more emigrants crowded into the hold, many forced to stand shoulder-to-shoulder near the entrance until those at the back gave up some of their claimed territory to accommodate the newcomers. The hatch was then closed and—by the sound of it—barred, leaving a total of nearly four hundred men stuffed into the windowless space. It was at that moment that the passengers realized—to their great discomfort, and to Chi-Yen's especially—that for the next month or more they would be sharing the same dozen buckets as their only toilets.

The tension was high with so many people packed together. Arguments and several isolated fights broke out, with men punching and kicking one another over slights both real and imagined. The circle around Chi-Yen remained calm, however, with her seated students facing her and repeating in unison, in muddled English: "A good day to you, sir. What a fine day this is, sir."

At that moment a group of men near the hatch, still the most densely packed area of the hold, began to laugh, and the laughter quickly spread, even absorbing some of the fighting. But one defiant voice rose up from it all.

"I am Tam Sin-Feng, apprentice to the great warrior Liu Kun. You say my master has pissed himself, but that is not true. He fell from the boat. Look, he is wet all over, not only in his pants."

The laughter in the hold doubled as the story was retold. The man had indeed fallen into the harbor and he had been so drunk that the boy had to fish him out. Surely he had pissed himself first, though, and gone for a swim to hide the evidence. Now he lay slumped against the bulkhead, unconscious again, oblivious to the amusement of his fellow passengers. Sin-Feng stood beside the man, defending him, the familiar canvas bundle clutched tight within his arms.

It wasn't until several hours later, with the ship cast loose from its moorings and underway through the channel, that Chi-Yen approached the boy. The sight of her amazed Sin-Feng—first because she was here at all, but even more because she was clean, well rested, and well fed, while his own haggard appearance betrayed his recent difficult circumstances.

The keeper of the opium den, who had protected Liu Kun from Malvenue but had also driven Chi-Yen away, had acted with the most selfish of motives. He had seen the satchel of gold and silver with which Liu Kun had attempted to purchase his safety, and although the man had been afraid to steal from someone who might very well be a formidable warrior, he had not been afraid to charge exorbitant rates for his services.

By the end of two weeks, the cost of substandard room and board and opium and protection added up to the exact amount that Liu Kun possessed, leaving the monk and his apprentice with not a coin to their names—only the two tickets and the mysterious box, which Sin-Feng guarded at all times.

Rousting his master on that final morning had been almost impossible for Sin-Feng, but after much effort he pulled Liu Kun from his bunk and supported him on their walk to the shore. And yes, Liu Kun had fallen into the water upon boarding the skiff, and Sin-Feng had fetched him out. It had only been by some miracle that Liu Kun managed to climb up from the skiff and onto the *Round World*.

Now they were together again with Chi-Yen, in much the same state as before, but at last free of the villainous Malvenue and on their way to America.

"Call me John," she said in a whispered voice. And then she brought Sin-Feng to her own sleeping area and introduced him to her students, announcing that he would be joining their lessons.

That day they learned the schedule that the ship was to follow for the rest of the voyage. They would be fed rice and vegetables once in the morning and once in late afternoon. They would be given rations of water for as long as supplies lasted. They would be allowed on deck in groups of no more than twenty for no more than fifteen minutes each. If they wished to relieve themselves at that time, they could go to the head of the ship and dangle their gear over the side. Otherwise they would use the supplied buckets in the hold and empty them overboard as necessary during deck visits.

The man who issued these instructions was the ship's second mate, who went by the name of Weldon. He was a tall, rough-looking man with a grizzled white beard and scarred knuckles. He spoke not a word of Chinese, but the passengers listened, hoping for something they could understand. When he finished and turned to exit the hatch, not seeming to care that nobody had comprehended a word he said, Chi-Yen clapped her hands together then translated the news. Weldon stopped short as he watched this curious sight: a boy who couldn't be more than thirteen years old commanding the attention of four hundred men.

"You speakee English?" he asked.

"I do, sir, yes," Chi-Yen replied.

The man nodded then left without another word.

By the time Chi-Yen was allowed on deck for the first time

early that evening, the mountainous islands of Hong Kong and the Kowloon peninsula were distant, indistinct silhouettes backlit by the setting sun at the ship's stern. A number of gulls stalked the ship above while several white dolphins paced its wake, breaking the surface then racing along just beneath it.

The captain had taken advantage of light but favorable winds and—according to shouts between men unfurling additional sails high in the rigging—there were high hopes for a quick and easy passage.

Chi-Yen and the others in her group took one long, last look at China—many of them, whether they knew it or not, for the last time in their lives—before being ushered back through the hatch and into the dark hold.

Liu Kun woke the next morning in a nasty mood, made nastier by the increasing height of the ocean swells as the ship was forced to tack against a change in the wind. Most of the passengers, including Chi-Yen, had begun to feel sick with this unsteady motion. It wasn't long before the first man vomited; and in the stifling, uncirculated air of the compartment, this began a chain reaction, with each man inspiring the next so that the deck beneath their feet became slick with spew.

Chi-Yen heard the monk yelling for his apprentice, and heard the complaints of men being stepped upon as Liu Kun stumbled with his first sober steps upon the wave-tossed ship.

"Sin-Feng! Where are we? What have you done?"

"Master! I am here!"

Liu Kun lurched in the direction of Sin-Feng's voice and fell to his knees, retching with the motion of the boat. Chi-Yen and Sin-Feng took him by the arms and guided him the rest of the way to their spot among Chi-Yen's students.

"You!" he said.

"Call me John."

"I will not! I will call you nothing!"

Liu Kun fell to the boards, sick again, and in this manner the days passed. The ocean provided no relief, but one by one the men in the hold began to gain their sea legs. They worked together to clean the floors that so many had soiled, returning some small amount of dignity to their awful space. Some days during their brief time above they could see land, while on others they saw only endless blue and gray as the *Round World* continued to tack north against the wind.

The monk suffered as much as any man on board, but less from seasickness than opiate withdrawal. In addition to the nausea and vomiting, he fought a mostly losing battle against stomach cramps and diarrhea. He sweated profusely and took more than his share of water. He could not sleep and trusted no one, always agitated and anxious. He lashed out at Sin-Feng and accused Chi-Yen of stealing his gold and his pipe.

"Do not listen to him," Sin-Feng advised her one morning as they took their allotted time on deck. "He is not himself. He has lost his brothers."

"His brothers seem to be less on his mind," Chi-Yen replied, "than the lack of opium on this ship."

"Our temple has been destroyed. You must try to understand. My master is a great warrior, but everything he knows is gone."

"Not everything," she said, for Sin-Feng still had not relaxed his grip on the canvas-wrapped box.

The boy flushed a bit, uncomfortable that Chi-Yen had noticed his prize.

"Everyone on board watches the way you guard that bundle, Sin-Feng—the way it never leaves your hands except at night, when you sleep upon it. Everyone wonders what great treasure is hidden inside."

"It is nothing. A token of our temple's history. I protect it for my master until he reclaims it as his own."

Chi-Yen knew better. But she also knew that Sin-Feng's loyalty would not be broken. And although he trusted her, it was not within his authority to reveal the secrets of his order—if he even knew what those secrets were.

Liu Kun, however, was another matter. After a week at sea he had improved physically, but his attitude was worse than ever. He complained about the food, he complained about the heat, he complained about the cold, he complained about the filth, his fellow passengers, the crew, the sea, the Chinese military, barbarians in general and especially barbarian generals, but more than anything else he complained about Chi-Yen—this freeloading orphan, this brothel thief, this half-breed mongrel whose wandering devil's eyes spent too much time fixed upon the last surviving treasure of Seven Dragons Temple.

"Take it," he said. "It is worthless."

"Master!"

"What, boy? If it had any power, would it have allowed China to be destroyed? Would it have allowed its own temple to burn to the ground?" Liu Kun grabbed the canvas bundle from Sin-Feng. He unwrapped the box—even in the dark of the hold it reflected an unreal beauty—and he tossed it to Chi-Yen. "If you can open it," he said, "you can take what is inside."

The box was as gorgeous as she remembered—more so, even—both delicate and strong at the same time, a union of opposites greater than either alone. She turned it round, admiring it for the second time until Liu Kun snatched it back.

"It will never open for you," he said. "In one hundred years you would never decipher the secret mechanism, which is known only to senior monks such as myself."

"What is inside?" Chi-Yen asked, her voice a hushed, reverent whisper.

"Nothing important. But in America I expect to sell a box

of such craftsmanship for a good price. It is worth its weight in gold, at least."

"Master!"

Liu Kun rewrapped the box and tossed it to Sin-Feng. Chi-Yen gasped at the careless handling. "Guard it well, boy," he said, "and we will eat well in our new home."

For the next two weeks the *Round World* made slow progress on days she made any progress at all. The captain cursed the crew and the passengers and the wind and ocean and his barbarian God. The rations proved substandard and many of the Chinese sickened with dehydration and dysentery. Even with constant carrying and dumping overboard, the buckets of waste in the hold filled too fast and overflowed or tumbled, reducing the compartment to a sweltering, fly-swarmed latrine. Two passengers died and their bodies were dropped into the sea.

The sickness had not touched Chi-Yen, and she continued her English lessons to the dwindling number of men who still cared to live and to learn. She relieved herself only at night, in the darkest hours, so that no man would see and discover her secret.

And then on the night of the seventeenth day, after creeping silently to squat over a bucket, she heard whispered voices.

"This way," said a man. "Follow me."

"I'm with you."

"How close are they?"

Three men at least. In the darkness they approached Chi-Yen. She felt one then another pass her by, the fabric of their trousers brushing her forearm.

"I counted the distance today. Thirty half-steps and then we stop, turn right, and five more steps."

"And then we attack."

The footsteps of the leading voice stopped until the others reached him. They were so near to Chi-Yen that she could smell the sweat on their backs, rising beyond all the other odors of the hold.

"The boy is first, with the box, and his master just beyond. Beat the master first, and then the boy. Hit them hard enough, kill them if we must, so that they fear us forever. Their treasure shall be ours."

Chi-Yen held her breath, afraid of being discovered and unsure what to do. As the footsteps moved away from her, in the direction of Sin-Feng, she prepared to call out a warning. But sooner than she expected she heard the sounds of fighting: the muffled thuds of fist against flesh, the snap of an arm, a cry of pain, a body slamming hard against the ship's hull. Amidst all the gasps and pained screaming, though, she heard not a single voice that matched her companions. Had these men attacked the wrong passengers?

It ended almost as soon as it began. Footsteps passed her by again, but more panicked shuffling now than stealthy creeping. A desperate moan rose up nearby from someone unable to move.

"Sin-Feng?" Chi-Yen called.

The boy answered with a voice full of pride. "My master," he said, "is a great warrior."

By the time the sun rose that morning, a rumored—and possibly exaggerated—accounting of the night's battle had spread throughout the hold. Liu Kun had taken out six men in under a minute. He had broken four arms and three legs. Eyes were blackened, teeth were pulled, ears were taken as souvenirs, and all in total darkness, as if he possessed the eyes of a bat.

He was a legendary hero, they said; you should never judge a man by the pee stains in his trousers.

There was little time to revel in this victory, however. During her brief time on the upper deck that morning, Chi-Yen had seen a squall on the horizon. She noticed the crew working with feverish, worried anticipation. By afternoon the ship was rising and falling and rolling more than at any time so far on the voyage. The hull's timbers strained with each hard return, sounding as if they might shatter at any moment.

The wide berth that his fellow passengers had offered to Liu Kun disappeared in the chaos as men were tossed through the air, colliding with one another and clutching for any handhold. Sin-Feng managed to keep one arm on the box and another wrapped around a bunk post. Liu Kun somehow slept through much of the turmoil, his body rolling forward and back with the motion of the ship. Chi-Yen braced herself between the ladder and the bulkhead.

How long this continued none could say. Day merged with night in the darkness of the storm. No food was delivered to the passengers and no announcement was made to explain its absence. The Chinese trapped in the hold began to wonder whether the barbarian crew had been swept away by the wind and waves. Several in the hold were dead and more were near death, and nothing could be done to prevent their bodies from surging forward to collide with the living.

The terrifying noise of the sea against the ship and the ship against the sea became tedious through endless repetition. And then, at just the moment Chi-Yen felt she could resist no more and would willingly collapse into helpless sleep even if it meant certain death, a new crash sounded above, a noise unlike any they had heard before that rattled the timbers of the ship, a cascade of creaking and snapping and half-imagined shrieks as the rain on deck turned from water to wood.

In the eerie silence that followed, the ship reoriented itself to the sea, listing to port and tumbling the passengers together in a heap.

The hatch opened and a single wave entered the compartment along with the mate Weldon, who slammed the door shut behind him. He peered into the darkness of the hold and called out, "Where be the English-speaking boy?"

"Here," said Chi-Yen.

"Bring ten strong men and come with me," he shouted. "No time to waste." He pointed to a group nearby. "You, you, you," he said, counting out his picks.

Chi-Yen translated and told the men they were wanted above. Although frightened by the prospect, it seemed better than where they were, and all clambered out the hatch with Weldon at the lead.

A mess of rigging, spars, and topmasts littered the deck and swayed in great tangles above. Chi-Yen and the Chinese followed Weldon's example and grabbed a rail, which served them well when the next wave washed over them.

Weldon passed out riggers' knives to his new crew. Their job was to lower the knots of sail and broken wood back to the deck—gently, gently—where it could be lashed down until they had ridden out the storm.

Chi-Yen relayed his orders and soon enough the lot of them were climbing up to the main course spar and then on to a break in the mast above the topsail. Ropes and canvas and upper beams snapped and whipped with the wind all around them and dipped down to drag the sea. Salt spray stung the climbers' eyes and the crack of the lines cut their palms.

Halfway up they passed the body of a crewman dangling from a rope wrapped round a single foot. His head and face were bashed in from slamming into the mast after being knocked from his perch.

Weldon called up from below, and Chi-Yen told her men to spread out across the topsail spar. The ship still listed to its side, canted by the anchor of mast hanging below them, dragging the sea. As Chi-Yen and the men inched out the wildly swaying beam they looked down and saw beneath them not the hard deck of the ship but a fierce boil of ocean. The cold wind blew hard against their wet hands and she and the men struggled to keep their grips, but there was no time to fear their precarious positions.

They worked quickly, lowering a guide rope to lasso the main topgallant yardarm, then another and another for broken bits of the main royal. Moving back toward the mast they used their combined strength to lure in the tangle. Below them waves washed the deck while other crew members fought to untangle and secure additional wreckage all about the ship.

Chi-Yen and her men at the main topsail spar fed more rope to those at the mainsail below, who guided it to the deck. Already the ship had begun to right herself. Then they climbed back down and helped secure the mess so that no loose pieces could careen as missiles against the men or the ship.

After that there was little more to do but keep watch and wait. Chi-Yen noticed for the first time how fast her heart was beating.

The volunteers were then offered cold food in the ship's galley—there would be no fire in the stove today—where the white sailors, the Indians, the Pacific islanders, and the Chinese all smiled at one another and laughed to be alive, brothers now in the aftermath of near disaster.

Chi-Yen learned that a wave the previous day had taken out the aft deck cabin along with the captain, the first mate, and several hands. That left Weldon in command of the struggling ship. The collapse of the mainmast into the mizzen topsail had taken several more lives.

The corpse in the rigging was an Indian named Singh, who was being cut free as they spoke.

Chi-Yen translated this information for her countrymen, along with the news that the shorthanded crew could use their help for the rest of the voyage if they were willing—at equivalent wages for the number of days worked—otherwise Weldon would seek alternate volunteers from below. The men all agreed, noting that this was an auspicious beginning to their lives in the new world.

The storm continued for another week, after which the seas became calm enough for the crew—including Chi-Yen and the ten Chinese—to re-rig the ship minus the main top-gallant and royal, and with none of the skysails or extended studding sails. In this condition the *Round World* limped at half speed west to east with the northern current across the Pacific, eventually coming within sight of land and dropping down the coast of California toward the Golden Gate of San Francisco Bay.

When not translating for Weldon, Chi-Yen worked with the ship's cook to help feed the passengers in the hold, who were in worse shape than ever. Seven more had died as a result of illness or injury. Both Liu Kun and Sin-Feng had become sick with fever, which was how Chi-Yen justified slipping the precious box out from between the two and carrying it on deck one afternoon, to where she could give it greater protection.

She had not forgotten what Liu Kun had said—that he planned to sell it for gold upon arriving in San Francisco. If that were the case, she was more fit to be its protector than the disgraceful monk. She could take it from the ship and escape into the city before they knew she was gone.

The Abbot had asked her to do what was necessary, and she supposed that included betraying his own men. Plus, the thing continued to haunt her dreams.

She remembered what else Liu Kun had said—that she could never in one hundred years open the box, that only a monk of the Dragon Temple could know its secret. And yet it had opened for her once before, the first time she had held it.

She sat in the shadow of the midship galley and unfolded

the canvas. She placed the box on the deck, the image of the dragon at its top looking directly at her, as if speaking to her, and she imagined noises coming from inside—scratching or clawing or tapping.

She raised the box and turned it about, seeking the hidden levers and latches that she must have tripped the first time, but there was nothing. She looked again at the dragon's head and brushed her fingertips across it. Nothing. She studied the carvings on its sides—the landscapes and peaks of China, the wild creatures, the warriors, the sea. But nothing.

With a sigh she returned the box to the deck.

And then it happened. As before, there was a hiss and a rush of sound as hidden gears dilated the iris and the lid opened up to her. She saw immediately, though, and with great distress, what was different this time. There was a flaw in the egg, a thin crack likely caused by all the rough handling during the voyage. The box and its contents had been tossed about as much as any man on board.

She picked up the egg and even that simple movement seemed to widen the damage, horrifying Chi-Yen with the thought that she might have caused this herself. How would she explain to Sin-Feng? To Liu Kun?

And then she heard the tapping noise again, and even more she felt it in her hands. In her initial surprise she almost dropped the egg, but then she recovered and peered in for a closer look.

She gasped when she saw a deeply curved bill pushing out from inside, spreading a web of fractures through the delicate shell. Not a bird—definitely not a bird—the bill was scaled but leathery, and as the crack widened she saw an eye blinking behind it, as if adjusting to the light.

The creature inside made a soft but high pitched sound—a *screeee*—and then the entire egg began to shiver and shake, as with muscles tensed to maximum strength, and the shell popped all at once, shattering into her hand, up toward her face, and raining down upon the deck.

Almost more quickly than she could see, the creature unfolded itself in her hand, stretching out to full size—about ten inches long but thin and snakelike, if not for the four sets of four-toed claws that dug into Chi-Yen's arm, piercing her flesh with its talons. She grimaced and the creature retracted its claws and looked around itself, taking in its surroundings with what Chi-Yen imagined to be some measure of surprise—the girl, the ship, the sea, the unfamiliar coastline distant off the port bow.

It was a curious looking creature, more like a lizard than anything else, light tan in color with a long, whiplike tail. Its oblong, crested head bore two large, dark, lidded eyes and gaping nostrils, and at each side of the neck a tufted, gill-like fan waved the air.

The beast looked up at the girl and rose on its hind legs so that they were eye to eye and—could this have been her imagination again?—it winked at her. What certainly was not her imagination was the sudden, blinding pain that came when the monster turned and bit her left hand hard between thumb and forefinger. Chi-Yen shook her arm to break its grip, only half unintentionally hurling the beast into the air and over the railing of the ship.

She gasped, horrified by what she had done. But any guilt she might have felt—along with any pain from torn flesh and any doubts about her mission in this life—fell from her mind in an instant as, in defiance of natural gravity, the young dragon rose up wingless on the wind, circled the *Round World* once, then soared high into the sky on a course for its new home.

Chapter Seven

Gold Mountain

Chi-Yen's hand was a mess of blood. She pressed it against the fabric of her dark pants to clear the wound, and upon examining it she found a track of deep punctures left by the beast's needlelike teeth. The U-shape of its jaw had clamped at an angle around both sides between her forefinger and thumb, leaving a tracked outline in the shape of a heart. She would need a bandage to stop the bleeding; the scars would be permanent.

She picked up the open box, kicked the broken eggshells overboard, and rushed to the galley in the midship deck house, where the cook stood cleaning the last of the breakfast tins and deciding whether to bother with lunch. By late afternoon, the man estimated, the ship would be within sight of San Francisco and every sailor not in sick bay would be jumping overboard to head for the waterfront saloons and gambling halls before they had even dropped anchor.

"Try not to get your blood in the food, boy," he said.

He tossed Chi-Yen the wet rag he had been using to dry

his pots. She wrapped it around her hand and tucked it into itself to secure it in place over the wound.

After fifty-eight days at sea the ship was low on most stores—and completely out of many—but the crew at least had been fed well and had eaten fresh meat up until the last week, when they had butchered their final pig. The galley even had a small but steady supply of eggs from the remaining live chickens, although these had been limited to the ship's officers—at least until the officers had been swept overboard with the aft deckhouse.

As Chi-Yen exited the galley she thanked the cook for the rag and—while the man's back was turned—she stole one of the eggs and slipped it into the box. As before, the weight was enough to trigger the lid into closing. The small egg was no match for the original, but she doubted Liu Kun would check it anytime soon.

It would be a mistake to tell him the truth—that she had broken the egg; that she had set the dragon free. Her punishment would be most severe if she were discovered. She recalled what the monk had done to the thieves that night, and her crime was certainly greater than theirs.

Chi-Yen returned below decks to the hold, moving silently through the hatch so as not to disturb the miserable, sleeping passengers. Sin-Feng and Liu Kun remained where she had left them, still sweating and feverish, their eyes closed. Neither had moved.

She returned the box to its place between them. But just as she began to withdraw, Liu Kun struck like a coiled snake, grabbing her by the left wrist and pulling her to his side.

"I smell blood," he said, noting the bandage wrapped around her hand.

"The mizzen course sheet flew loose. It tore my grip."

Liu Kun eyed her suspiciously, then glanced to the box at

his side. "Watch yourself, boy," he said, adding heavy scorn to that last word. "You are less clever than you think."

Chi-Yen was on deck later that afternoon as the ship sailed through the Golden Gate into San Francisco Bay. The veteran crew had taken over the duties of preparing for harbor, pulling up the anchor rode and anchor from its locker. The ten newly forged Chinese sailing men stood on deck as well, idly watching the spectacle of new land, while the rest of the Chinese passengers remained confined to the hold to keep them out of the way of the work.

Chi-Yen, though, kept her eyes on the sky, scanning gull to gull between fast blowing clouds, searching in vain among birds both familiar and unfamiliar. Her wounded hand pulsed with each beat of her heart. Nothing in the air indicated that the world had changed—that now there was magic where before there had been none—but Chi-Yen knew better.

As the ship rounded the peninsula, her companions along the rail grew excited.

"Gold Mountain!" they shouted, "Gold Mountain!"

That was the name that hopeful Chinese immigrants had given to the city of San Francisco, gateway to the immense riches that had been discovered in this land of America not yet a dozen years earlier. Within a year of those first flakes of gold being plucked from Sutter's Mill, the population of this tiny town had grown from less than one thousand to more than twenty-five times that number, with countless many more spreading throughout the Sierra Nevada mountains and up and down the newly admitted state of California.

The city had been built in a rush. Supplies had arrived by ship and both passengers and sailors had abandoned their ships in the harbor, heading out to strike it rich while leaving the bay and the wharves clogged with clippers and barques and whalers, with nobody willing to man them. Ships without crews were cut down at the docks and their timbers were taken for hotels, gambling halls, storage facilities, and jails. Some were dragged ashore and new doorways were cut into their hulls, converting ships into buildings in a single afternoon. Yerba Buena Cove was slowly filled in with sand and dirt, landlocking derelict vessels. Shops and warehouses were built upon their decks, turning their holds into basements and erasing all memory of what and where they had been. Fires were a constant threat, with many of those first frail structures burning to the ground several times over in the span of just two years.

By the time the *Round World* dropped anchor off Goat Island in March of 1858, nearly 80,000 people filled the city's tightly packed homes, boarding houses, and tents. The rush to the gold fields had slowed as the reality of hard, dusty labor won out over rumors of easy wealth, but for many the urge to strike it rich or start anew remained, and newcomers continued to arrive daily.

The harbor pilot, in fact, advised acting captain Weldon that he would have to wait for two days to unload his battered ship, as empty space at the bustling wharf could not yet be found. As expected, though, none of this stopped the eager crew from forfeiting their duties now that they were so close to their destination. The anchored *Round World* soon found herself surrounded by small skiffs offering shore transport to any willing crewman desirous of strong drink in comfortable environs—and most every crewman was willing.

"Bottle-headed bastards." It was Weldon shouting from near the wheel. He called out to Chi-Yen: "John, you'll keep your men away from those crimps if they want what's good for 'em."

But as the rest of the crew clambered down rope ladders to the enterprising boats below, the Chinese stood their ground, not having been invited, or at least not invited in a language they understood.

"Damn'd shanghaiers," Weldon said. "Men ought to know better, seein' that's how half 'em ended up shippin' to sea in the first place."

The situation, as Weldon explained to the young Chinese boy who had shown such aptitude as a sailor and translator, was this: With so many seamen arriving in San Francisco, and so few willing to leave, a lucrative relationship had developed between captains and certain less savory local businessmen. Any man willing to drink was a man able to be drugged, and any man able to drug a man's drink could easily transport his unconscious victim to the captain of a departing ship, who in exchange for the favor would hand over the unwitting sailor's first two months pay in advance—a false "debt" owed by the sailor to his persecutor. By the time the unconscious man awoke the next morning, he would be out to sea and well on his way to Shanghai, the first stop on a one-way trip around the world.

"Poor fools ha' not been home in a year," Weldon said, watching helplessly as his crew with their seabags deserted ship en masse, "and on the morrow most'll be dead drunk and bound back for China 'gainst their will."

Chi-Yen might have felt sympathy or even empathy for men forced into lives not of their choosing, but to repeat a mistake was to take at least some responsibility for your fate. And her own fate, at that moment, was most prominent among her concerns.

A dragon? Truly? Whose life was this? Whose dream?

But it was no dream. Chi-Yen could hear the cheers and the laughter of the crew in the skiffs below as they pulled away from the ship; she heard the water lapping against the boards, the birds crying out overhead, the crash of terns and brown pelicans hitting the bay. In the distance, at the wharves that fed the city, men carted goods from ports near and far, the fortunes of a lifetime passing through their hands in the space of an hour. Behind them the grid of streets was an anthill of activity, with people moving here, there, and everywhere, everywhere grading new roads and erecting homes and factories and banks, their hammers and chisels and saws singing a constant song of progress.

And somewhere out there, hidden among it all, an incongruous stranger in this strange new land, was Chi-Yen's dragon.

But that would be presumptuous. The dragon was not Chi-Yen's. The dragon was not even Liu Kun's—the monk was merely caretaker of an egg. And now that the creature was hatched and free? Did Chi-Yen's responsibility end here? Did Liu Kun's?

She laughed out loud. Responsibility? Responsibility had nothing to do with it. There was a dragon out there, and she wanted to see it again.

And so two days later, her pockets filled with fair wages for her work before the mast, Chi-Yen disembarked at the Pacific Street Wharf along with Liu Kun and Sin-Feng and all the rest, ignoring the insults from the local longshoremen that she alone among her fellow passengers could understand.

"You will know those words soon enough," she remarked—in English—to her former students as their feet felt land for the first time in two months. "I wish you the best of luck in your new work. Goodbye, Sam. Goodbye, Joseph. Goodbye, Edmund."

"Goodbye, John," the men said, shaking hands with her in the American style as she had taught them.

She had to hurry to catch Liu Kun, who had not bothered to wait, preferring to lose the girl to fend for herself. Chi-Yen would not have minded that at all, since allying herself with the monk meant she would spend more time solving his problems than her own. But he was the one man with knowledge that might help her find what she was looking for, and so she grabbed her bundle and slipped through the crowds and soon enough was walking just behind Sin-Feng as Liu Kun unfolded and consulted his letter from the Abbot.

San Francisco was alien and yet familiar at once. The rutted streets were wet with mud and livestock dung, while the sidewalks often consisted of little more than planks laid side by side across the deeper puddles. Wood-sided houses rose two or three stories high, with peaked roofs and dormered windows looking out upon flat-roofed brick banks and dry goods shops, while additional residences climbed the steep sides of Telegraph Hill to the north, stacked almost one upon another like the ingenious rice paddies of Longsheng. With so many structures packed together so tightly, it followed that the people within them spilled into the streets in density equal to what Chi-Yen had known in Canton.

And what people they were! Alongside the stream of fellow Chinese immigrants she heard speakers of Spanish, French, Russian, Italian, rough-hewn American English, and numerous languages she had never before imagined. She recognized sailors by their demeanor, but also the familiar watchful eyes of working pickpockets, of more desperate petty thieves scouting open shop windows, of drunken cutthroats, of pimps and prostitutes and gangs of thugs surveying the newcomers for opportunity. And yet also there were families—fathers and mothers and children walking hand in hand, out for a stroll in their exciting young city, enjoying their normal lives. How strange that would be!

Liu Kun and Sin-Feng continued to study the Abbot's letter, puzzling over their destination. They muttered between themselves, turning round to look for signs, lost amid unfamiliar landmarks. Chi-Yen held back, listening, watching, until at last her patience wore out.

"Excuse me," she said, addressing a passing gentleman. "Might you direct us to Dupont Street, please?"

With his tailored jacket, vest, and pants, and his graying hair, the man could have been a doctor or a respected publisher. He patted his pockets, verifying that his valuables had not yet been stolen.

"Fresh off the boat, boy? Your English is better than most natives."

"I learned many exciting new words while working alongside the American sailors during the voyage from Hong Kong."

"For the sake of civilized society, let's keep those secrets bottled up, shall we?" The man gestured with his thumb back over his shoulder, jogging it just a bit to his right. "Dupont is the next cross street," he said. "You'll feel right at home."

But in truth, the city so far was much better than home—so young, so unformed, so full of opportunities for a fresh start unencumbered by history.

Chi-Yen thanked the stranger, and in her excitement to see more she almost forgot her companions. She rushed ahead to the corner and scanned the new views for any signs of her dragon—for if the dragon were seeking out familiar sites and sounds from old China, there was no place better in the New World than Dupont Street in San Francisco in the year 1858.

It was almost as if Chi-Yen had never boarded the *Round World*. The buzz of language now was all Chinese, the street filled with dark-haired men, their long queues hanging down their backs, their shaved scalps protected from the sun by broad-brimmed conical hats woven far across the sea. They gathered together to read the latest from Chinese newspapers pasted to building walls. They haggled at food stalls and in brightly colored shops full of carvings and curios. Banners and signs indecipherable to English speakers advertised medicines and hardware, camp supplies and gambling halls. There were joss houses and Chinese opera and buyers of gold. There were District Association headquarters and money lenders and fortune tellers. There were poor Chinese men and very, very wealthy Chinese men and—Chi-Yen now realized—not a single Chinese woman in the street.

She checked again, scanning the crowds: no women and, other than herself and Sin-Feng, no children. She was, as far as she could see, as rare as the dragon she sought.

"Is this our destination?" asked Sin-Feng. "Have we arrived at last at our new temple?"

As if put out by having to explain such matters, Liu Kun grunted his reply. "There is no temple, boy. The temple is finished."

"But master, we are Guardians of the Seven Dragons. The temple is central to our mission."

The monk scoffed. "Our mission is burnt to ash. All we seek now is a bed in a warm room and sympathy from distant cousins of our dear departed Abbot."

"But master—"

"Enough!" Liu Kun held up his hand, putting an abrupt end to the discussion. He turned his head rapidly side to side as he scanned the surroundings. Then he rushed forward into the crowd, anonymous as any other among countless immigrants teeming the street, but more than any other now with a determined, driving purpose.

Chi-Yen felt her heart skip. Had Liu Kun's training in the ways of the dragon brought something to his attention? Had he somehow sensed the beast? Sin-Feng at first refused to follow his master, but Chi-Yen grabbed the boy by the wrist and pulled him forward.

They passed a bunkhouse and an apothecary and then paused outside a narrow alleyway between two buildings. A pair of possibly drunken Americans, solid men with large knives sheathed in their belts, loitered upon a pile of broken bricks just inside the alley entrance. Liu Kun looked past them, deeper into the dead end corridor littered with rubble and rotting, discarded timbers, and they in turn ignored Liu Kun. They gave him little more than a glance as he moved past them into the alley, just another Chinaman among thousands, trailed by a couple of beggar boys.

Chi-Yen scanned the shadows high and low, looking for any indication of her dragon, but upon entering the alley she felt trapped and uneasy. There were several basement entryways leading into windowless buildings on either side, but the unmarked doors were closed and probably locked. As Liu Kun stopped before one and descended the steps, Chi-Yen looked back up the alleyway. The two foreigners had vanished, but something felt wrong about this.

"Master Liu Kun," Sin-Feng said, "are you sure this is the place?"

Liu Kun ignored the boy. He knocked twice on the door and in that instant Chi-Yen recognized the danger. The smell gave it away, a smell to which the addict Liu Kun, in his late stage of withdrawal, must have been even more attuned than she, who had grown up in the presence of the drug.

"Liu Kun," she said. "You have no money. How do you expect to pay for opium?"

"I have property to trade. Valuable property." The man smiled as if proud of having outwitted the girl. Sin-Feng clutched the wrapped dragon box tight to his chest, protecting it from his own master, but Liu Kun shook his head. "Not the box," he said. "Not yet." Then he pointed at Chi-Yen. "Her."

Before she could step back, Liu Kun grabbed her by the forearm and pulled her to his side, and in that instant the basement door opened. Chi-Yen tried kicking and even biting to escape the monk's grip, but despite the obvious flaws in his character he remained a strong man and a skilled warrior who could subdue any enemy—especially a young girl.

He pulled her through the doorway and into the building, which—unlike Old Mother's and even Mei-Xing's clean and open establishments—was dank and dark, with stained mats and pillows spread about the floor and streaks of black mold staining the damp walls.

Liu Kun immediately launched into negotiations with the establishment's owner—a See Yup man from poor coastal counties southwest of Canton, judging by his accent—and Chi-Yen quickly realized that the monk was not very good at it. She could not help but think that she could argue a much better price for herself.

"How much would you pay me for this filthy girl?" Liu Kun asked.

The man smirked and spat onto his own floor. "You are mistaken, sir. The child is filthy, yes, but he wears his hair in the style of a Manchu man. A queue must dangle between his legs as well."

"She is a diseased whore. She disguised herself to stow on board our ship."

"If, as you say, the child is female, then one as devious as this is more trouble than she is worth. You could not pay me to take her."

The man turned his back to Liu Kun as if returning to more important business. Liu Kun was fast becoming desperate, distracted by the scent of opium around him and by the sight of other men on the floor already lost to dreams.

"A pipe, then," he said, his voice a bit too loud, too pleading. "For the cost of a pipeful I will give you the girl."

The man reluctantly turned back to Liu Kun and gave Chi-Yen a closer look, going so far as to press his finger to her cheek and study the light scar left behind by Mei-Xing's lash.

"I suppose she is not entirely worthless," he said, "although inferior to every other courtesan in my possession. Can you load a pipe, girl? Load this one for your former master."

Liu Kun released his grip at last and Chi-Yen stumbled forward, rubbing her arm where it had begun to tingle from lack of circulation. The man gestured to a table upon which rested a tray containing a simple bamboo opium pipe with its octagonal ceramic bowl, a lamp for heating, and a needle for manipulating the drug. Chi-Yen knew the process, having seen it countless times at Old Mother's, and having even helped on occasion during busy nights when the rest of the girls were otherwise occupied.

Liu Kun took his place upon an empty floor mat, reclining on his side and resting his head upon a simple wooden block. Chi-Yen took the tray and knelt with it beside him. She checked the level of oil in the lamp, trimmed the wick, and lit it, bringing it to the proper temperature. With the steel needle, she transferred a small, sticky pill of black opium to the bowl of the pipe, and she held the bowl above the lamp, massaging the opium as it warmed and turned a sweet, bubbling, golden brown. At just the right moment she shifted the drug to the small hole in the bowl and extended the pipe to Liu Kun. He inhaled, taking in every last wisp of vapor.

"Enjoy," Chi-Yen said. "You deserve no better."

This was an unfortunate turn. She had travelled to the far side of the world only to find a fate the same as she had left behind. She had been teased by the good fortune of a dragon, only to land in a dingy cellar under the command of a whoremaster as bad as the awful Mei-Xing. Her hand still ached as if the beast had only just removed its teeth, but its distance from her was as far as could be.

Sin-Feng, meanwhile, remained less than helpful, having retreated to a corner with the dragon box, his arms wrapped tight around it as he watched his master slide back to his old ways. Liu Kun remained on his side on the mat, his eyes and mind relaxed, the cravings of his addiction satisfied at last after months at sea.

Chi-Yen considered kicking the man in the stomach if she found the chance, but knew he would not feel the blow. And anyway, her new owner now had his hands upon her and was pulling her to her feet and toward a doorway in the back of the hall, promising a thorough examination of his purchase. She did not even resist, finding herself in a state of such disbelief at this unfortunate turn of events.

And so it was with mild amusement, and with the feeling that she was standing outside herself, watching from another angle, that she became aware of a series of resounding blows against the basement entrance door. The timbers shook and the hinges bent and the See Yup man dropped her arm as he shouted for assistance from two servants, who rushed to his side with knives drawn. They stood with him, facing the hammering onslaught until an almost explosive force knocked the door free of its frame and sent it hurtling into the room. The heavy door fell upon the legs of a sleeping customer, who woke to gaze curiously, painlessly, at his flattened limbs.

A dozen men poured through the breach and into the room, clearing a fog of dust and crumbling grout. Chi-Yen thought she recognized the two foreigners who had stood in the alley, although to be honest they looked much like the other ten men who had joined them, and soon enough she could tell none of them apart as they went to work with their clubs and knives, smashing and slashing everything that stood in their way—object and man alike—until they stood alone, with all Chinese resistance either beaten, bloodied, and cowering or fled out the door, the See Yup man among them.

And then, in through that bright, broken opening, stepped Basil Malvenue.

"Liu Kun?" he asked, rather upbeat and polite, quite pleased with the scene before him. "Which of you is the monk Liu Kun?"

He walked straight to the monk and, with the toe of his boot, rolled him over so that he could see into his vacant, opium-shadowed eyes.

"At last, the mighty China warrior," the Englishman said. "Pathetic." Then he addressed the armed gang that had done his dirty work: "Patriotic citizens, you have performed your duties well. The mongrel invaders have learned an important lesson today about the strength of the American character. And now … where is the boy Tam Sin-Feng?"

Sin-Feng, as Chi-Yen had been, was in shock as Malvenue pried the bundle from his arms. The man pulled the box free of the canvas and held it to the light streaming through the doorway. He was speechless as he admired his treasure. Then he turned at last to the girl, and here he switched from English to his flawless Cantonese.

"Ah, Chi-Yen," he said. "Lovely Leung Chi-Yen. I should thank you for this side-trip to these rebel colonies. Primitive cultures have always fascinated me, but I would not have had the opportunity to visit if not for you. Your bumbling companions would never have made it half as far without your help."

Chi-Yen said nothing. There was no point in speaking to this man when any careless words would be used against her.

"Mei-Xing sends her regards, by the way. And Old Fong. And your mother."

She made her face a stone mask, giving him nothing.

"You should learn from their examples," he said. "If we need to meet again"—and here he held up the bundle in his arms, as if reminding her that it was his now, and no one else's, and he smiled as if relishing the thought—"I dare say it will be an unpleasant reunion."

Chapter Eight

Fifty-Niners

But Chi-Yen was not afraid—especially not after seeing the dragon again one week later.

Even after a full year in the gold fields, the memory of those few minutes on the bay was enough to pull her through the most difficult of days—and the days were difficult indeed. That spring and the following winter she would spend countless hours knee- to waist-deep in icy rivers, hands numb and blue from repeated plunging into fresh, fast-rushing snowmelt, while in the high heat of summer and fall she broke hard, dusty ground with shovels and picks, hammering holes into rocky hillsides and swallowing as much broken granite, horse flies, and pine sap as air.

Sin-Feng and Liu Kun worked alongside her, hauling earth to the sluice boxes where the flow of water washed away the lighter sand and gravel, leaving smaller but heavier gold flake trapped against the wooden riffles—in theory, at least. In practice the gold was harder and harder to come by in plots that had been dredged several times over by earlier miners.

They worked from before sunset until after sundown six

days a week, splitting each day's earnings with the others assigned to their crew. In the first days their hands blistered and bled, but soon the scabs and calluses toughened and it was as if their tools had become extensions of their bodies, forged metal fists for cracking the earth and drawing out its wealth.

The boy Sin-Feng enjoyed the toil from the start; he grew stronger with it by the day. Relieved at last—thanks to their new poverty—of having to scrape his master from the floor of every alehouse and opium den, he put all his effort into the task at hand. He was rewarded with a body that, over the course of the year, grew leaner, more powerful, and taller than many of the undernourished adult men in the camps. Liu Kun, in contrast, became fat with long naps and breaks each day, although he never ceased his complaining.

"This food is not fit for a goat," the monk shouted.

Without a reply the camp cook served him a second helping of rice and roast pork, and Liu Kun ate it as greedily as he had eaten the first.

"The bankers pay us only half what our gold is worth," he said, lying on a rock slab in the afternoon sun, watching as Chi-Yen and Sin-Feng and the others bent low in a dry creek bed, overturning heavy boulders to get at the sand and silt beneath.

Nobody said a word.

"I am Liu Kun! I fight for Seven Dragons! How dare they charge me ten dollars to replace a broken shovel!"

Sin-Feng clenched his jaw and kept his mouth shut, but Chi-Yen read his thoughts in the ever-so-slight narrowing of his eyes. In the mind of the apprentice, the master had given up all rights to his Order when he had failed to pursue the Englishman Malvenue and the stolen dragon box. Sin-Feng knew what Liu Kun could do—every man in the camps knew, the legend of his nighttime battle in the hold of the *Round World* having been told and retold from the moment the ship docked, so that now wherever he went, honest and dishonest Chinese alike stepped aside to avoid crossing the lazy monk—and so the boy could not forgive his master's easy surrender.

"The box was worthless," Liu Kun said. "Only a relic for superstitious fools."

Chi-Yen could hear the anger in Liu Kun's voice, though. But which did he feel was the greater tragedy: that he had lost faith in his own life's work, or that the stolen artifact might have been traded for opium? Both in equal measure, she decided.

She had tried to convince Sin-Feng of the truth—that she had seen the dragon, that it was free, that they would be in grave danger when Malvenue discovered that his stolen prize contained nothing but a rotten chicken's egg—but he would hear none of it.

"You lie!" he said. "You mock the Temple of Seven Dragons. Do not speak of this again."

But she spoke of it again repeatedly and urgently, because she had to make the boy understand. The dragon was out there somewhere, and it needed the protection of people who knew its ways—even if those people were nothing but an inebriated monk and his abused dog of a servant.

Chi-Yen had told her secret to Sin-Feng that very first night in San Francisco as they huddled together for warmth in the gutted opium den. While Liu Kun lay passed out on the floor and the boy fought back frustrated tears of both rage and despair over Malvenue's victory, she had unwrapped the bandage from her hand, the ring of raw wounds barely visible in a room lit only by the glow of fog through the shattered doorway.

"This is no rope burn," she had said. "This is the bite of a dragon."

She confessed her entire story—how she had twice stolen and opened the box, how she had lifted the egg and felt something living inside it, how the beast had hatched and flown.

"Nothing you say is true," Sin-Feng said. "Only a master of Seven Dragons can unlock the dragon box."

"I can prove it. I can describe the egg. It was like no other I have seen. The color of bleached earth, with a gritty, sandy shell, and strangely heavy for its size—"

"No living man but my master has seen this egg. I know nothing of its appearance."

"It bit my hand!"

"If the dragon had truly hatched, it certainly would bite the hand of such a lying fool as you. But the dragon we protect reveals itself only to princes and emperors, not to whores and the daughters of whores!"

And so the next day and every day for the following week Chi-Yen had set about scouting the city of San Francisco alone, roaming the dense streets and empty surrounding hillsides, from the isolated Spanish mission near the Lady of Sorrows creek all the way to the northern tip of the peninsula. She had exhausted Chinatown and the Spanish quarter and ventured into the threatening shanty blocks of the Sydney Irish, who found that pelting a lone John Chinaboy with bottles and rocks was the greatest of sport. She even paid a visit to the address in the Abbot's letter, which turned out to be an ordinary apothecary run by an ordinary old man who tried selling her a packet of herbs that would help her grow strong and put hair on her chin.

In the end she found nothing. Not a glimpse, not a sound, not a shadow of the beast. If it were there, someone would have seen it, and if someone had seen it, the streets would be buzzing with the news in every language.

"Where have you been?" Sin-Feng whispered angrily as she rejoined her companions after one final sleepless night wandering the waterfront warehouses and shipyards. "We have not eaten in days. He stole a bottle of rum from a barbarian sailor. We ran for our lives."

"He is not my master," Chi-Yen replied. "He tried to sell me for opium, and he will try again."

They stood among a crowd of fellow immigrants at the foot of a pier in the dim pre-dawn hour. She opened her satchel and removed an orange that she had bargained from a street vendor the day before. She gave it to Sin-Feng, and the boy peeled it greedily.

For work in this new land they had signed on with a crew headed for Chinese Camp in the foothills of the Sierra Nevada mountains. She recognized many of these men from their ocean voyage. Most would be serving their home District Associations, which had loaned them money for the trip. With luck they might pay off the debt within a year.

"The white men believe there is no more gold," Sin-Feng said. "We Chinese believe the barbarians are too lazy to dig."

"You are both right. The real gold comes from selling supplies to the diggers. Rice, shovels, nails, picks, tents. You pay for these things whether you find gold or not."

"What do you know? You are only a girl."

Not for the first time, Chi-Yen considered punching the ungrateful beggar in his smug Manchu face. But before she had a chance to clench her fist, a deckhand shouted at them in heavily accented, rural Cantonese.

"Here! Here! Join the others!"

He pushed them from the dock onto a waiting ferry, its steam-pumping heart rattling the boarding planks, ready to drive the large rear paddlewheel that would propel them across the bay, up the Sacramento River, and into the delta that fed this new land.

And anyway, Sin-Feng had a point. This was a man's world, and she was a girl. That fact was becoming harder to hide each day, although she hoped to keep her disguise for as long as possible. She hated to admit it, but she needed the protection of Liu Kun's and Sin-Feng's company as much as they needed hers.

Within half an hour the ferry was underway, headed on a course that took them not far from the tall ships anchored at harbor, the *Round World* prominent among them.

It was odd to see it again from this angle, as Chi-Yen had become so accustomed to the views from the foredeck and in the rigging of the masts. As the morning sun rose it lit the ship low, and as they passed south of it during an outgoing tide, she was able to see the sharp V of the bow head on. It was, or had once been, a beautiful ship, although she wondered if it would ever again take to the seas.

The full extent of the damage from the voyage was now on display, or at least evident by what was missing: the aft deckhouse, half the mainmast, any valuable ropes and fittings already stripped away. There was no crew on board, and perhaps there never would be again. But—and she realized this with a sudden shock—not only was there no crew, but unlike all the other ships in the bay, which seemed to be colonized by gulls and cormorants and pelicans the moment the last sailor stepped off deck, the *Round World* was free of avian escorts. Chi-Yen's heart raced as she scanned the rigging, redoubling her efforts in a search not for birds but for—

There!

She saw it halfway up the foremast, halfway out the port side of the topsail spar. Something sat there swaying along with the gentle bend of the ship in the tide. It was brown in color, almost the same shade as the wood itself—or a rich, fertile soil—and it was definitely a living creature, for dangling beneath it was the carcass of a young herring gull. Chi-Yen could not quite make out the head of the predator, but she could tell it was feeding by the periodic rain of feathers and blood that burst from the dead seabird and showered the deck and water below.

She looked about her own boat. Her fellow passengers were also intent on the surrounding views, but most either looked back to shrinking Gold Mountain or ahead toward the long-dreamed-of mountains of gold. None had seen what she had seen. Liu Kun appeared to be asleep, with his rice mat hat pulled low across his face, while the boy watched only his master as if awaiting the next inevitable bout of trouble.

"Sin-Feng," she whispered as loudly as she dared. "Sin-Feng!"

But the boy ignored her and Chi-Yen returned her attention to the creature in the rigging. If only it would raise its head, she would know for sure. Its movements were unbirdlike, although it was not much bigger than the gull it had killed. It was much more slender in the body and, unlike a bird, it was rending the flesh of its victim with a pair of clawed forearms rather than its bill.

The ferry sounded its sharp steam whistle—a salute to an oncoming skiff—and the Chinese on deck startled at the unexpected noise. The captain in the wheelhouse laughed with his mate at the discomfort of their passengers. He cranked the wheel hard to starboard and the ferry pitched, but the Chinese—accustomed as they were to the much greater vagaries of the Pacific crossing—merely shifted their weight and rode the deck without complaint.

The distance from the *Round World* was increasing by the minute, and this new heading gave Chi-Yen a much less advantageous view. It took her a moment to locate the proper spar and the object upon it. When she did, however, there could be no mistaking it. The creature had raised its head and was staring back at her—straight back and into her eyes, as if it knew her—and with all her being Chi-Yen welcomed the reoccurrence of the pain in her palm, as if teeth had only just entered flesh. This time she would not cast it away.

"Sin-Feng!" she said. "Come look! The dragon!"

But again the boy refused to turn.

Chi-Yen raised her injured hand in salute and stared unblinking at the beast, prolonging the connection long past the time it became an indistinguishable spot in the rigging as her own boat beat on against the current. How long it watched her she could not say, but she knew now with an unshakable conviction that, no matter how far she traveled, no matter how long, she would see it again.

And then spring turned to summer turned to fall turned to winter turned to spring.

From their first base at Chinese Camp they worked their way higher and higher into the mountains, then down and up again, gradually making their way north as each new dig proved unprofitable. On those few occasions when they managed to uncover decent amounts of gold, they were soon enough forced to abandon their claims when gangs of white miners invaded their camps, firing warning shots over their heads.

Chi-Yen did not mind the movement. The more ground they covered, she figured, the better her chances of crossing the dragon's path. And constant movement, likewise, seemed the best way to stay steps ahead of Basil Malvenue. She remembered his last words to her:

"If we meet again, I dare say it will be an unpleasant reunion."

The threat was clear then, and now—for by now he must know he had been duped—she imagined he planned an even greater unpleasantness.

All the daily digging and hauling dirt and rock allowed her plenty of time to contemplate this inevitable showdown. At each new campsite she strategized her best escape routes should the moment come. But also, more and more, she wondered about Malvenue's greater plan. Why did he want the dragon so badly in the first place? Was this nothing more than the typical barbarian urge to conquer and collect? Was the egg destined for nothing more than a crowded shelf in some dusty London museum? If he captured a living dragon would he kill it and stuff it and mount it for display in his Queen's drawing room?

Or was there something more?

"What good is a dragon, anyway?" Chi-Yen asked late one cold April night.

She had at last coaxed from Sin-Feng a few secret tales of his Order. She had learned that he was an orphan himself, but that he had been raised for as long as he could remember to one day become a Warrior of Seven Dragons. It had been his destiny to be a guardian like Liu Kun—in fact he had been marked at the age of seven as Liu Kun's designated successor, the latest in an unbroken line going back almost six hundred years to the last—

"The last what?" Chi-Yen asked, encouraging the boy, who had fallen silent.

Sin-Feng looked toward the canvas tents, toward the sound of snoring from Liu Kun and the other men. It had been a wet, filthy week in the diggings, with no profit to speak of, but somehow Liu Kun had procured a bottle of whiskey that afternoon. As a result the monk now slept soundly but with occasional bursts of half-wakeful violence.

"Since the last what?" Chi-Yen repeated.

A great horned owl sang out from a twisted foothill pine shadowing the camp in the light of a waxing moon, while tree frogs and crickets barked a raucous chorus, stopping and starting together as if at the cue of some unseen conductor.

Sin-Feng spoke in a whisper. This was secret knowledge.

This would have been a betrayal of his Order, had his Order still existed:

"Since the last hatchling," he said. "Since the last dragon."

"So you know it is true? You do believe?"

"Only a fool denies the dragon's truth."

Chi-Yen bit her tongue. He was talking now, and she did not wish to shut him up by reminding him once again of what she had seen.

"The dragon is the source of all good in the world," he continued. "The dragon brings us the rivers and seas and mountains and rain, and brings good fortune to those who are worthy."

"What kind of fortune?"

"A bountiful rice harvest. A dutiful wife. Healthy sons."

"Is that all?"

"What more can a man want?"

"Did the Englishman steal your egg because he wants to feed rice to his sons?"

Sin-Feng glowered at Chi-Yen. She would have to pull back on the sarcasm if she wanted to wring useful information from the boy.

"What happened at the last hatching?" she asked. "What good is a dragon?"

"This is not your concern. This is for the men of Seven Dragons only, and you are the daughter of a diseased whore."

That was enough. The crack that rang into the night when Chi-Yen slapped Sin-Feng across the face was loud enough to again silence the crickets and frogs and birds, so that when he returned the favor and slapped her even harder, that noise echoed alone back from the nearby tree line and through the camp.

Chi-Yen staggered from the blow but barely registered the pain of it beneath her anger at Sin-Feng's arrogance. Where would he be without her? Likely in a garbage dump on the far side of the world, nothing but scattered, rat-plucked bones. Their situation had not much improved since China, but thanks to her they at least remained alive and free in a land of opportunity.

And what had she gained for her trouble? Not even the trust of a disgraced monk's garment washer.

For the course of an entire year she had hidden her true identity, disguising herself for safety as a boy among the men of this wretched place, even as her body rebelled more and more against the uncomfortable wraps and as the rough miners laughed at her modesty when she hid behind the willows whenever it came time to urinate. She had set aside her dignity. She had lost her savings. She had saved their lives and protected their secrets. And the boy repaid her with nothing but insults.

So she hit him. And he hit her back. And when she recovered from that strike she turned again and rained her fists upon him, a fury of blows that carried them both to the ground, where they scrambled and kicked and cursed and within minutes were surrounded by the half-naked men of the camp, who emerged from their bedrolls and quickly set about taking bets on the outcome of the fight.

"Two dollars, Sin-Feng! Sin-Feng, two dollars!"

"Give me two-to-one, I take John Leung!"

The guttural shouts of the men urged on the fighting, encouraging a punch to the groin and a bite on the ear. The long queues of the combatants swung wildly as they grappled, and their eyes teared from the clouds of fine dust billowing up from the ground.

It soon became apparent, though, that Sin-Feng's new size and strength gave him the advantage, and as Chi-Yen wore herself out with her attacks, he defended each strike with minimal effort until at last her arms hung from her sides, exhausted. He grabbed her by the shoulders and pinned her down, straddling her waist. Then he leaned forward and kissed her hard on the mouth.

This understandably changed the tone of the evening.

Some of the men in the surrounding crowd laughed uproariously while others began to argue that Sin-Feng's action implied submission, and that their own long-shot wagers should prevail.

Chi-Yen, though, was disgusted by the unexpected turn. Had Sin-Feng bloodied or broken her nose, she would have understood. She had thrown the first punch, after all. But this—this clumsy tenderness—she could not forgive. He was supposed to be on a mission. There was no room for distractions.

She spat in his face, sticking the gob of saliva just below his right eye.

"I thought you would be better than your master," she said. "But you are the same. You care only for your own pleasure and pride. You do not deserve the dragon."

As she spoke, her usual calm control of her own voice wavered, and the rising pitch of her words confirmed for the gathered crowd what a few had begun to suspect.

"John is not John!"

"John is not a boy!"

"John is a girl!"

There were indignant shouts of "Impostor!" and "Liar!" and then "Cheat!" and "Thief!" despite a complete lack of basis for these latter claims.

Sin-Feng stood, leaving Chi-Yen to rise to her elbows in the dirt as the men tightened the angry circle around them. She began to fear what might happen next. Several of the men had lit gas lamps by now, and in the fresh light she could see the boy's face still flushed with exertion and possibly embarrassment as he wiped the spittle from his cheek. But he too feared the mob's intentions. He raised his arms in protest as one man and then another moved in to deliver a kick to Chi-Yen's side.

"No!" he shouted. "No! Leave her alone."

But they pushed him away and pulled Chi-Yen to her feet.

"See what she has! See what she is hiding!" encouraged lanky Chu Siew Choh, whose wound Chi-Yen had cleaned and dressed just a week earlier when he had cut his palm on a broken camp stove.

Chin Hao Li, normally jolly and easy going, held her by the shoulders while angry Deng Tsan-Tai ripped open her shirt, revealing the strips of wool wrapped tightly around her chest. Those, too, he pulled away. Chi-Yen trembled as the night air found her young breasts, still slick with sweat from the fight.

"Nothing to see there," joked another in the crowd. "She might be a boy after all. Check for a teapot spout."

But as the men began to pull at the waistline of her pants, another shout rose up, louder and fiercer than all the rest:

"I demand silence! I am the great warrior Liu Kun!"

The men halted their fun as the monk stepped—or rather stumbled—forward, his soiled shirt askew. He reeked of alcohol and vomit, and none could remember the last time he had bathed.

"Tam Sin-Feng! You disturb my sleep with your games."

"I apologize, master."

Chi-Yen stood alone now, the men having released her, and Liu Kun looked her up and down.

"The whore has revealed her true nature at last," he said.

"She was attacked."

"As she deserves to be. A girl in a camp full of men gets what she came for."

Chi-Yen gathered her torn garments and held them together across her chest, shielding herself from the night's eyes. This was most definitely not what she had come for. This was what she had traveled so far to escape, and yet the same fate awaited her at every turn—men, unwashed men with their greasy hands grabbing at her, striking her, trying to own her. She thought of Xiao-Niao dead in the street, and the other girls at Old Mother's and Mei-Xing's, and Mei-Xing with her switch and Old Mother in a spreading pool of blood. This was her reality.

Perhaps Sin-Feng had spoken the truth. Perhaps the dragon had never intended to reveal itself to her; perhaps it had been nothing but a dream, a fever dream as she lay sick in the hold of the ship, and she had never opened the box or touched the egg. Perhaps the scar on her hand truly was nothing but a rope burn—

The scar. It hurt. She could feel the beating of her heart through her hand as the blood pulsed its way beneath the ring of hardened, fibrous tissue. She had not felt a pain like this since the *Round World*, and no pain at all since the original scabs had fallen away a few weeks after. She raised her arm into the moonlight to check that she was not bleeding once again, that the fighting had not reopened the wound after all this time.

She *had* seen the dragon.

She would not deny it.

She could not forget.

Liu Kun was shouting nearby, alternately boasting of his own many accomplishments and then berating Sin-Feng and the miners. He slurred his words and the through-line of his thoughts was lost to the whiskey. The men feared him—in his current state even more than when he was sober—but Chi-Yen only half listened, already growing beyond this place and this night.

The dragon was real, and through the dark it was calling to her.

Chapter Nine

Enter the Dragon

It took only a few moments for Chi-Yen to gather her belongings and tie them into a bundle that she could carry on her back. Having marched several hundred miles up the state during the past year, in and out of the mountains with each change of season, she had no reason to dread another night's walk. Her shoulders were tough and her legs strong.

Sin-Feng followed her into their tent to protest: She could not leave; It was not safe; She was but a girl. How would she live?

"I will be away from this camp," she replied. "I will be away from these people. Worry more about how you will survive without me."

Liu Kun, drawn by the commotion, stumbled through the canvas flap door, muttered something about a magical carp, and tripped hard forward, snoring even before his face hit the ground.

With nothing more than a disgusted glance, Chi-Yen stepped over the fallen warrior and forced her way past Sin-Feng and into the night. Most of the miners still milled about outside the tent, hoping for more of a show, but they made no move to approach as she turned from them and left the camp circle.

Sin-Feng, though, grabbed her by the arm.

"Leung Chi-Yen. Please come back. I need you."

"I do not need you." She twisted her shoulder to free herself and pushed away.

"But," he said, "but—"

As she moved onward she heard his feet shuffle and halt, and she felt the distance and darkness between them increase. She was ten steps ahead, twenty, thirty, disappearing into the shadows beneath the trees, unable to see her own feet.

"But how will I get our master into his bed?"

The voice was smaller and weaker than expected. She paused, holding back her fury, clenching her fists. Somewhere out there was a dragon, and all the boy could do was insult her and worry after the useless Liu Kun. Forget them, she told herself. She set off alone into the dark woods.

Her scar still hurt, but not with the same sharp pain as before—more of a dull, almost pleasurable ache. She massaged her hand as she stepped lightly through the forest. The night belonged to the animals—the raccoons and bears and lions and owls, the silent hunters—and she would respect their home by disturbing it as little as possible.

For an hour she traveled this way, maybe more. The darkness slowed her progress. More than once she dropped to her hands and knees to touch the ground, to make sure she had not strayed from the worn trail. The canopy of incense cedar and black oak overhead blocked much of the night sky, and after some time her other senses took over for the missing light. She heard a river to her left, sometimes distant and sometimes near, sometimes muffled by dense willows and twice amplified by short, steep falls. She could feel the brush of leaves against her cheek even before they touched her skin, allowing her to duck and avoid the occasional low branch that blocked her path. She smelled subtle shifts in the soft breeze, becoming aware of unseen gaps in the trees by nothing more than the increased density of pollen from nearby meadows.

And then something else—not a sight, not a sound, not a touch, not a smell—but an intuition that electrified her entire nervous system and froze her in place, too alert to move for a full five minutes.

At last she called out: "Who is there?" She attempted a threatening voice but she sounded like nothing so much as a frightened, squeaky girl.

No answer came.

"Who are you?"

Silence.

Which was the worse enemy? The one that spoke or the one that did not?

She realized with regret that she had left her mining tools at camp. The pick or even the shovel might have made a valuable weapon. In her mind she inventoried the contents of her pack: her bedroll, a change of clothing, cooking utensils, and a small amount of food. Perhaps she could blind an attacker with a handful of rice.

She lowered the bundle from her shoulder and knelt beside it on the ground. She untied the bindings and opened the flap, listening all the while for any unwelcome approach. The trail was clear for as far as she could see in either direction—although that was not far—and dense with brush on both sides. She felt through her gear and found a short, sharp blade used mostly for cutting vegetables.

When she looked up again, with her hand wrapped around the hilt of the knife, two large, unblinking eyes returned her gaze from the middle of the path ahead. They glowed as if lit from within. They held steady and unwavering as their surrounding silhouette shifted and changed shape, at one moment hugely imposing, the size of a grizzly, and then the next narrowing to something proportionally more slender, like a cougar.

But Chi-Yen knew the truth.

She stood and tried to speak but no words would come. Her mouth hung open, rendered useless by awe and wonder.

The eyes turned slightly down and Chi-Yen followed their direction to the knife in her own right hand. She dropped it immediately, embarrassed that she had thought to bring such a vulgar tool to an audience with a dragon.

As the blade hit the ground, the eyes blinked out—or no! They turned away as the entire shadow writhed itself off the trail and vanished into the brush.

"Wait!" Chi-Yen shouted. "Stop!"

Without a second thought she ran after it through a stand of snapped manzanita, the foliage still rattling from the creature's quick passage. But Chi-Yen's third hurried step snagged a limb or root and she tumbled forward, her palms hitting loamy soil that gave way beneath her as she slid and rolled twenty feet down a steep bank, collapsing at the end into a pile of river-carved boulders.

She recovered as quickly as she could, rising to test her scraped knees and possibly strained wrist. She had landed just short of a bank where the water was wide and shallow, the trees far apart. The unexpected moonlight was almost too bright at first, but as her eyes adjusted she saw the dragon standing halfway across the river, casually looking back.

Just a glimpse of the creature would have been enough to satisfy Chi-Yen for the rest of her life. It would have been all she had dreamed of, more than she could rightfully ask. But the dragon cocked its head curiously, patiently, as if posing to allow her all the time she needed. In the silvery, blue-gray light it was difficult to pick out colors, but she could see all the details of scale and ridge and filament that made up the magnificent beast.

It was perhaps eighteen feet from snout to tail tip, although at the withers, with all four clawed feet flat against the shallow river bottom, Chi-Yen could have draped her own arm across its back. Its thin, snakelike body waved rapidly side to side and up and down, sending both sharp and gentle pulses of S-curve along its length.

"Are you real?" she asked. "Am I awake?"

The beast gave no indication that it heard or understood. Its great horned head remained motionless, and those eyes—she was certain now that they glowed from within. At last it turned and leaped lightly, silently, to the far bank. It looked back just once, as if to make sure that the girl would follow, before disappearing into the forest.

Chi-Yen hurried across the river. She jumped from rock to rock and more than once lost her footing and slipped into the cold water. At the far bank she increased her speed, running as fast as she could back into the forest, heedless of the branches and limbs that slapped at her face and sides, desperate not to lose the trail of the creature.

"Wait!" she called again. "Dragon! Wait!"

The forest floor rose steeply here and she slipped and scrambled as she climbed, sometimes needing all four limbs to maintain momentum. But each time she thought she had lost the beast she caught a glimpse of its silvery tail breaking a trail ahead. Her lungs burned with effort against the cold air. Brief glimpses of sky through the canopy told her that sunrise was less than a few hours away.

She seemed to have been climbing forever when at last she collapsed, exhausted, near the shadow of a large granite outcrop, able to climb no more. As she turned to sit, though, she saw that at least part of the outcrop was not granite at all, but dragon—seated motionless upon its own tail, looking out over the vast expanse of valley. The river cut a distant ribbon of light through the trees far below.

"You do not make this easy," Chi-Yen said.

She slept that night in a shallow cave with the beast's cold-blooded coils wrapped around her, protecting her. She slept secure in the dragon's safekeeping, free of care for the first time in her life. She relaxed fully—something she had never done before, not with Old Mother, not with her own mother, not with the warrior monk, not during nights alone in the slums of Canton or San Francisco—and she released herself to dreams. She dreamed dragon dreams—dreams of flight and fire and ice and water, dreams of great births and deaths and the ends of the world.

In her dreams she became the dragon, or many dragons, and she flew through the earth and the sky and the sea. She witnessed armies rising up against her and others battling valiantly for her, the terrific power of their weapons churning her dragon blood. In her dreams she saw the past as it was and the future as it might and as it could be, and it frightened her and exhilarated her at the same time—monumental cities of metal and glass, monstrous machines ripping the land and water, challenging the sun, casting the world in shadow.

Chi-Yen dreamed all this and more and she dreamed until she woke, a circle of light from the cave entrance warming her bare foot, and she smiled as she drifted back to consciousness. She opened her eyes and saw standing above her the silhouette of the boy Sin-Feng.

"What are you doing?" she exclaimed. "Why are you here?" And then: "Do you see? Do you see now I spoke the truth?"

"I found your gear on the trail," he said. "I followed your path."

He dropped her bundle—her change of clothes and her bedroll, her cooking tools and knife and bag of rice.

"You slept here?" he asked.

"What—" She sat up and looked about, disoriented. "Where—"

She was alone except for Sin-Feng. There was no dragon.

"We thought you were dead," he said, then corrected himself: "They thought you were dead. I thought we should look."

"Thank you for your concern." The irony behind her words was lost on the boy. Had the dragon hidden itself at his approach? She stood and hurried past Sin-Feng into the light outside the cave entrance. She scanned the nearby tree line for any sign of the creature. A red-shouldered hawk called out its repeated *keeer-keeer-keeer*, then flushed over the valley. The sky was cloudless and clear. Chi-Yen's anger rose now, and it all focused on the boy.

"Do you know what you have done? Do you know how long I waited for this? And now you come along and ruin everything. You foolish, ignorant, flat-headed simpleton. The dragon brought me here! I was safe! I was happy!"

She shouted until she ran out of breath, her anger never diminishing. She had turned on the boy so that she yelled only inches from his face, jabbing his chest with her index finger. But oddly Sin-Feng did not cower from all this. In fact he did not notice it at all. He stood slack-jawed, staring at Chi-Yen with his eyes unnaturally wide and unblinking, not even hearing her words. When at last she paused to refill her lungs with air, he spoke.

"Your back," he said. "Look at your back. It is beautiful. Look at your sides."

He reached out to touch her. His voice was soft and hushed, almost reverential. He spoke as if he were in awe of what he was seeing, as if he were witnessing some wondrous, glorious thing. Chi-Yen knew that he liked her—the kiss had not been quite so unexpected, after all; it was an unfortunate and incontrovertible fact that men and boys were often drawn to the women who liked them least—but this was too much.

"Do not touch me. Never touch me again." She slapped his face. "I hate you. I despise you. You and the idiot Liu Kun. You can both—"

But the boy reached out to the arm that had struck him. He caressed the sleeve. He laughed joyfully. He fell to his knees and held his hands cupped together in the air to catch a gentle cascade of sparkling dust.

"Gold," he said. "You are covered in gold!"

And it was true. The layer of dust on her shirt and pants glittered and flashed as she turned to examine herself. She ran her fingers through her hair and shook her head. The flakes fell forward, catching on her eyebrows and lashes. The gold was everywhere, but especially heavy on her back and the backs of her legs.

"The cave," he said. "You slept in the cave."

He ran inside and Chi-Yen followed. They stopped at the entrance to let their eyes adjust. It was not deep—maybe ten feet at most—but it was tall enough to stand inside, with smoothly carved walls of rock and compressed soil. Thick tree roots, some recently severed, hung from above. The ground was soft and loose, and they sank an inch into the soil as they stood upon it. The boy scooped some into one hand and let it fall through his fingers. It was pure gold.

"We are rich!" Sin-Feng was ecstatic. "And look!" He picked up a fist-sized nugget that flashed even in the shadows. Countless more of these, many much larger, littered the space. "The emperor of China himself has never seen such treasure."

Chi-Yen felt uneasy. The gold was not theirs to take.

"Never steal from dragons," she said, half to herself, knowing the boy would never listen. But to her surprise, he became thoughtful. He set down the gold and surveyed the cave itself more closely, paying special attention to several great parallel scratch marks on the walls. He nodded.

"This place bears the signs," he said. His voice quavered. "Do you speak the truth? Have you seen it?"

"Do you believe me at last?"

"We must tell my master. He will know what to do."

His master. Chi-Yen had known it would come to this. The monk must find out eventually, but she had dreaded the day. The dragon had been her secret, her mission. As soon as Liu Kun learned the truth, all that would change. Whether it would change for better or worse, she could not say—although knowing Liu Kun as well as she did, better was unlikely.

Sin-Feng insisted. As much as Chi-Yen disliked the idea, she knew it was the right thing to do. Liu Kun was the expert. If anyone knew how to protect the dragon, he did; and the dragon deserved protection.

Still, she insisted on staying at the cave while the boy went to fetch the monk. Perhaps the dragon would return while he was gone. Chi-Yen could at least warn it that its true guardian would be a bitter, angry drunkard.

She waited all morning and into the afternoon. The sun rose high in the sky and baked the earth around the cave entrance. All day long she listened to raucous jays and woodpeckers in the surrounding forest. She watched a family of marmots going about their marmot business in an old rockslide. Clouds came and went, shadows shifted, and she grew famished. She hadn't eaten in days, but she refused to leave her position to search out water for cooking rice.

As the hours progressed she grew more nervous and worried. What if the dragon never returned? What if she had betrayed it by revealing its existence to Sin-Feng and Liu Kun? What if this were a test, and she was failing miserably?

At about three o'clock she heard a distant commotion rising up from the trail below. She heard branches snapping and metal clanking metal, and the sounds of many feet shuffling and stumbling, and voices—many voices, one rising above them all:

"I am Liu Kun! I am a mighty warrior! Drink your allegiance to me, and great fortune shall be ours!"

Someone smashed a bottle against a rock and a dozen men laughed, and Chi-Yen knew she had made the greatest mistake of her life.

Chapter Ten

Fools and Their Money

Liu Kun did not believe in stories for children, and neither should you. This was the real world and it was hard and ugly and cruel, and no dragon would swoop down to rescue you from your fate. Accept your humble place and serve your master gratefully. Open that sack; fill my pipe; fetch me my flask.

The prospect of immeasurable wealth had improved the monk's mood to the point that he was at least jovial in his cruelty, mocking Chi-Yen's fanciful tale with a smile. He told her that she was young and female and thus incapable of understanding the complexities of life. And so fantastic fables, Liu Kun explained, had been invented to guide her.

"We speak of handsome princes and dragons and talking monkeys and the spirits of ancestors," he said, "to free your girlish mind of its petty, greedy concerns. Learn from these stories but know that they never come true."

The miners banished Chi-Yen from the cave as they began their work. Shoveling gold was not suitable labor for a girl—never mind that she had proven herself by breaking rocks and dredging creek beds alongside them for more than a year.

Instead, they sent her down the mountain to fetch buckets of water from the river for cooking their afternoon meal. This was no easy task. Three times she made the steep half-hour climb, and by the end of each trip at least half the heavy load had sloshed and spilled onto the trail. By the time she had lugged up the third bucket, the miners had loaded all the gold into a pile of small sacks and were taking turns sitting upon it as they would a throne, laughing and grinning like feeble-minded kings.

Chi-Yen could not help but scowl.

"Watch yourself, girl," one of the men warned. "I will bend you over my knee if you even think of looking at my gold."

"How can you let this happen?" she asked Liu Kun. "You were a warrior of Seven Dragons temple. Now you rob your own masters."

"A man does the job he is called to do. When that job comes to an end, he is wise to seek the next great opportunity."

"You once believed."

"I was a fool."

With those words his mood darkened again—whether because of the memory or the alcohol, Chi-Yen could not say. Either way, she wished nothing more than to be far from this awful man.

"Do not look to the skies," Liu Kun advised. "There is nothing there for you. Or for me. Help Sin-Feng to collect wood for a fire. Prepare my meal."

Sin-Feng could not look at her as they gathered fallen kindling from the edge of the forest.

"I tried to convince him," the boy said. "But he tells me this gold is the result of natural geological processes, not the hoard of a mythical beast."

"Do not believe that."

"I wish for dragons. Truly I do. But this is no easy land. For a year we have eaten like beggars. With this fortune our men will repay their debts. Many will return home to invest in new opportunities for their families. This gold will help many, many people."

"It is not our gold to take."

"The decision has been made."

"I want no part of it."

"They do not intend to offer you a share."

And so that was that. Chi-Yen stood aside and watched with despair as Liu Kun sent two of his men to the nearby town of Weaverville to purchase a string of mules. This was a luxury the hard-working miners could never before have afforded, and was perhaps not the wisest investment. The mule seller, upon learning of the men's great good fortune, had immediately doubled his asking price, but no matter—they were rich beyond knowing. After a night in town they returned with half a dozen unsightly, flea-bitten animals and two brain-splitting hangovers.

Under the monk's direction the camp was emptied, the beasts of burden were loaded with gear and gold, and the troop began its proud procession down the mountain.

The men were not shy of their good fortune. They laughed together and boasted of the lives they would lead, of the many sons their wives would bear. They were eager to celebrate and ready to do so with great enthusiasm. They bragged as they passed strangers on the trail. Poor white men, Chinese, and Indian alike stepped aside to make room for the lumbering parade. Chi-Yen noted that a good number of the Americans carried guns. These men narrowed their eyes as they focused on the bulging sacks of gold. Several seemed to divert from their original course, curious at least if not yet menacing, just keeping an eye on things in case an opportunity arose.

Inevitably, it did.

As they reached the outskirts of Weaverville that afternoon they passed through a bustling frontier Chinatown—hub to the thousands of immigrants living and working in the surrounding Trinity Alps range. There were cabins and shops, a joss house, open air markets and gardens, all tended by men far from home who had come here seeking their own fortunes, or at least a chance at a better life. The mule train and miners brought with them a cloud of fine-grained dust rising up from their feet, coating the rough-timbered buildings and rough-visaged citizens.

"A drink!" Liu Kun demanded. "We must honor our luck with a drink!"

They tied the mules outside one of the more notorious local establishments and left Chi-Yen and Sin-Feng outside to guard them. Chi-Yen sat in the shade, leaning her back against the building. Sin-Feng paced outside the doorway, sneaking glances inside at his happy, boisterous master, watching the man down a first shot of liquor then a second then a third.

"We must prepare ourselves," he said to Chi-Yen. "This will not end well."

"It has already ended badly."

The voices inside grew louder and the crowd increased as locals joined the fun. Before long came the shakes, rattles, and snaps of a new game of fan-tan. The gambling had begun. Liu Kun stepped outside to liberate a sack of gold from one of the mules, then an hour later came back for another and then another again. As the day wore on and the sun dipped in the sky, the voices inside grew more and more raucous as the wealth was distributed and the drink continued to flow. Punches were thrown and bottles broken. Several fights spilled from the bar. Sheriff's deputies arrived on horseback but stayed in the street, content to watch the show and let the Chinese work out their own disputes. At last one voice rose above the rest.

"I am Liu Kun! I am a warrior of Seven Dragons!" The

words began as a shout and ended as a roar. "How dare you cheat me of my gold!"

"Brace yourself," Sin-Feng said.

He and Chi-Yen ducked beneath the front-facing window as it exploded from the inside. A constellation of glass fragments propelled by one three-legged wooden stool rained down upon them. The seat of the stool clipped Chi-Yen's forehead, sending her staggering, concussed. She stumbled mindless of direction, only trying not to fall, as a mass of arms and legs and torsos came roiling through the doorway. She saw the angry, blurry face of Liu Kun as he pushed her to the ground. She screamed in agony as a boot—perhaps Liu Kun's, perhaps some other man's—came down hard on her ankle, wrenching her left foot farther to the right than it had any business turning.

"Chi-Yen!" she heard Sin-Feng call out. But by that time there were two dozen men in the street striking one another with fists and bottles and broken bits of furniture.

She rose to her hands and knees and watched the dirt beneath her fade in and out of focus. Each time it came back she noted with curiosity an increasing pool of spattered red.

"Chi-Yen! Chi-Yen! Show me."

Sin-Feng looked into her eyes now, held her face in his hands, and brushed and pressed her forehead with a folded cloth from his pocket.

"My master is a difficult man."

In the chaos of dust and shouting it was difficult for Chi-Yen and Sin-Feng to spot their own companions within the crowd. Only Liu Kun stood out from the rest as he stumbled drunkenly through the brawl. Despite his condition, no man could put a hand to him. He ducked and leaped and struck back with furious vengeance against any who dared approach. Men staggered and fell in his wake even when Liu

Kun moved so quickly that his fists or feet could not be seen to make contact.

It had not taken long for a large crowd to gather at the outskirts of the fighting. In the beginning, depending upon their inclinations, Chinese and whites alike had sorted themselves by either running from the riot or into it. Others crowded the periphery to cheer and place bets. Many dollars rode upon the exploits of the wild monk at the center of it all. Eventually, though, Liu Kun grew bored and sat for a nap while others continued to battle around him. Afterward he let himself be carted off with a dozen others to spend the night in the warm town jail.

It had lasted for only twenty minutes. The final casualty count was eight concussions, two broken arms, numerous cuts and bruises, and the destruction of every chair in the saloon.

After all the excitement, people cleared out quickly. Evening was fast approaching and there was no point standing in a cold, empty street.

Chi-Yen teased the cloth from her scalp. The gash had begun to coagulate, but still the blood fell in slow drips past her eye and down her cheek. A dull throbbing engulfed her ankle. With Sin-Feng's help she tried to stand, but as she shifted some of her weight to her left leg a hard jet of pain shot from foot to knee. She gasped as half her support gave out beneath her.

"Can you walk?" Sin-Feng asked.

She could not. He lowered her to the ground.

"You can ride one of the mules," he said.

"The mules are gone."

From the railing to which they had been tied hung the short ends of their leads, cut clean with a sharp blade.

"No," Sin-Feng said in disbelief. "No!" He looked up the street and down, into the deepening shadows between buildings. "It was our duty to watch the mules. What will my master say when he discovers our failure?"

"Who cares about your master?" Chi-Yen painfully worked her foot free of its boot to reveal an ankle swollen to twice its normal size. A large, dark bruise had already appeared. She pressed it with a fingertip. It felt numb to the touch. "Those mules carried our blankets and gear and the last of our food. Think of that if you wish for something to fear."

The boy hung his head for a moment, his shoulders slumped. Chi-Yen wondered if the strain of it all had finally gotten to him. He seemed broken at last.

"I hate him," he said. "I hate them all. I never want to see them again."

"It makes no difference to me."

But then he brightened a bit with the beginnings of a hopeful new idea. "We can find the dragon. We will leave tonight. Just the two of us." His voice was strained, as if he could not quite bring himself to believe his own words. "We will dedicate a new temple."

"You forget I cannot walk."

"The mules must still be close by. I will find them. I will bring them back."

"The dragon wishes nothing to do with us."

He shook his head, brushing this off as a minor inconvenience. He rose up and stood taller than ever before.

"I am Sin-Feng," he announced. "I am a warrior of Seven Dragons. No dragon has roamed the earth in the last six hundred years, and yet my people have never wavered from our mission. I shall not waver now."

And with that he departed.

Chi-Yen waited as night fell. Temperatures had not dropped below freezing for several weeks, but without a blanket or even a coat there would be no comfortable sleep—if sleep came at all. And besides, the pain in her ankle and the worry over whether she would be able to walk in the morning made rest impossible.

At one point the saloon keeper came out to strike her across the back with his broom. "No sleep here!" he said. "Customers only. No drunks, no vagrants!"

He tried to sweep her from his stoop, hitting her again and again with the bundled straw. She was too tired to resist. She dragged herself through the cold dirt, clenching her teeth against the jolts from her useless leg, until the man at last relented and she stopped to sit again just ten feet from his doorway.

"This is what you get for fighting," he said. "Trying to steal from honest workers. Begging in the streets. We cross the ocean to work hard and make good business in this new land, but your kind gives Chinese a bad name."

Where was Sin-Feng? He had been away for more than an hour. It took less time than that to walk the length of this town. She was sure he had not found the gold. That would be long gone—the blankets and gear as well.

She trembled now, her arms clenched against her chest. Her teeth chattered. She wished for a hat, a fire, a bowl of rice. She remembered the comfort of the dragon's embrace, of sleeping within its coils. She remembered all she had gone through to get there—from the slums of Canton across the ocean to San Francisco to the hard life of the gold fields—and how quickly she had fallen again to this. Liu Kun slept peacefully in jail tonight, and for all she cared he could rot there for the rest of his life. But where was Sin-Feng? Had he found the thieves who had taken the mules? Had he attempted bravery and paid dearly for it? For the first time she felt she needed him more than he needed her. Where could he be?

Across the street stood a hardware store, closed for the night and unlit. Beside it was a barber shop, empty as well, and then a hotel catering to Chinese miners. She wondered if any of her own party were there, although she knew she would never be welcome among them. Even men whose injuries she had recently washed and dressed—Chu Siew Choh with his cut palm, Ho Gee Hee with two broken fingers—would turn blind eyes to her now, not even offering a dirty bandage to wrap her ankle.

She would never see the dragon again. She had failed it, she knew. It had asked nothing of her, had treated her only with kindness, and yet she had allowed Liu Kun and the others to invade its home and steal its treasure.

She deserved her fate. She deserved to die here cold and alone and forgotten.

She waited another hour for Sin-Feng and then another and another. The hotel porch light burned itself out, leaving the street unlit except for the starry night sky. There had been no customers at the saloon since the fight that afternoon, and the saloon keeper had either slipped out a back door or fallen asleep amidst the rubble of his furniture.

Chi-Yen tried again to stand. Her foot was numb now as long as she put no weight on it. She hopped into the street to retrieve a broken chair back, which she dismantled to fashion a short cane. With this she could hobble slowly and with a small degree less pain.

She did not call out for Sin-Feng, hoping not to draw attention to herself, but she paused often to listen. The night was still with no breeze to rustle the pines. She heard distant night birds and the rustling of rats or cats on a roof. The squeak of hinges and the slam of an outhouse door sounded nearby, followed by a cough and a long fart. There were snores from several directions and at least one man talking in his sleep.

At last she heard a snort from a mule. She followed the sound and located all six of the animals standing loose in a field behind the apothecary. How had Sin-Feng missed this?

The gold was gone along with most of the gear. The saddlebags had been dumped or slashed and scattered in the grass. In the debris she found an empty rice sack, several crude chopsticks, and a dented cooking pot. She pulled a soggy woolen bedroll from a low stand of manzanita and wrapped it around her shoulders for warmth. There was also a long-handled shovel—if only they had left her a saw blade she might have cut it down for a better walking stick. But best of all, she found a rusty knife blade. She used it to cut a burlap sack into narrow strips, which she then turned into a compression wrap for her swollen ankle. Then she laid down in the middle of the field to sleep.

She knew it was a mistake not to concern herself with Sin-Feng's whereabouts, but she was too tired. There would be time in the morning. In the morning she would find him and they would sell four of the mules. They would use the money to resupply themselves and they would leave this town behind—in the morning.

When she woke at sunrise, though, she rose to a circle of six riders on horseback looking down at her with guns drawn. Her head ached at its wound and deep within. Her neck and shoulders ached. Her leg ached. She was wet from sleeping under the dew-sogged blanket and probably from fever as well. The new sun blinded her eyes. She shut them and opened them again, squinting and taking in the world around her.

Yes, six guns—two long-barreled single-shot rifles and four short range Colt revolvers, each more than capable of doing her in, all aimed at her helpless form half tucked under the filthy bedroll.

"This the one?"

"Looks to be. Ain't no other Chinese filly within a hundred miles, I reckon."

"You sure that's a girl under all that dirt?"

The men spoke to one another as if she could not understand their words—or as if they did not care whether she could. One wore a star badge on his chest, but other than that they looked like most any other white American men she had seen in the mountains—calloused from the work, weather-burnt skin, never recently shaven. Their horses told her they had seen some success at one time or another; the fact that they had volunteered for a posse told her they were bored and dangerous. But they relaxed a bit and lowered their guns when she made no move to fight or run.

"You speakee Engrish, girl?" asked the deputy, not bothering to tip his hat.

She nodded.

"What do you call yourself?"

"Jane," Chi-Yen said, hesitating only a bit as she tried out this new version of her name. She could be John no more. "Jane Long."

"You a friend of the boy Tom?"

Tom? Tom? It took her a moment to process, and then she could not help but blurt, "Tam Sin-Feng! Have you found him? Is he all right?"

"Oh, he's all right, all right." The deputy smiled but not at Chi-Yen and not especially kindly. "String her up, boys," he said. "She's the one."

And with that a noose dropped around Chi-Yen's neck and pulled her to her feet.

Chapter Eleven

Wanted

As soon as Chi-Yen was upright the deputy and his posse ordered their horses forward. She clutched at the noose and hopped twice in a desperate attempt to follow, but the rope lost slack and yanked her from her feet. She fell hard, wrenching her shoulder on impact. The horses dragged her several paces through the field before coming to a halt.

"I can't walk," she said, coughing through a mouthful of earth. "My ankle."

The deputy dismounted and lifted her up and slung her over his saddle as if she were a sack of rice. It was the first time she had been on a horse and she wouldn't call it comfortable. Saddles were not meant to be mounted face down. The deputy took the reins and walked ahead of the animal, leading it through the streets of town. The other men rode alongside and behind.

"Don't fall off," one of them warned. "Gonna hurt."

They all laughed.

There was not a limb on her body that did not hurt already, but she pressed herself as tightly to the horse and saddle as she could. The empty stirrup swayed just out of reach with far too much space between it and the hard ground below. She smelled the musky, musty scent of the stables and watched as splashes of mud caked to the horse's legs flexed and fell with each step.

They stopped at a small, thick-walled log building, where the men tied their mounts to a rail at the front. The deputy pulled Chi-Yen down, stood her outside the open front door, and pushed her through. Again she fell, this time bracing herself but still scraping and bruising an elbow on the hard wooden floor.

"This the one they call Lung Chin?"

Chi-Yen looked up to see a man seated behind a desk near the door. He wore an elaborate blonde mustache and his hair was slick and combed tight to his head. She could see the impression his hat had made across his sunburned forehead. When he spoke her name it was almost unrecognizable, butchered as it was by the American-accented English.

"She claims the name Jane Long," the deputy said.

"Never can tell them Chinese apart," said one of the men behind her. "Buncha yella Injuns."

"But this one here's only half as ugly as the rest of her kind," said another.

"Least maybe once you scrape off the dirt."

The seated man—Chi-Yen saw by his badge that he was a sheriff—looked at her more closely. "She's got the blue eyes," he finally said. "Doubt there's another."

The deputy and all five members of his posse had crowded through the doorway now, towering over Chi-Yen. She felt several arms lift her from behind and heard the sound of a wooden chair scraping across the floor. She was deposited into it, facing the sheriff, and heavy metal chains were clamped round her wrists and to the arms of the chair.

"Can't move much," said the deputy. "Twisted ankle, looks like."

"That so, girl? You not about to turn tail?"

Chi-Yen shook her head.

"Because we can't put you in a cell just yet. Wouldn't be civilized what with all those savages. But I won't hesitate if I need to."

Two cells lined the entire rear wall, separated from one another and from the front half of the building only by closely spaced bars rising from floor to ceiling. It looked as if the jail was intended to hold only a dozen men comfortably, but that number and half again as many crowded the wooden bunks and floor.

"I will not run," she said. "I could not if I tried."

All the men in the cells were Chinese. She recognized many from yesterday's riot—they were tough, scarred men who looked to be familiar with the inside of a jail—along with most of her fellow miners. The few white men arrested at the fight must have been released with warnings. Liu Kun snored alone on one bunk—no man dared invade his space—and Sin-Feng squatted weeping in the center of the floor, hiding his face in shame.

The sheriff took a metal box from a desk drawer and from it removed a handful of dollar coins. He paid out several each to the posse members, who collected it with arms outstretched.

"Not bad for a half hour's work," he said. "You boys have a drink on me."

He slid a bottle across the desk and the men took turns drinking from it. One of them pulled a deck of cards from his pocket and they took seats around a small table to begin a game.

"Excuse me, sheriff?" Chi-Yen asked. "Have I committed a crime?"

"You tell me. What are you guilty of?"

"I only want to sell my mules and be on my way."

"Ain't gonna happen. Those mules were bought with gold from a claim that don't belong to you."

In the cell behind them Sin-Feng sobbed a little louder.

"But we have no gold," Chi-Yen explained. "Our gold was stolen from us."

"Lost, stolen, gambled away. Makes no difference to me long as I get my share."

The sheriff no longer bothered to look at her as he spoke. He put his feet up on his desk and closed his eyes, signaling an end to the short interview. The deputy pulled up a chair of his own opposite the sheriff's desk and sat to read a week-old San Francisco newspaper.

Chi-Yen took stock of her injuries. Her ankle still would not support her weight. There was blood or mud crusted in her hair. Her shoulder was sore but would recover. Her shirt was torn at the sleeves and her trousers at the knees. Her elbows and knees stung where the skin had scraped away. What she wanted more than anything else was a bath and something to eat, but she knew better than to abuse the sheriff's hospitality by asking for that.

"Sin-Feng," she whispered, "what happened?" She spoke Chinese to test her jailers, to see if they would object, but they did not see her as a threat.

Sin-Feng did not reply, though; he only doubled his weeping. Liu Kun had not moved but Chi-Yen suspected that the monk merely feigned sleep, as was his habit when avoiding responsibility.

"They plan to hang your friends," said a jailed man she did not recognize. "They will hang you as well."

"You lie. Why would they?"

"They say you stole gold from the sheriff's claim. He has a deed. A judge signed it this morning."

That is how the world works, Chi-Yen understood. The

men with power wait for poor men to earn a living, and then they steal it away.

"It is true," Sin-Feng said, speaking at last through his tears. "But it is worse than that." He pointed to the wall behind the sheriff's desk. "Can you read the English?"

Chi-Yen turned to look and immediately felt sick to her stomach. A number of notices printed on heavy parchment were tacked to the wall beside the door but one stood out from the others. In large bold print across the top was the word WANTED followed by three crude drawings. The pictures were simple caricatures of a Chinese man and two children, not recognizable as actual people. But the names LIU KUN, TAM SIN-FENG, and LEUNG CHI-YEN underlined each drawing, along with the corresponding Chinese characters. No crimes were described but there were separate rewards offered for each of them along with a bonus for the capture of all three together. The poster promised one hundred dollars for the leader Liu Kun, described as a habitual drunk and a fierce and eager fighter. The girl Chi-Yen, also worth one hundred dollars, was noted for her odd blue eyes, devious nature, and for possibly traveling in disguise as a boy. The simpleton Sin-Feng, whose bounty was half the other two, would at least have knowledge of their whereabouts if captured alone.

"He has found us."

Chi-Yen scanned the jail once more, this time with an eye for avenues of escape. The building walls were windowless and too thick. There would be no removing or squeezing through the bars. There were no keys in sight; they would be either in the sheriff's desk or his pocket. And then there were the seven armed men guarding the door—the sheriff, his deputy, and the five card players.

"What does your master say to this?" she asked Sin-Feng.

"He is Liu Kun. He is a warrior of Seven Dragons," the boy

replied. "He has not stirred from his rest except to lick his plate clean and demand a second serving."

Chi-Yen saw that Sin-Feng had not touched his own plate or his cup of water. Her stomach rumbled at the sight of the food but she dared not ask him to pass it through the bars. She expected someone would take the plate away before it reached her. For now she would have to eat vicariously through the boy—at least one of them should have some strength for a journey.

"Drink," she said. "Replace your tears. And eat your beans. You will need the energy."

"But what are we to do? They say the Englishman is nearby. He will torture us before this sheriff hangs us."

"Then let us be gone before he arrives."

She had spoken the truth when she told the sheriff she could not run away. Her ankle would not allow it. But she could not stay here, either. Malvenue had promised her that if they met again it would end badly. She believed that to be true and she feared him far more than any small-town peace officer.

"Sin-Feng," she said casually, almost as an afterthought, "the sheriff has not learned of our second strike, has he?"

"Our second strike?"

"This is no time for games. The rest of our gold. We must not let the sheriff or his men discover it."

Sin-Feng was puzzled by this—and not just puzzled, but nervous. Although Chi-Yen had spoken softly, and although she had spoken Chinese so that their jailers would not understand, several of the prisoners nearest to him overheard. The looks these men gave him now were less than welcome as they sidled closer.

"And Liu Kun as well. He must never know about the great fortune we have hidden from him."

At this mention of his name, the monk opened one eye and

aimed it at Chi-Yen. She pretended not to notice. Instead she switched to English—playing up her best British accent—and addressed the sheriff.

"Pardon me once again, sheriff, but I believe there has been something of a misunderstanding. My companions inform me that you have been in contact with my father."

"Wouldn't know about that," the sheriff replied, less than thrilled by this interruption of his nap. "Can't imagine even a Chinaman claimin' a dirty runt like you."

"My apologies, sir. I do not wish to mislead. While Mr. Basil Malvenue is my father—having known my mother well at the appropriate time and place—he has no intention of claiming me as his own."

That got the sheriff's attention. "The Englishman?" he asked, swinging his feet from desk to floor and turning his chair to face Chi-Yen. He was curious now. "No surprise you're a bastard, I suppose—or that he fathered one."

"I am his daughter but also his servant. My companions as well. At least that is what he calls us since it is against the law to own slaves in your country."

"In California that's true," the sheriff said.

"So you will set us free?"

"Why would I do that? You got your own uncivilized laws where you come from and it's none of my business 'cept to collect on the bounty. It'll be a happy time for your Englishman and for me when he finds you tied to that chair. Three less Chinese to worry about is a good day's work, I'd say."

A crash and clatter sounded from the prisoners' cell. Without turning to look, Chi-Yen guessed that a tin plate had been hurled against a wall.

"Easy in there," the deputy warned.

Chi-Yen could not make out the whispered Chinese words intended only for Sin-Feng, but from the boy's renewed sobs she could imagine what they were.

"Is Mr. Malvenue expected soon?" she asked.

"I left word at his hotel. He's in the field now. Could be back today, could be next week. Who knows?" But now the sheriff—along with his deputy—was distracted by the commotion in the cell. "What're they up to?" he asked Chi-Yen. "What're they jabberin' about?"

The voices were growing louder now and she heard several men hectoring Sin-Feng about his hidden treasure: *Where is it? How much? Tell us!*

"It is nothing," she said. "A minor disagreement."

"Don't sound like nothing."

The card players laid down their cards and turned their chairs for a better view of the show.

"No, no, no! Chi-Yen! Tell them!" The pitch of Sin-Feng's voice went higher as he became more and more agitated. "There is no more gold! It was taken from us!"

"They say they do not like the boy's manners," Chi-Yen said, pretending to translate for the sheriff. "But really, it is a Tong dispute. They are Young Wo. The boy is Ah You. Not a concern for white men."

"It's a concern when it's in my jail," the sheriff said. "Any of you savages spills any blood in there, you're cleaning it up—not me."

This was the attitude from the authorities toward Chinese-on-Chinese violence. Only a few years earlier and less than a mile from this jail, the Young Wo Company had defeated the Ah You in a battle of several hundred miners armed with pitchforks, scythes, and a few bayonetted muskets. It had begun as an argument over mining rights. Weaverville's city fathers had looked the other way, some even offering their services as paid consultants to the competing Chinese gangs. White miners had gambled on the outcome and even spurred on the fighting when the Chinese began to have second thoughts. In the end there had been dozens of casualties and a number of deaths, which local law enforcement refused to investigate.

"I doubt there will be blood," Chi-Yen said. "But if the boy is injured, I do worry my father will not pay you your full reward for our capture. He is very unhappy when his property is damaged."

Two of the prisoners grabbed Sin-Feng by the arms and held him up against a wall. Three more crowded round, ready to take their turns with punches to the gut. But before the first could strike, Liu Kun rose up from his bunk.

"Leave the boy," he said. "His gold belongs to me. If you want it, you must first defeat the great warrior Liu Kun!"

"This should be good," said one of the card players.

"Any bets on the first broken nose?"

The men holding Sin-Feng released the boy and were joined by several others—men from Liu Kun's own crew—who had long ago had enough of the monk. They figured the odds were finally in their favor. They charged. The momentum of all the men together knocked Liu Kun from his feet and back onto his empty bunk, which cracked and collapsed to the floor.

At first it was a dog pile of churning fists and knees with Liu Kun on his back somewhere underneath. There were grunts and shouts as he worked his way clear. One man rolled away and lay on the floor clutching his groin. Another retreated to a corner with a broken finger. Liu Kun took several blows to the face and suffered a wide cut beneath his left eye.

The sheriff sighed and stood from his desk. He patted his pockets and pulled out a ring of keys. "All you," he said, addressing his deputy and the posse. "Guns on the wall. Let's put this down. Try not to hurt the boy or the crazy drunk too bad—unless you have to."

The men hung up their guns and armed themselves with heavy wooden cudgels as the sheriff unlocked the cell door.

They grinned in anticipation of the fun they were about to have.

"Chi-Yen!" Sin-Feng shouted, as panicked as ever. "Chi-Yen! Do something!"

"I did," she said.

One advantage, Chi-Yen conceded, to being an undernourished Chinese girl—as opposed to a full-grown adult American male—was that her wrists were relatively slender. The manacles that bound her arms to the chair were rather loose. And so in the less than fifteen seconds that it took for Liu Kun to disarm and lay out the white men entering his cell, she was able to slip her bonds, rise from her chair—careful to keep her weight on her one good foot—and, with surprise on her side, knock the arm of the sheriff as it rose from his belt, pistol at the ready. This bought her only a second or two, but that was more than enough time for Liu Kun to spy the threat, cross the room, and neutralize it. The sheriff lay sprawled on the floor, half conscious and unaware of what had hit him. The only drawback to this fortunate turn was that Liu Kun grabbed Chi-Yen by the throat and lifted her six inches off the ground.

"My treasure," he growled. "Take me to it."

"Gladly," she croaked.

The six horses were still saddled and ready in front of the jail. Stealing horses was of course a hanging offense, but so, she imagined, was attacking a sheriff and imprisoning him in his own jail—at least as the code of criminal justice was applied to the coolie class.

"Can you ride?" Liu Kun asked.

"I will learn."

And so Liu Kun, Chi-Yen, and Sin-Feng mounted three of the horses and spurred them toward the end of town, leading the other horses away as well. They rode slowly at first to avoid attracting attention. Having been helped onto her saddle due to her injured ankle, Chi-Yen discovered too late that her feet could not reach the stirrups. She clung with one hand to the saddle horn and wrapped her knees and legs as tightly to the animal as she could. This only spurred it on, which caused her to tighten her grip even further. Soon enough her horse pulled ahead of Liu Kun's at a hard run.

The monk and the boy shook their reins and shouted out "heya" in imitation of the Western riders they had seen, racing after Chi-Yen and keeping close pace, not quite outrunning the thick dust clouds at their backs. They left the town of Weaverville behind.

There had not been much of a plan beyond this. Chi-Yen had been improvising all morning, taking things one step at a time just to free herself from jail. Now her new problem—aside from not getting thrown from the horse—would be to appease Liu Kun and put as much distance between herself and Malvenue as possible.

"They will hang us if they do not shoot us first," Sin-Feng said, twisting to look back over his shoulder at the empty road behind them. "They will shoot us and then they will hang us."

"Shut up, boy," Liu Kun commanded. "Take me to my gold."

"But there is no—"

"Shut up, boy," Chi-Yen said. "You heard your master."

They were on the same road they had taken into town just the day before, which was good. It would keep Liu Kun's suspicions down as long as they stayed on familiar ground. If they could make it as far as the river crossing beneath the dragon cave, Chi-Yen thought, then perhaps they could afford time for an argument and a tantrum from the mad monk—but not here, not so close to town.

Also, the horses remained a problem. They were remarkable animals, strong, young, and in fine condition—and recognizable by any who knew their true owners. The saddles alone were worth more than Chi-Yen had earned during a year in the gold fields, but they bore distinguishing brands that would make them difficult to sell. If not for her ankle, she would have set the beasts free and headed out on foot across country.

Chi-Yen relaxed her grip and her horse responded by slowing its pace. Liu Kun and Sin-Feng pulled up beside her so that they rode three abreast. She discovered a handful of dried venison in a satchel attached to her saddle. She ate it and felt her strength returning. Next she raised a leather water bag to her mouth but came away choking and coughing fumes.

"Mine," said Liu Kun.

He took the bag, sniffed it, and savored the whisky for the next two miles.

Sin-Feng dropped back from Liu Kun's right side and came up again on Chi-Yen's left. He uncorked a glass bottle filled with water and passed it to her. He gave her a small loaf of bread and a hunk of cheese that he found in his own saddlebags. For the first time all morning she allowed herself to relax. Then they rounded a narrow curve in the road and came face to face with seven riders headed in the opposite direction—chief among them the Englishman Basil Malvenue.

"Well, well," he said. "If it isn't the disgraceful Liu Kun and his two adorable moppets."

"Who is this man?" Liu Kun asked Sin-Feng, genuinely confused. Having never seen Malvenue while sober, the monk's memories were dim.

"He is the one who stole our dragon box," Sin-Feng replied.

"You owe me an egg," Malvenue said in his flawless Chinese.

"He intends to kill us all," warned Chi-Yen. "Do not trust him."

"Shut up, girl," Liu Kun commanded.

"Do not be so hard on poor Leung Chi-Yen. How many

times has she saved your life? Also, she speaks the truth. I do plan to kill you."

And with that, Malvenue pulled a rifle from its saddle scabbard and raised it toward Liu Kun's chest.

The shot that rang out, though, grazed the Englishman's own bicep, causing him to drop his weapon to the ground. For a moment everyone, Malvenue included, was too surprised to locate the source of the quick draw. Had the rifle misfired? Then Chi-Yen smelt the gunpowder wafting from the barrel of the sheriff's pistol in Sin-Feng's outstretched hand.

"Thief," she said, smiling at the boy. And then she took advantage of the brief confusion to shout "Heya!" and spur her horse forward. Sin-Feng and Liu Kun followed her lead. They forced their way through narrow gaps between the horses blocking their path as Malvenue's men struggled to decide whether to draw their guns or turn their mounts.

"After them," Malvenue shouted. "Kill two. Keep one alive. I don't care which. Ya!" He kicked his own stallion, which reared and turned and tore off in pursuit.

Once again Chi-Yen found herself in fear of being thrown from a speeding horse. But now there were other fears as well. She heard several rifle shots but dared not look back to see whether anyone had been hit. No unmounted horses passed her, which was a good sign. Neither did she hear any voices, either from her companions or her pursuers. It was all she could do to hold her reins and saddle horn; talking would have been one task too many.

Without her feet in the stirrups to allow her legs to act as supporting springs, each step of the horse tossed her into the air. Each next step slamming her back to the saddle. At least there was a rhythm to it. She leaned as far forward as she could to distribute the blows across more of her body. If she survived this, she knew, she would be sore for weeks. Despite hanging free beside the horse, her ankle hurt more now than ever. The saddle horn slammed her sternum. Her palms began to blister. Her head ached, her elbows ached, her shoulders ached, her knees ached.

It was almost calming, meditative, to focus on the pain. But there was no way she could keep this up, not ahead of experienced riders. She considered surrender. Her words were her most powerful weapon, after all. Perhaps they could save her again.

But no—Malvenue. He knew too much. He knew what he wanted. He knew more about the dragon, even, than she did. And so it was escape or die. Those were her options. She very much preferred the former.

And besides, in that catalog of aches and pains she had felt a glimmer of hope. What was it?

She ducked to avoid a series of overhanging oak limbs. In doing so she caught a glimpse of Liu Kun's horse running alongside her. She ducked again for a better look and spotted Sin-Feng not far back. The boy grimaced, all his focus on the road ahead. Malvenue followed another ten paces behind—and closing that gap—with his own men not far back.

But the pain—it was her hand, her left hand between the thumb and forefinger. The one spot on her body that had survived the last twenty-four hours unscathed now ached more than any other, and the pain was growing worse, calling more and more attention to itself.

She was not even sure she recognized the spot in the road. She had been there only once at night and then again yesterday morning, but yesterday she had been facing the opposite direction. She recognized no landmarks but the pain—and the pain she trusted.

Without thinking twice she reined the horse to the left, sending it through a gap in the trees. It leaped a fallen trunk and came down on the far side in thick duff. The horse lost its footing and stumbled, throwing Chi-Yen over its shoulder.

She was fortunate enough to land at a glance on a sloping hillside, tumbling and rolling as she slowed to a stop at the riverbed bottom.

She may have lost consciousness. She wasn't sure. But when she opened her eyes, up was down and down was up and her world was spinning. It took her a moment to understand that she was lying on her back in cold mud. She heard voices. People were shouting nearby but the sound faded in and out as her ears buzzed. She could not make out the words but the excitement was palpable. She reached up with one hand to caress the dragon's cheek as it leaned down toward her, nuzzling her hair with its long snout. She saw Sin-Feng and Liu Kun running towards her from upriver. Several mounted horsemen were chasing them down. Several more paced the hill above, looking for a route to the river. Malvenue called out orders to his men.

"No guns," he shouted. "Ropes only. We need it alive."

The dragon? She tried hard to focus her eyes, to stop the sky from spinning. Yes, the dragon. She felt calm and at peace and without a care. Liu Kun fell to his knees in the mud beside her and kowtowed to the beast, pressing his face so far into the mud that she was not sure he could breathe. Sin-Feng did the same. They held the pose until the dragon, with some subtle gesture seen only by the monk and the boy, signaled them to rise. It accepted their offers of service.

Chi-Yen tried to sit up but the dragon breathed gently on her face and she knew it was not yet her time.

A lasso glanced off the side of its head as a horseman behind it missed his first throw. The dragon looked back as if noticing these men for the first time and taking stock of the threat. It hissed and their horses trembled. Then it rose up on its four feet and ran alongside the river, its tail whipping side to side as it disappeared into the forest.

"After it," Malvenue shouted. "Don't let it get away."

In an instant he and all his men and their horses were gone. They would not return any time soon. The dragon would see to that. Chi-Yen was safe now. She could rest.

She heard gentle crying beside her. When she turned her head she was surprised to see that this time it was not the boy.

"No fool in all the world is a greater fool than I," said Liu Kun.

Chapter Twelve

The Searchers

For the next seven days the monk carried the girl on his back. They retreated through the mountains to the east—away from the dragon but also away from their enemies—traveling mostly at night, forging their own trail to avoid people whenever possible. Liu Kun marched without rest or complaint. In the mornings and evenings he foraged and hunted for food. He taught Sin-Feng to set snares for small game. During a midnight thunderstorm at Lewistown they snuck across a toll bridge over the roaring Trinity River. The boy stole food and supplies from a nearby trading post—not too much, no more than they could carry—and they disappeared again into the wilderness.

The jumbled mountain ranges were thick with trees—a mixed forest of fir, pine, oak, madrone, maple, and dogwood—which gave them cover as they followed deer trails across the slopes and over the crests. They climbed to a ridge and spotted the settlement of French Gulf in the distance. They turned away to the south and likewise swung wide around the town of Shasta, avoiding the diggings to the north where they might have been recognized.

By the end of the first week Chi-Yen's ankle had recovered enough so that she could walk on her own for short distances. Liu Kun, though, insisted on carrying her over the more difficult stretches. He carved a walking stick for her from a fallen oak limb. They forded cold streams and soaked their feet in pools beneath icy waterfalls.

Soon the mountains became shallower hills and then leveled to a wide plain. They hid themselves in a dense stand of willow trees on the bank of the Sacramento River and watched as four Indians drifted silently by in dugout canoes. One of them locked eyes with Chi-Yen. She could not imagine how he had spotted her through the thick vegetation. He held up a hand in silent greeting and she raised hers in return and the men glided away with the current.

Liu Kun excused himself. He asked Sin-Feng to watch over Chi-Yen while he scouted this more exposed, unfamiliar territory. They would travel again at night when he returned.

"Rest until then," he said.

"Do you trust him?" Sin-Feng asked once the monk had gone.

"I do. Do you?"

"Yes. Now. But can it last? Can he change from the man he was?"

"He saw what you saw."

Sin-Feng thought on this for a while—what he had seen. He had thought of nothing else for days. He had seen a dragon. A dragon had looked into his eyes. And yes, that was enough to change a man.

"But why is Liu Kun taking us into the east?"

"It is not safe where we were."

"The dragon went south."

"The dragon knows how to find us."

They slept without leaving the shelter of their natural bower. In the evening they woke to a soft splashing and looked to see Liu Kun rising up from the river, wet from head to toe, with a large rainbow trout writhing in his hands. They cleaned it and cooked it over a small fire.

"An Indian camp lies three miles south of us on this side of the river," Liu Kun told them. "They will ferry us across. We continue east from there. A military fort not far to the south has been abandoned, but patrols still enter the valley. Most of the people we encounter will be emigrants arriving from the east. They will be tired and happy. They will not trouble us."

It was as Liu Kun said. They followed the river in darkness until they reached a small band of Wintu people waiting on the bank. There were men, women, grandparents, and infants, but no more than two dozen in total. They were malnourished and fearful, whispering in the dark.

"Voices carry on the river," Liu Kun explained. "And not all ears are kind."

He communicated with the natives in hand signs and broken English. Liu Kun spoke the language much better than Chi-Yen had realized. He offered their hosts a rabbit he had snared that morning; in exchange he accepted a bundle of dried fish for their journey.

"These are bad days for their people," the monk later told Chi-Yen and Sin-Feng. "Not many years have passed since three of every four died from the white man's smallpox. Their people have been poisoned and shot. Their food now goes to feed a stranger's cattle and sheep. This is their end of days."

A few weeks later Liu Kun, Chi-Yen, and Sin-Feng descended the eastern slopes of the Sierra Nevada along with the melting snows. They dropped into the Black Rock desert, traveling against the current of incoming hordes of people and wagons and oxen and horses. From a distance they surveyed the banks of the Humboldt River, which swarmed with tired but hopeful European American families. Hundreds at a time bunched up there to rest and bathe before small groups broke off one by one for a final push into the new state of California and the future.

Chi-Yen's future lay elsewhere, however. In the coming years she would travel with her companions as far north as the Snake River in the Idaho territory, as far east as Salt Lake City, and as far south as the northern Mojave. Liu Kun declared the land in between—the entire Great Basin desert—as ideal country for their dragon. They looked for it always, climbing mountains and scanning the skies and staking out brackish watering holes in desolate no-man's-lands. They spent time with the Washoe and the Paiute, the Bannock and the Shoshone, and they heard the tales: A mysterious cave had appeared overnight in the shadows beneath Black Mountain; A thin coating of gold dust on a high boulder in the Antelope Range revealed faint, four-clawed footprints where a great unknown beast had perched; A strange new bird had been seen crossing the moon at night.

They avoided white men when they could. There was not much knowledge to be gained from other newcomers to this land, and they did not know what sort of rewards might have been placed upon their own heads. But from the natives they learned the secrets of survival in this strange, harsh desert. In the local dialects they were known first as the People Who Seek the Dragon and later—since Liu Kun insisted on using the Chinese word long for dragon—they became Followers of the Long Way.

They lived like their desert friends, hunting and foraging to survive, traveling great distances for food and stashing their stores beneath the earth. Summers were hot and dry while winters were bitter cold. They huddled together in rabbit skin capes as hard winds from the north blasted snow and hail at their low shelters. Liu Kun made himself a bow from a strip of juniper backed by deer sinew. He taught Sin-Feng and Chi-Yen to do the same.

Chi-Yen received several proposals of marriage from Shoshone warriors, with one offering four horses to Liu Kun in exchange for the girl.

"We are guardians of the earth," Liu Kun explained. "Our lives are not our own. We do not marry. We do not mate."

Sin-Feng was both relieved and distressed by those words.

They marked time by seasons rather than days or months or years. They turned away when they could from the ever-lengthening ribbons of dust in the near distance—the aerial tracks of settlers and soldiers—but more and more they felt the tensions rising between the warring parties who each claimed the land as their own. As new towns and forts and fences rose up, the natives were being cut off from the food and water sources they had relied upon for hundreds of years. There were rumors of massacres at Mud Lake and Cache Valley.

It was a harsh, difficult, and often monotonous life, brightened only by their mission and—for Chi-Yen, at least—one new passion.

During their second summer in the desert they discovered an abandoned Conestoga wagon sunk to its axles in a salt flat. It had been stripped of perishable goods and all else of use for a desert crossing, but left behind was a library of books. Chi-Yen was excited at first until she discovered that they were all written in German—a language she knew only well enough to recognize. The only other reading materials in the wagon were yellow strips of the New York *Tribune* newspaper used as insulation. She peeled away what she could and spent the next few days piecing together fragmented old shipping reports, political diatribes, and battlefield tales from a distant, bloody war in the southern states.

"The white men kill their own brothers," Liu Kun noted. "They are not the first to do so and they will not be the last."

But reading the words awakened something in Chi-Yen—a hunger for knowledge of the world beyond her desert borders, of lives beyond the life she lived. One morning she snared a jackrabbit and ventured alone to the trail of the migrant settlers, holding the animal up as the wagons passed, finally trading it for a book of poetry. Later she would trade that for a Bible, that for the tragedies of William Shakespeare, that for Cooper, for Austen, for Dante. She read jumbled, partial, disordered fragments of Dickens. She studied a dictionary of the English language. She followed Ahab to his last breath spitting after the white whale. A well-thumbed edition of *Frankenstein* fell apart beneath her fingers as she turned the pages. Whatever she could get her hands on, she read.

From a distance she made quite a sight, dressed in native rags, her hair grown long again and tied at her back, standing to the side of the deeply rutted path with a book in her hands. The travelers who saw her from afar expected some sort of Indian trickery and they fingered the stocks of their guns. But then closer came those eyes, those blue eyes, and the perfect English she spoke—

"There but for the grace of God," the women muttered, shielding their children and imagining some long-ago savage raiding party that had ended in murder and the kidnap of a good Christian wife. "Your mother?" they asked.

"Dead many years," Chi-Yen replied.

"I'm so sorry. Would you like . . . ?"

"Thank you. No. Just a book? To trade? I have *The House of the Seven Gables* by Nathaniel Hawthorne. It's quite good."

She would watch the wagons depart and wonder again what it would be like to live a normal life—men and women building their new homes and cities and empires, finding love and raising children, striving, succeeding, failing, striving again.

Of course she had Liu Kun and Sin-Feng. They had become like brothers to her—like family. But this was no *normal* family. She knew very well that this was not a normal life.

Not a day went by without new lessons from the monk—and not just lessons in hunting and survival, but in the history, science, and philosophy of dragons and their servants. He had wasted many years to alcohol and opium, but now he worked with unceasing effort and dedication to teach to Sin-Feng and Chi-Yen all that he knew. Liu Kun seemed to be working against a clock that only he could read, urgent to pass along his knowledge while he still had time. There was no arrogance in these lessons. He spoke humbly and welcomed questions and admitted ignorance when he lacked answers. He separated fact from conjecture. He understood that his old temple and masters were gone forever and it was up to the three of them to carry on in the New World with new rules, the first being this: The dragon had chosen Chi-Yen. There would be no questioning that fact, no second guessing—at least not by Liu Kun.

Chi-Yen, however … a year passed without seeing the dragon again, then two, three, four, five, six, seven. She was no longer a girl. Sin-Feng was no longer a boy. Liu Kun was no longer plump and drunk, but wiry and lined and his hair streaked with gray. For seven years he had held nothing back—neither of dragon lore nor of fists and feet as he taught Chi-Yen to fight, for there would be fighting in her future. He taught her to kill and maim from a distance and to do the same in close quarters, with and without weapons. He taught her to recognize the strengths and weaknesses of her foes and to play one against another. And he taught her to use her own weaknesses—the perceived size and powerlessness of a woman—to her advantage.

What he did not—what he could not—teach her was *why*. Why had the dragon chosen her of all people? What did it want from her in return? And why had it vanished from her life as suddenly as it had appeared? She began to wonder if perhaps—

"Can a dragon be killed?" she asked Liu Kun one day.

"No weapon made by man has ever defeated a dragon," the monk replied. "But why would a man wish to do such a thing? Dragons created the earth and the seas and the sky. The dragon is the wellspring of life. The dragon is to be revered, not destroyed."

"What about the Englishman?"

A sadness came across Liu Kun's face—not anger at all the destruction, displacement, and death brought about by their tormentor, but true sadness that the follies of men inevitably lead to such fate.

"The Englishman does not understand what he seeks," Liu Kun said at last. "He believes that if he captures the dragon, he can control it. But a dragon is owned by no man. A dragon cannot be contained."

"But can he hurt it? Is that not why there are monks and a dragon temple? To protect the dragons?"

"The answers to some questions are lost in time, Chi-Yen," the monk said. "I suspect the purpose of the dragon temple is less for the dragons than it is for the men. I cannot say whose folly is greater: Basil Malvenue's or ours. The dragons do well enough without men."

"And yet I fear they do less well *with* them."

Even so, there had been no sign of Basil Malvenue in all this time. Had he given up his pursuit? Had he been killed by the dragon? Or perhaps the dragon had led him far, far south into Mexican territory, leaving him to wander aimlessly among the hot sands, cactuses, and gila monsters. She had no way of knowing. All she had were her books, her two companions, and vast, lonely expanses of sage brush, salt brush, rabbit brush, and no brush at all.

The year 1868 marked Chi-Yen's birth year according to the twelve-year cycle of the Chinese zodiac. That made her twenty-four by Western measure—an unmarried old maid by the standards of the young Deseret brides now homesteading the lands around her. Chi-Yen did not wish for a husband for herself, but all the years of dust and sun and searching had become oppressive, and food was harder and harder to come by. The same difficulties that had beset the Indians were making it harder and harder for their small band to survive this desert banishment.

The distant American Civil War had ended, freeing even more migrants, former slaves, and soldiers to head to the western territories. Fortunes in gold and silver were being pulled from the earth every day in mountains to the west, east, north, and south. There was less and less unclaimed territory that they were free to roam, and they were less able to travel unnoticed in the increasingly partitioned land. Piñon forests had been felled for timber, taking away the staple pine nuts that had been a large part of their diets. Livestock had stripped the land of its fragile vegetation, and native game was being slaughtered for sport.

And then one day something new appeared on the horizon: a line of men with picks and shovels and hammers not digging into the earth, but smoothing it, building it up, turning it into a bed for wooden beams and iron track.

The men appeared first in the distant haze, imagined figures dancing through the desert's familiar watery mirage. Liu Kun and Chi-Yen and Sin-Feng held their place on a low rise through the day and watched as the men stitched their new road into the earth at the pace of a slow walk. It grew several miles directly toward them over the course of an afternoon.

As the sun shifted and the first of the men drew near, it

became clear that the laborers were Chinese—hundreds if not thousands stretching back beyond the rim of the earth. By late evening they were within shouting distance. Then voices sounded below as a cook's wagon halted and a portable kitchen was prepped. Rice was put on the boil and there were mushrooms and dried fish and as darkness fell the aroma spread through the dry air and rose up the knoll and the three gasped together at the rush of memories—not all of them good—brought on by this unexpected hint of their former lives.

Chi-Yen's mouth watered. She imagined every detail of the steaming pots below. In the glow of firelight, workers squatted beside the wagon and passed around a bottle—frontier whisky by the looks of it—as they waited for their meal.

The monk took a deep breath, held it briefly, and exhaled a sigh.

"In the beginning," he said, "the dragons created this world. We can never know what compelled them to do so, or why they abandoned their creation for so many centuries. But lately men have spread like a plague across the earth and the seas, making them their own. And now, here, they have conquered the last untamed wild. These railroads—these iron dragons of man's own making—have enchained the earth at last."

He opened a pack to survey their meager remaining rations. He tore a strip of dried rattlesnake meat into thirds and they ate it with sips of water from a shared leather flask.

"Never approach your enemies with an empty belly," he advised. "Let them see your strength, lest they play on your hunger."

Chapter Thirteen

The One-Armed Man

They found the man face down in the mud, or so they told him. He was lucky they had found him at all, they said. He was alive, he would survive, but how that was possible none could know. Stronger men had died from less.

He spent weeks, maybe more, at the mercy of some self-styled frontier physician. There were tinctures and salves and laudanum for the pain and his bandages were changed whenever the smell made the room unpleasant for visitors—not that any came other than that incompetent Weaverville sheriff again and the mistress of the house, who had taken a liking to his pocketbook.

He asked after the men who had ridden with him. Names and whereabouts unknown. Had they survived? No matter. He remembered what he had seen and he bore the scars to prove it.

When at last he was able, he requested paper and pen and a writing desk and chair. He started a letter, but training himself to write with his left hand was more difficult than he had anticipated. The characters trembled and jerked and sloped the wrong direction and smeared beneath his palm as it pushed across the page.

Sacramento, 23 June, 1861
My dear Lord Madden,
I beg forgiveness for the late gap in my correspondence. Your two most recent letters settled upon my night stand without a reply due to an unfortunate—albeit rather astonishing—turn of events.

Rather astonishing. That was an understatement. But understatement was his duty as an Englishman at the edge of empire—stiff upper lip and all that.

Let me simply say that what we have sought for so long is real. I have confirmed it with my own eyes—and not the inert artifact so long secreted by the abbots of the Dragon Temple, but the creature itself. It lives. It moves upon the earth. As proof I offer you the example of my missing right forearm, devoured by the beast's own ungodly mouth. The fiery heat contained therein cauterized the wound, otherwise I would not be here today struggling to put pen to these words. Suffice to say I have told no one of these events. None know the details of this encounter save the few who assisted me in the failed hunt—ruffians all, drunkards whose tales will not be believed.

And his own tales? Who would believe those? Likely not his lordship, the doddering toad.

Of our opponents in this matter I have revised my opinion. The boy Tam Sin-Feng remains a dullard and a fool, easily dealt with. Likewise the base addictions of the monk Liu Kun continue to be our best weapon against him. The strumpet Leung Chi-Yen, however, a mere sapling of a girl, is a greater threat to our mission than we knew. I now suspect it was she who deceitfully slipped the hen's egg into the box after the original had hatched. The beast seems to have formed a sort of bond with this child, as these creatures in the old accounts are wont to do.

How many years of his life had been invested in this quest? He had been a young man when he was granted that first innocuous assignment from the Company. An old cache of scrolls pulled from the wreckage of some Bengal palace needed translating. A curiosity, nothing more—fanciful stories. But there were grains of truth—consistencies with other tales from other places and other eras—that lodged in his memory, scratched at his thoughts, growing and hardening over time into less a pearl than an obsession.

He had visited libraries, temples, castles, tents, and bazaars from London to Bombay to Baghdad, from Calcutta to Tibet to Nanking. He met with scholars and princes and monks and merchants and pirates, all of them far more interested in his opium than in his silly questions about dragons.

"Dragons? Yes, certainly, sir, once there were dragons. And now if you would kindly land your ship near midnight at this point on the map, my men would be happy to replace half your cargo with generous quantities of tea and silver."

Business had been good, information less so. But over time he had pieced together the outlines of a history—the truth of a legend—and the compasses had all converged on one particular set of coordinates: Canton and the Seven Dragons Temple. That the city at that time had been closed to foreigners was only a minor obstacle. His interests there converged with those of his Company masters, and before long pressures were applied to officials of both governments and to traders on all sides, and the happy objective of war had been achieved.

Ah, the good old days.

Despite this latest setback, I am inclined to find favor with my new understanding of the girl. While it would have been a relatively simple matter for us to take possession of a single egg, a living dragon poses difficulties. However, a living dragon with loyalties to a child ... well, the implications are clear: Control Leung Chi-Yen, and we control the beast. I propose to do exactly that.

In fact, he proposed to take great pleasure in doing just such a thing, although it would be unseemly to confess as much to a sitting member of the House of Lords. The constitution of the ministers was a delicate thing. There was no cause to bother them with details. That is why men such as Malvenue were brought into the game. Someone's hands had to get dirty, and God forbid it would be a nobleman's.

In any case, Basil Malvenue very much looked forward to wrapping his remaining five fingers around Chi-Yen's delicate throat.

He thought back to the day he had last seen her. It had been a pleasant surprise, after all that searching, to meet the girl face to face there in the road. There had been such fear in her eyes. The chase had been nothing but fun, slowly closing the distance between their horses, watching her flop about on the saddle like a trout thrown to shore. He could have pulled his own stallion up beside her and reined her in, but he had let it play out. He let her dance on the line, waiting for her to tire or fall.

And then the world had changed.

The dragon was beautiful. How long had he stared at the creature? He, his men, the monk and the boy—they all watched in silence, in awe, in witness to this most fantastic of creatures. It was twenty feet or more from tip to tail, not yet fully grown, although its length was difficult to judge due to the constant side-to-side slithering even as it stood with feet planted in the river bottom. Its long, slender ears drew back, twitching as they listened to the arrangement of the men ahead and behind. Its eyes, though, its great black unblinking eyes, were only for the unconscious girl beneath it.

Was it about to devour her? That would be a sight. But no. It nuzzled her; it kissed her; it woke her from her slumber.

The dragon had the head of a horse and the antlers of a first-year stag. The scales dominant across its body were plain brown above although in changing light they shifted from pale wheat to tan to umber to the color of rich, fertile soil. Its belly shimmered like rainbow quartz. A flat plate of horn covering its forehead and part of its snout was said to be a source of great magic.

This was the beast that the monks called Earth or Clay or Sand—there were so many names, so many translations, so many stories. Malvenue had suspected as much back when he first studied the carvings on the egg box. But only after seeing the living animal with his own eyes could he know with certainty which of the seven dragons the monk Liu Kun had been assigned to protect—and what its hidden powers would be.

"No guns," he shouted down to one of his men, who had crossed the river and was moving into position behind the dragon. "Ropes only. We need it alive."

The monk and the boy ran splashing downstream and dropped to their knees, obsequious as any base peasants. The girl tried to rise. She smiled. A lasso was thrown and the chase was on.

You will appreciate the need for subtle diplomacy in the handling of these revised circumstances. If the Americans discover the great source of power residing within their borders, the game is up—our empire will fall, theirs will rise. There will be no stopping them, as there will be no helping us.

Could he make it any clearer? This is what they were playing at; this is what they risked. He had been on the front lines of this battle for much of his life, while those who benefited from his tough decisions grew soft and weak-willed. One little mutiny in the backwaters of India, a few sob stories from the missionary class about orphaned Chinese babies, and suddenly the beef-witted ministers back home—Lord Madden chief among them—were caving to the concerns of the common people. Armies were being withdrawn, trade charters nullified, loyal servants disavowed. It all turned his stomach.

He looked at the stump three inches past the bend of his elbow. He had sacrificed an arm for his country—and the arm only a small part of all he had given—and he would do so again if it would guarantee success. Meanwhile back in England, the homeland he had not seen in a dozen years, his lordship sipped tea from fine China cups and decided the fates of better men with no more care than a coin toss.

He set his pen aside. His left hand, unaccustomed to the grip, had begun to cramp. His missing wrist itched where he could no longer scratch. In his mind he flexed fingers he no longer had. He remembered how it had felt that night, looking up into the maw of the great beast as its jaw clamped down upon his forearm.

They had pursued it for weeks, following river courses up and down valleys, over hills and into mountain passes, always just out of reach, just one more bend in the path ahead. They learned to read the signs: light sprinklings of gold dust where it had rested, occasional flakes of diamond glitter, a peculiar aroma not unlike smelted ore. Sometimes they caught a glimpse through the trees as the beast paused, turning to look over its shoulder as if it were playing a game with them.

The Earth Dragon. The legends all agreed that it ate base metals for breakfast and shat out gold, diamonds, and rubies at lunch—but that was nothing. If Malvenue could harness this creature's powers he would be able to move mountains. He could create land where no land had been before and he could pull the soil out from under his enemies. What use was mere gold to a man able to stop the Earth in its tracks?

But the beast was in control of the chase. Each night they would camp and in the morning they would wake to find the dragon no further than it had been, and no closer. The dragon was leading them on this wild course, not at all afraid of them, but for what reason?

Malvenue had been so busy with the hunt that he had taken no time to consider until one evening it struck him all at once.

"That little bitch," he said.

"Eh? What's that?" His men, unaccustomed to hearing him speak at all except to issue orders, had been half asleep around the campfire.

"Leung Chi-Yen," Malvenue replied, more to himself than to them. "The girl. I need her."

"Don't we all? Can't remember the last time I had a piece."

The men laughed.

"We could stake her up right here. Take turns," said one. "They say with these Chinese you gotta go in sideways. But they say it's worth it."

Malvenue ignored the vulgarity. Words meant little to him except in the service of action. "The dragon protects its precious pet," he explained. "To catch the beast, we must first catch the girl. She owes me a debt and I intend to collect. She will pay dearly."

What happened next, though, remained hazy in memory. He had a vague recollection of sleeping beside the dwindling flames of the campfire, of pulling up his bedroll and closing his eyes. Whether he woke minutes or hours later, he could not say. There had been a snap, a muffled gasp, a scream. Which sounds came first, which had awakened him? There was a spray of blood—not yet his own, he was sure—and two men were running half-dressed toward the trees. At least one body twitched on the ground nearby. The horses reared up, broke free of their restraints, thundered their hooves.

Malvenue tried to sit but before he rose even halfway it was on him. He lifted his right arm to push it away and the arm was gone, severed in an instant. He felt no pain, not at first. He only cursed himself for being so ill-prepared, for not having a net ready to snare the dragon while it was so close. He looked into its near eye and saw nothing, just deep black emptiness, not even his own reflection. And then he collapsed.

They found him on the bank of the Sacramento river, not far from the city itself. They identified him from his papers, found his most recent address in Weaverville, and contacted the sheriff there, who made the long trip as part of his inquiry into the riot at his jail.

"We hung two Celestials over this already," the sheriff said, "as an example." He stood uninvited in the doorway of Malvenue's room, hat in his hands. The Englishman made him nervous, but his investigation had stalled and here was his last lead. "I'd very much like to get my hands on that monk you was looking for."

"I do wish I could be of service," Malvenue replied, not bothering to sit up in his bed, "but as you can see I'm half the man I was." He paused to raise his helpless palms—one real, one imagined. "Or more than half, I suppose, but I do seem to be suffering a certain lack of symmetry."

"He tore up my jail and now his trail's gone cold as a dead whore."

"A dead prince is just as cold. Is there no sign of his two young friends?"

"Not a thing. Nobody's seen 'em or nobody's talking. Hard to tell with these lying Chinese."

"It's a damn shame," Malvenue said, shaking his head and

clucking his tongue in an approximation of sympathy. "Some day these heathens might learn from their betters the benefits of civilization. But I fear that day is beyond our lifetimes."

Malvenue was happy to learn that the three had disappeared. That they were safe from the sheriff meant that they were still out there somewhere, a treasure just waiting to be snatched by a man who knew what he was doing—a man such as himself.

But first things first. For all his reassurances to Lord Madden, loose tongues were still a danger to the mission. He finished his convalescence and paid his debts to the doctor and the brothel madame—recovering from illness in a whorehouse had been expensive, but worth every penny—and then he went in search of the men who knew too much.

The first was easy. He found him several weeks later drunk in a Stockton bar, telling tales of the giant lizard that had killed his companions. Nobody was listening, which pleased Malvenue in that they did not believe a word, but displeased him in that his secret had already been told too many times.

"Mr. Malvenue, I … I …"

"Yes. You did."

That night as the man lay unconscious beside a rubbish heap in an alley, with a sky full of silent stars as the only witness, Malvenue choked his life away.

One month later he waylaid two more of his former employees as their horses were taking water from the Salinas River. They relayed news of other survivors, of their suspected whereabouts, and then Malvenue shot them both in the chests and watched them bleed out into the dirt.

That left two, and one of these he found on the grounds of the abandoned Spanish mission in San Miguel, dead by someone else's hand—convenient but less than satisfying. The final man he sliced deep through the throat, ear to ear, as he prayed for release in a stinking San Luis Obispo outhouse.

It had taken only four months to see five men dead. Malvenue was good at his job.

Still, if the trail to Chi-Yen had been cold before, it was nonexistent by the time he set out for her again. It was as if she and her companions had never existed. Malvenue visited congregations of Chinamen large and small throughout the state. He bribed merchants and foremen. He paid for spies in all the trade associations. He haunted opium dens and followed their supply lines from ship to hovel. Nothing.

Since the dragon had first tried to lure him south, Malvenue headed north, convinced it had been a diversion. He searched the new state of Oregon and into the Washington territory, finding little but dismal rain. He then turned south again all the way to the backwater of San Diego, where Indians and Mexicans wasted his time with ignorance and lies.

It was hard going for a one-armed man. The years took their toll. His skin darkened and toughened from long hours under the bare sun. His right shoulder slumped from lack of use while his left bulked up with the constant reining of his horse. He continued to write to Lord Madden and he continued to receive his annual pay—not because anyone but himself still believed in his project, but because his budget was a relative piss-drop in the Company ledgers. He suspected they would rather have him marching some distant wasteland than returning to England to sully their hallowed halls with his mismatched deformity.

He shifted his search into the Sonoran desert, where there were plenty of venomous reptiles but none that left trails of gold. He shot a few Apache in skirmishes that may or may not have been justified—he didn't give it much thought—and then he headed up into the Great Basin. The place was filthy with migrants and settlers and Mormons, but not a Chinese among them. While it was good country to hide a dragon, or at least this particular dirt-loving species, he needed the girl first if he wanted any hope of controlling it. And so he made his way back across the desert, up and over the Sierra Nevada, and down again into California.

In San Francisco he ransacked the home of an old Canton herbalist. The man had been a friend to the dragon people, had even expected a visit from Liu Kun years ago, but claimed the monk had never graced his doorway. He had heard rumors that Liu Kun was less than reliable. He knew nothing of the apprentice Sin-Feng and seemed surprised to hear mention of a girl. All this information was provided under great duress, and when Malvenue increased the pressure the old man volunteered to say whatever words he would like to hear—anything, anything, anything to stop the pain. But he knew nothing that would help in the search. In the end Malvenue wedged the old man's mouth open with an iron rod and stuffed his throat full with leaves and roots and liquids until he found the right combination of poisons to finish the job.

Then he sat in the wreckage of the apothecary and wondered: Was this the end? Was his quarry off the map? Were they nothing now but windswept dust and bone, or had they united with the dragon and found their escape, set up a new temple behind some inaccessible mystic cloud?

For the first time he experienced doubt. He had explored more of this American frontier than any grizzled trapper and he had seen not a single encouraging sign in three years. Quitting was not an option, but where could he go from here?

At about that time it happened that grand plans for the nation's first transcontinental railroad were at last being put into action. Thousands of laborers were needed for the hard work of grading and laying tracks from California into the Utah territory, where they would connect with another line of tracks approaching from the east. Construction officials had been skeptical at first about using Chinese workers until it was pointed out that the Chinese had already engineered their own Great Wall. They were certainly capable. And anyway, at wages of only thirty dollars per month, where were the white men willing to do the job?

This was as good an opportunity as any. Basil Malvenue offered his services to the Central Pacific Railroad Company as a man who knew both the terrain and the language of their new workers. He was granted the position of floating foreman and arbitrator all along the line of the project—a position that put him eye to eye with the greatest single gathering of Chinese in the western hemisphere. At least one of them, he was sure, had to know something.

He was a stern but solid master. The men worked hard around the clock in three eight-hour shifts every day—the labor never ceasing—and there was no need to force the issue with prod or whip. Daily they shoveled and blasted with black powder, carted the rubble by wagon and horse, leveled cuts and filled gaps. They pushed up, into, and through the mountains, boring near a dozen tunnels through solid rock. When winter snows built up, making work at higher elevations impossible, they shifted men further along the line until the ground was clear again.

Malvenue spurned beef and beans with his fellow supervisors, choosing instead to dine on rice with his underlings. He spoke in their native language and shared dried oysters, abalone, mushrooms, and bacon. He gambled with them often, winning to earn their respect and losing to earn their love. He made sure that their barrels of tea never ran empty during their work shifts and he personally delivered their wages each month.

It took a full five years of labor, from 1863 to 1868, for the rail to climb from Sacramento over the summit to Reno, Nevada. Only 130 miles of track had been laid, but that included a crest of the Donner Summit at 7,000 feet elevation. As much a trivial side project as this was next to Basil Malvenue's quest to capture a dragon, he remained proud of his Chinese workers. They were dedicated, loyal, and industrious. Their vices were moderate. They would make for good subjects when the rule of Britain expanded to cover every inch of the globe. And they were more than happy to share with him any information they might come across related to the whereabouts of his missing friends, the monk Liu Kun, his assistant Tam Sin-Feng, and the girl Leung Chi-Yen.

After the passage through the mountains, the push through the desert was some of the easiest work the men had faced. They made up for it by picking up the pace, adding new miles of track as quickly as supplies could be carted to the front of the line. They crossed forty miles of scorching desert then followed the Humboldt River, cutting their way through Palisade Canyon, building the railroad town of Humboldt Wells, and then pushing into more desert.

It was here early one evening that he woke to a clamor near the cook's wagon. It wasn't arguing or fighting—just voices raised in excitement. He listened but it was too distant to pick out the words. His own tent door parted and a man entered with a simple message.

"Forgive, Mister Malvenue. Your friend? The monk? Liu Kun? He is here."

Malvenue nodded, pulled on a pair of pants, and loaded his Colt Army revolver with powder, ball, and cap. He left his tent and walked through the dark toward the commotion. He saw the monk hunched over a bowl of rice, looking more like a tired, ragged old Indian than a proud dragon warrior. Still, Malvenue was cautious. He moved behind Liu Kun, staying in the dark outside the range of firelight. There was Sin-Feng and Chi-Yen as well, so much older now, blinded by their own hunger. Were they lovers, he wondered? Could he use that against her? A crowd of Chinamen surrounded the three, alternately staring and asking questions, which went mostly unanswered.

Malvenue waited for a gap in the crowd. He stepped a few feet to the left for a better angle. He aimed his Colt and fired once and Liu Kun lurched forward at the shoulder. He lifted the gun overhead and pulled back the hammer, clearing the cap to prevent a jam, then brought it down and fired again. Liu Kun fell. Once again Malvenue pulled back the hammer as he raised the weapon overhead. He stepped into the crowd and looked down at the fallen, motionless monk. He sighted down the barrel once more and fired a shot into the man's head, just to be sure.

Three more shots waited in their chambers. He turned the weapon to Chi-Yen and he smiled. In his mind he was composing his next letter:

Nevada desert, 15 Septr, 1868
Dear Lord Madden,
She is ours.
Yours most truly / B. Malvenue

Chapter Fourteen

Bad Company

Chi-Yen was tired. She had never felt so tired in her life. And there was a bed in the room—a true bed with a wooden frame, padded linen mattress, clean sheets, and fresh down pillows. She was exhausted and it was the most luxurious piece of furniture she had ever seen, and yet she refused to sleep on it. Instead, she curled up in a corner on the floor and stayed there with her eyes wide open, staring at the locked door.

Liu Kun was dead. She had heard the shots, had seen him fall, had seen the Englishman put the final bullet into his head. The monk had offered no resistance. He had not fought. Chi-Yen could not say with certainty that he had not seen it coming, that he had not allowed it to happen. Liu Kun had been tired as well.

And Sin-Feng—where was he? In the stunned seconds after Liu Kun's collapse, neither Sin-Feng nor Chi-Yen had moved. A crowd of men had grabbed them both by the arms and legs, bound them with ropes, lifted them to their feet, and neither had spoken a word. They had put her into a horse-drawn cart and driven her miles to this place, and the last words she heard had belonged to the murderer Basil Malvenue.

"Do not harm the girl," he commanded. "Do not hurt her, do not threaten to hurt her. Treat her well, feed her, let her bathe. As for the other one—I don't care. Only keep him alive."

She had eaten their food but—still bearing in mind her mother's old advice—she had refused the soap, warm water, and soft towel they offered her. She did not recognize the woman who looked back at her from the mirror; she had not seen herself so clearly in more than six years. She traced the faint line on her cheek from Mei-Xing's lash. It was almost invisible now unless you knew to look for it, but it would always be with her. She combed her hair with her fingers and tied it back using the same filthy strap of antelope leather she had relied on for the past eight months.

When the time came, she could smash the mirror and use a shard as a blade. But not yet.

She curled herself up in a corner and tried to sleep, ignoring the soft feather bed and clean white sheets in the center of the room. That was a gift too far from a man she planned to kill at the first opportunity. His death would make the world a better place even if it were the last thing she did.

As for Malvenue, though, she saw and heard nothing. She passed four nights and three days in solitary confinement. Her door opened only three times each day for a young serving boy—about six years old, Chinese or at least partly so—to deposit a tray of food and to take away the previous meal. At first he would not answer when she questioned him. He kept his gaze low. He turned away as if afraid of her or—more likely—afraid of the man who gave him his orders.

"Where is my friend, Sin-Feng?" she asked.

Nothing.

"Where is my enemy, Basil Malvenue?" She repeated the question in both Chinese and English.

Nothing.

"What is that banging sound?"

Silence—except not silence, for the banging continued. Banging, digging, sawing, footsteps on the roof above, hammering against the walls outside. She could not have slept even if she had wanted to. It continued without pause twenty-four hours a day. There was no window in her room, but bright artificial light for the workers shone at night through a square ventilation hole high in the wall. The vent was low enough that she could jump and reach it, hang from it, and pull herself up to look, but through the louvered slats there was no clear view of the activities outside and no way to squeeze herself free.

She knew this was the town they called Humboldt Wells. She had seen the silhouette of the prominent water tower on the way in. Much of this place was still under construction to accommodate the influx of thousands of new railroad workers, but that could not explain the constant hammering just outside her attic prison. Were they building a gallows for hanging? A rack for torture? A coffin for her body?

It could have been any or all.

She concentrated on the sounds to learn what she could of her surroundings. Two Chinese men stood in the hallway outside her room at all times. They knew nothing and were curious about nothing; when they spoke, they spoke of food and little else. She guessed by the weight of their footsteps that they were strong, as men must be who haul rocks and iron beams for a living. Still, with her years of training as a dragon warrior, she doubted they could match her if she took them by surprise. Once outside the building, though, she would face an army of men carrying hammers, saws, and probably guns. She might be able to slip past them, but then what? Even if she could outrun every last one, she could not outrun the horses stabled less than a block away. No, if she were to escape she would have to do so with subterfuge, under cover of darkness, with at least a fifteen-minute lead to allow her to steal a horse of her own. And then? She would be back in the desert, alone, hunted, hungry, friendless.

Better to stay put, to kill Malvenue in this very room as soon as the opportunity presented itself. Sin-Feng, wherever he was, would then be free to continue the mission without her. She was ready to make that sacrifice.

The boy came again with rice and tea. This time he watched her eat. She saw where his pants had been mended, mended, and mended again, and how the legs had been hemmed but were still too long for him. Men's pants handed down to a child.

"What is your name?" she asked.

"Louis."

"Does your father work on the railroad?"

He said nothing.

"Ah. Your mother provides comfort to the workers."

He nodded.

"My mother did the same. For the fishermen."

The rice was good. She had been malnourished for so long, but she could feel the energy returning to her limbs.

"Be strong," she told the boy. "The world is difficult, but there is magic in it."

At last on the morning of the fourth day she woke to silence. The work outside had stopped. A knock sounded on her door, followed by a man's voice speaking crisp, proper English. "Miss Leung Chi-Yen? May I enter?"

As if she could have forbidden it.

In keeping with the typical English reluctance to admit discomfort, he was dressed in a dark wool suit and topcoat despite the lingering summer heat. His black silk vest was buttoned top to bottom, accented by a drape of gold chain for a hidden pocket watch. He removed a black bowler hat from his head as he stepped into the room, palming its crown with his left hand—his only hand, Chi-Yen realized with a start—and he bowed to her.

"Forgive me for not calling sooner," Malvenue said. "I do hope the accommodations have been to your satisfaction."

His face was leaner and more deeply lined than it had been. His neatly trimmed beard had gone to gray in the seven years since she had last seen him. And what game was he playing with his courtesies and politeness? She knew what was in his heart—a demon, a killer—and this pretense only put her more on guard.

She had been squatting in the corner. Now she stood, Malvenue between her and the door. He closed it and looked around the spare room. For lack of a better location, he placed his hat upon the untouched bed.

For more than a minute, neither spoke. They studied one another, reading the hidden signs, taking in the details of the last seven years, conversing with their eyes alone.

He was not wearing a gun and there was little in the room that could be used as a weapon unless she were to drive his head into the papered walls or timbered bed frame, or if she were to shatter that mirror. The chain of his pocket watch was too fragile for use as a garrote. The watch itself could gouge out an eye if she could get hold of it. But no matter how she did it, to kill him now she would have to use her hands. She had heard at least four men standing just outside the door, though, ready to intervene at the first sign of a struggle.

"We have much in common, you and I," he said. "Show me."

She would not.

"I won't bite," he teased. Then, seriously and sincerely, deeply curious: "Please. Show me yours and I'll show you mine."

She knew what he wanted, and in truth she was as curious

as he. She raised her left arm. With her permission, he took her hand in his own. He bent to her, leaned close, turned her hand palm up, then palm down, then palm up again.

"First blood," he whispered.

The ring of scar tissue was no longer as prominent as on the day she received the dragon's kiss, but the mark was there for all who could read it. The track of the triangular puncture marks—hardened now with glossy, pale skin—formed a heart-shaped tattoo across the webbing between her forefinger and thumb.

It sent a tremor through her body when Malvenue traced the brand with his fingertip. He noticed. He smiled.

He released her hand then removed his topcoat and laid it upon the bed. His jacket followed. Then he unbuttoned and unfolded the sleeve that contained his own severed appendage. He pushed back the fabric and held out the withered arm to Chi-Yen. It was a pale, feeble thing, the skin slack around atrophied muscle and bone. She was both disgusted and fascinated.

May I?

He nodded.

She took hold of the stub and touched the faint zigzag line that marked the meeting place of the dragon's upper and lower jaws. She could see the shape of the teeth and their size, she could almost picture the moment of the bite. Malvenue seemed to be doing the same—his eyes had closed and he trembled, as she had. Not wanting to give him the pleasure, she dropped her hands and stepped back. Malvenue exhaled and kept his eyes closed for a moment, composing himself.

"We have much in common," he repeated.

"We have nothing in common."

"We share the mark. We both seek the dragon."

"You seek it. I protect it."

"I seek to protect it as well. Every day this world grows more dangerous. You know it. You cannot do this alone."

"I had companions until you murdered one and imprisoned the other."

"Liu Kun was a drunken scoundrel. He deserved his fate. And the boy is weak in the head. I could hire ten better men tomorrow."

Chi-Yen said nothing. The Englishman did not know—he did not know what Liu Kun had become, how the dragon had changed him, restored him. He did not know how Tam Sin-Feng had trained his own mind and body every day to become a warrior almost as skilled as his master. And there was no reason to tell, no reason to argue—let it be a surprise.

"The dragon is of no use to you," she said. "It does no man's bidding."

"And no woman's?"

"No."

"Have you never asked?"

"Asked what?"

"You disappoint me. For all these years I imagined you as my great nemesis—as a girl, a woman now, perhaps the equal of a great man—and yet you remain as ignorant as the day we met."

As he stared at her his expression soured to real disgust.

"Look at you, dressed in those filthy rags. Stinking like a feral squaw. Crawling through the desert like a savage, feasting on grubs while the world burns. That dragon would shit gold for you, and yet you live your life like a coward, hidden away in some spider hole with your worthless friends. Empires are colliding and armies are crashing. Entire nations are dying. New machines are rising up from the earth to choke the sky. The power to ease this pain lies within your grasp, and yet you do nothing."

Chi-Yen did not know what to say to this. She was just a

girl—a woman now, it's true—and all she wanted was to live a normal life.

"You never asked," he said contemptuously. "It is time I asked in your place."

He called for his men and in an instant they were in the room—four of them, and stronger than Chi-Yen had imagined. She tried to fight back but they had her pinned, each with their full weight on an arm or a leg. Malvenue tied each limb to a corner of the bed so that she lay spread-eagled with no slack. He was rather expert at the task for a man with a missing arm. The ropes dug into her skin at the ankles and wrist.

"The dragon will protect me," she told him.

"I know it. I'm counting on it."

Young Louis then wheeled in a portable brazier glowing with hot coals. He leaned several branding rods against a wall and turned to leave without a word, without looking at Chi-Yen on the bed.

"My knife, boy," Malvenue said.

Louis stopped and turned back. He unclipped a sheathed knife from his belt and handed it over. This time he dared a helpless glance in Chi-Yen's direction. She could see that he was about to burst into tears. She could only smile back at him. Be brave, she thought. You're about to see something amazing.

She hoped it was true.

Malvenue dismissed the men and the boy. He told them to wait downstairs. He would call if he needed them.

"And if you value your arms," he added, raising his right half, "stay inside the building."

He closed the door, picked up the long metal rods one at a time, and pushed their ends into the glowing coals.

"I am the ugly instrument of a noble cause," he said. "I am a necessary evil."

"You are a killer."

"I bring order to a cruel, chaotic world. Sacrifices must be made."

"Like you sacrificed Xiao-Niao?"

"I did not kill Xiao-Niao," he said, flashing brief, unwished-for anger. "I adored Xiao-Niao. Xiao-Niao put herself in *your* crossfire. If not for you—" He turned away, back to the coals, composing himself again. "I do the things I do in the sincere hope that my actions will bring about a world that has no use for men like me. I do appreciate the irony."

He lifted one of the rods by its handle, examined the heated tip, and returned it to the coals.

"This dragon will be mine. I've studied the texts. These creatures have been captured before, and I know how to do it again. The traps are rather ingenious. Those were some clever little engineers, those ancestors of Liu Kun."

He was just biding his time, Chi-Yen could see, rambling on until the iron was hot enough to sear her flesh. Where would he stick it first?

"What do you mean?" she asked, just hoping to delay the pain.

"You think seven magical dragons just volunteered themselves as servants to a bunch of yokel monks? No, they were captured one beast at a time. It took centuries. But I've got to hand it to them, they got the job done. We are only just getting started."

"We? Who is we?"

"Like I said, I'm just one man working for the good of many. And there are others like me, out there right now, tracking those other eggs. We are a company. *The* Company, we call it."

Her head was spinning. This was news. This was something she had to share with Sin-Feng, with Liu Kun if only he were alive, with … no one else was left.

Malvenue kept talking, relieved after all these years to

have someone he could tell his troubles to—someone who wouldn't be around much longer to spill the secrets.

"I have to say, your dragon would not have been my first choice. Not that I'm complaining, considering how well things are turning out, but Earth? What's a fortress full of gold compared with the power to extend life or hasten death? Now there's a dragon for you. Or Sky? To soar high above the tallest mountain and have dominion over all you see? Well—"

He pulled the iron from the coals and this time the brand was glowing red.

"Here we are. Now, I don't know how long this will take. I don't know whether I'll have to do this once, twice, or a dozen times before your savior finds its way into my trap. But we have to start somewhere."

He looked her up and down, examined the length of her, picking his spot. He had to set the brand down one more time to draw his Bowie knife, exposing the long curved edge. He pressed the back of the blade against her belly, cutting side up, and ran it up over her chest, between her breasts to the base of her throat, slicing her deer hide vest in half. With the point of the blade he pushed the severed sides to her shoulders, leaving her naked from the waist up. He sheathed the knife once again, picked up the hot brand, and waved it just above her torso to let her feel the heat.

"You might want to close your eyes," he said.

The pain was unbearable. She screamed so loudly that it must have pierced the walls and echoed through the town. She writhed on the bed with all her strength, trying to break free of the bonds. And then came the strange realization that the pain was not on her belly at all, but on her hand. The brand had never touched her. It had fallen to the floor, where she could smell it smoldering against the wood.

Chi-Yen opened her eyes and turned her head and saw Malvenue backed against the far wall, screaming as loudly as she had, tears streaming from his eyes as he grasped at the empty air before him—at the space where his missing arm would have been. He dropped to his knees and leaned forward. He seemed to be gagging through his cries, but when he looked up at her she saw the smile on his face and knew it was laughter.

"It's here," he said. "It's here."

The building shook. There was a rumble and crash downstairs. Chi-Yen expected to hear the footsteps of Malvenue's men retreating up to join him, but they must have been braver than she thought—or dead already.

The pain in her hand had not subsided. It was the scar telling her not to worry, that help was on the way. But still she worried. It was a trap. The building shook again. Was the dragon caught in Malvenue's web?

She could hear panicked shouting from outside. The wind was picking up and men were running for cover. She heard the words repeated: *dragon, dragon, dragon. Long, long, long.*

Malvenue rose to his feet, grimacing, and stepped toward her, but then they both screamed together again as the pain in their scars sharpened. She clenched her teeth and he fell to his knees. Her vision went black. She could still hear the screech of the timbers in the floors and walls as they rubbed against one another, but she saw nothing through her blinding pain. She felt the vibrations of her bed as the floorboards rattled.

The sound of sand blasting against the walls outside was non-stop and deafening, and within it came a crack and a roar that she could only identify as half the building collapsing into the street.

The wave of pain relaxed and she opened her eyes just in time to see the boy Louis leaning over her, Malvenue's knife in his hand. He first sliced the ropes holding her arms, then those around her ankles.

"No!" Malvenue shouted. He stood and shoved the boy hard toward the wall. The concussion knocked the knife from the boy's hand and it flew through the air, landing somewhere beside the bed. Malvenue turned to Chi-Yen. "Stay where you are."

She wasn't moving yet—the blood was still returning to her hands and feet—but she was finished obeying this evil man. She sat up just as another wave of pain hit her hand, just as Malvenue doubled over once more and fell to the floor. Then yet another gust of storm hit the building like an earthquake, throwing her from the bed. The brazier fell and spilled, scattering hot coals across the room. Malvenue's coat began to smolder and burn.

They both lay side by side, waiting for the pain to subside, waiting for the wave to wash over them, waiting until they could move again. When they were able, each grasped for the nearest weapon. Chi-Yen came up with the knife and Malvenue screamed as he wrapped his fingers around the still-hot end of the branding rod.

Her years of training, her fighting instinct, put her on him in an instant. She pushed the blade against his throat. But the look of sheer, tear-stained bliss in his eyes as he stared past her—no longer seeing her—caused her to hesitate. She looked up. The entire ceiling was gone along with the roof above it. The open sky was a twisting funnel of dust and sand, impenetrable save for the eye, and in the eye was the face of a dragon.

The creature was too large to fit into the room—its back half remained hidden within the storm—but it lowered its head into the space, its forelegs hovering a foot above the floor. It nuzzled Chi-Yen and all the pain and anguish was gone. She dropped the knife from her hand and it stuck the floor inches from the Englishman's head.

Chi-Yen placed an arm over the dragon's shoulders then

swung a leg across to seat herself bareback on the great beast. In that moment the entire building collapsed, its four walls falling away like petals from a flower. The floor dropped beneath them, breaking Malvenue's revery. He reached up with his one arm, grasping for the dragon, mouthing a noiseless "No!" as he fell.

As for the boy, Louis, he clung to the rubble and watched with great delight as the girl who had promised magic disappeared into the sky.

Chapter Fifteen

The Lair

They shot up, up, up into the air, out of the sand storm to a height of several hundred feet above the town. Chi-Yen clung tightly to the dragon's neck at first, but relaxed her grip as she realized she felt no fear. The ride was smoother than any horse, with no bucking or jarring, and the dragon's scales were softer than she would have imagined, providing a seat more supple and comfortable than a saddle.

This is what birds see, she thought. The snow capped Ruby Mountains and the East Humboldt Range, which began their combined hundred-mile southward march just west of town, seemed even closer from this vantage, and taller and longer. Beyond them she saw the stretch of the Humboldt River watershed, the river itself a flash of silver ribbon in the morning sun.

Directly below, her former prison was still in the process of collapsing, exhalations of dust and debris coughing up and thickening the air with each falling timber. The rest of the town was untouched by the chaos, but the streets were filled with men—and a few women—drawn out of doors by the noise. They stood now, mouths agape, staring at the great beast twirling in the sky above.

Chi-Yen felt a sudden impulse to wave at them. She was carefree and untouchable atop an animal with the powers of a god—an animal that flew without wings, that summoned storms from the earth, that plucked her to safety always at the moment of her greatest need.

A pair of red-tailed hawks circled on an updraft nearby. She could see the detail of feather flexing against breeze; she could have reached out to touch them. The smell of bread rose up from below and she wondered if the baker knew how much aroma he had lost to the sky. In the near distance a railroad engine steamed along the straight line of track bisecting the plain, lugging supplies of timber and rail from California. All her senses felt like a dream.

And then they dove swiftly, steeply to the street, and with a swoop just before impact they were running along the ground—or perhaps gliding just above it. The dragon accelerated block by block. One by one a few townspeople tried to give chase, but always too late and too far behind. When Chi-Yen looked back she saw them gathered together, jabbering and gesturing, excited beyond belief.

Had they seen what they saw? They had. Hoo-whee!

Chi-Yen did not know such speed was possible. The dragon moved faster than a horse, faster than a train, faster even, she imagined, than a diving falcon. The ground was mere feet below her now—in fact she suspected the dragon's own feet were somehow in the ground, propelling them forward like a duck's in water. There was no churned trail behind them, though, no dust cloud, not a sign of their passing. The sagebrush was a blur beside them, just a green-gray streak of leaves and stem.

It took only minutes to travel a dozen or so miles into the foothills at the base of the range. The town of Humboldt

Wells was now a distant haze behind them, while ahead rose steep granite inclines leading to the first of many jagged mountain peaks. Wide swaths of piñon pine and juniper splashed green upon the gray ridges and plateaus. The peaks themselves were white with ice and snow—beautiful and enticing from a distance, deadly up close.

They approached a looming cliff side, a sheer wall of extruded rock blocking their path ahead. Chi-Yen had only a moment to wonder where they were going, if they were about to take flight again or turn—should she tighten her grip?—when, unexpectedly, inexplicably, they did neither. They dove straight into the mountain, still racing, not slowing one bit.

Had there been some gap she had not seen? She looked forward, up, down, back, to the sides, and all she saw were shadowed cavern walls—hanging boulders, veins of ore, flashing red garnets. They raced past the bones of the mountain, never once turning or twisting. How was this possible? This was no natural cave—not a cave at all, even. The earth opened up before them and closed again behind, parting for the dragon like water for a ship.

She realized she was holding her breath so she inhaled once, cautiously, then exhaled and inhaled again. The air was clean and cool but she felt no breeze.

A shift of her weight on the beast's back told her they had turned upward. She wrapped her arms around its neck to keep from sliding back toward its tail. And then without warning she found herself blinded by the bright ball of sun and sky. She shut her eyes then blinked repeatedly, adjusting to the light.

The dragon stood still now, unmoving. She slid off its back and was unnerved by the feel of solid earth beneath her feet. They were standing on the rocky shore of a small subalpine lake. The water was deep blue but clear as crystal, fed by melting snows and contaminated by little else. There were patches of snow higher up on the valley rim, but here there were flowers in bloom among the rocks. A large stand of mountain mahogany dominated the slope on the far side of the lake.

Chi-Yen found herself taking deep breaths of the cold, thin air as she adjusted to this new elevation. She looked up toward the nearest mountain peaks, trying to pinpoint her location. She had traversed this range several times during the past few years with Liu Kun and Sin-Feng, but from this angle she recognized nothing.

The dragon was staring at her. She remembered the state of her clothing—the vest that had been sliced in half by Malvenue's knife, so that it covered little, and the meager rags that decorated the rest of her body—and she flushed with embarrassment. She covered what she could with her hands and—was she imagining things again?—that seemed to make the dragon smile.

It waded into the lake, beckoning her to follow. And why not? How long had it been since her last bath?

The water was so cold that it stole her breath. She dunked herself, came up gasping and laughing, and then went under again. She grabbed handfuls of silt and gravel from the lake bottom and used them to scrub her skin and hair. It was the closest thing she had to soap. Invigorated and emboldened now, she pulled off her clothes and let them float on the surface of the water. Then she rinsed and rinsed again. Her fingers and feet were numb, her entire body trembling, but she felt alive and fresh and new.

Again the dragon was watching her, again beckoning her to follow, but it was moving toward the far side of the lake now—swimming or floating or walking, it was hard to tell.

Chi-Yen swam naked across the short distance toward it, arriving just in time to witness the dragon diving beneath the surface. She took a quick, deep breath and followed, a sharp pain stabbing her ears as she descended. She swam hard to keep up underwater, surprised that such a large creature could mostly disappear from sight in such a small lake.

Then the dragon's tail leveled out and headed toward the nearby shore, except the shore was not quite as near as she expected it to be. She swam and swam and was sure she should have reached it. Her breath began running low and so she started to rise—only to collide with the ceiling of an underwater cave.

Chi-Yen fought the urge to panic. She could return the way she had come—she had just enough breath left to make it back—or she could continue on after the dragon, no longer visible in the darkness, trusting that after all she had been through, the creature was not now leading her to a pointless death.

She kicked hard and pulled with all her strength, chasing the tail. The pain in her ears returned as she went deeper. Her lungs burned. The water grew pitch black—she wasn't sure if it was the lack of light in the depths of the cave or if she was starting to lose consciousness—and then she was coughing, breathing water but breathing air at the same time.

She crawled, dripping onto damp, dark soil, gagging and heaving the lake from her lungs, flushing it from her eyes and ears as well. It took almost a minute of this before she could even raise her head to view her surroundings. And when she did—

Well, dragons are wondrous creatures, and courteous to their guests. Chi-Yen found a warm towel waiting for her on a clean boulder. She patted herself dry and wrapped herself in it, discarding her old rags.

She was in an underground passageway with no light from outside. A torch fixed to the wall cast flickering firelight across the water behind her and the tunnel ahead.

"Dragon?" she called.

A large cedar chest sat propped open just a few steps away.

She looked inside and found it filled to the rim with folded clothing—men's trousers, shirts, and jackets, women's dresses and bonnets, miscellaneous shoes, belts, gloves, socks, undergarments. It was an odd collection of sizes and styles that must have been scavenged from desert travelers. There was even a Chinese-style straw field hat.

She removed several dresses from the box and could not understand how these women got anything done. So many buttons and straps and layers, so much weight, so many impediments to movement, so much lace for collecting dust.

She pulled one on over her head. It was simple cotton in a green calico print, without adornment at the hem or sleeves—something basic for a prairie wife to wear while sweeping the porch. She struggled to fasten the buttons at the back and then she pulled her long hair free and let it fall, still damp, around her shoulders. She pulled on a pair of men's socks and a sturdy pair of women's leather boots that laced up the insides.

Once dressed, Chi-Yen continued down the corridor. Several more torches lit the way. The walls and floor here were not ragged like a naturally formed cave, but smooth and polished as if the space had been bored by some perfect machine. She ran her fingers along the surface, marveling at the cool, clean marble.

—*Enter,* a voice said. But it had not been a voice. It had been … something else.

She took one step forward and then another and another, and then she saw it. The lair was immense—a circular room ringed by several dozen torches, with high, vaulted ceilings that the light could not quite reach. There was a ring of seven columns for support, equidistant from the outer wall and the center of the room. The size of it all was entirely appropriate, however, perfectly to scale, considering this place was the home of a fully grown, thirty-foot dragon. Like the corridor she had just passed through, the stone walls and columns here were hard, smooth, and reflective, glazed by the heat and pressure of creation.

The dragon rested in the center of it all, coiled in its nest as it watched Chi-Yen. The nest itself was an impossible pile of precious metals and jewels—gold dust and nuggets as large as a human head, silver and platinum bricks, rubies and diamonds capturing the light of the torches and reflecting it back out and up so that it seemed the dragon sat on a bright, sparkling sun.

It was not this wealth of nations, however, not even the dragon itself, that captured Chi-Yen's attention. No, what drew her eye was back at the periphery of the space, where rows of shelves lined the entire circumference save for the torch gaps and the arched entryway through which she had passed.

The shelves were filled with books. Thousands of books. Tens of thousands. More.

She looked from the books to the dragon and back to the books again. She could spend a lifetime in this room—many, many lifetimes. There were books of history and science and philosophy, studies in languages she knew and many more she did not. There was fiction and there were books of art and there were hand-written manuscripts seen by no eyes but the authors' own. The dragon had even dedicated one shelf just to books that Chi-Yen had already read.

I could stay here forever, she thought.

—Forever is not in our stars.

She turned back to the dragon. Had it spoken?

—Eat.

The words were in her head even though the beast had not moved a muscle, had not opened its mouth. And there was food, she realized—a sheep roasting on a spit beside the dragon's nest—along with a knife, a plate, and chopsticks. There was a bowl of steaming rice.

—You must eat for the journey.

"Where am I going?"

—There is much to see. There is much to know.

"I have a thousand questions."

—And every answer will lead to a thousand more. Eat.

Chi-Yen sliced off a small portion of meat from the roasting sheep, cut it on a plate, and mixed it with her bowl of rice. She was starving, she realized, and there had never been a more delicious meal in all the history of the world.

—We have time for one question. Choose wisely.

She did not even have to think: "Why me, now, when so many others have worked so hard for so long?" she asked. "Why is this my fate?"

—Fate is an illusion, she heard. *One man turns left and meets his life's love; another turns right and collides with a mortal enemy. There is luck, and there is putting one foot in front of another, and there is being ready and able to meet your own fortune. You found us, and we found you interesting.*

"We?"

—There is much to see. There is much to know.

Twenty minutes later Chi-Yen was once again seated on the dragon's back and hurtling through the heart of the earth. Her cumbersome new dress required her to sit side-saddle at first, which gave her a crooked neck from turning her head. In frustration she hiked the dress up around her waist and swung a leg over the creature's neck so that she sat facing forward again.

They traveled for hours through a monotony of geology, the highlight being a passage into molten metal. Protected as she was by her shield of dragon magic, she watched with fascination the swirl and glow of liquid iron all around her. After a while, she grew tired and slept. When she woke again she was cradled in a loop of dragon, the journey continuing unabated.

Then the scenery began to repeat itself in reverse. They moved from core to mantle, from mantle to crust, and then rapidly through familiar rock and fossil layers, emerging into a warm, humid night beneath a sky full of unfamiliar stars. She dismounted onto ground thick with vegetation. They were in a clearing surrounded by a forest of strange trees. A slow-moving river sounded nearby and a fierce jungle cat cried out in the distance.

As her eyes adjusted to the darkness she saw the outlines of a crude reed hut. She stepped forward and looked inside. A man lay there on the floor, trembling, a thin blanket cast aside. She could see that he was Chinese. He wore his hair in the Manchu style, shaven at the top with a long queue behind, but it had been some time since he had last used a razor.

He was not an old man, but he was getting there. He was emaciated and shivering, awake but only half-conscious.

"Who?" he asked.

She held a hand to his forehead. Fever.

—*Step aside.*

Chi-Yen did so and the dragon's head entered the hut, hovering over the man, whose eyes went wide. The dragon exhaled a breath onto the man's face and he relaxed at once. His shaking stopped. He even found the strength to pull himself to his knees and then kowtow before the beast.

Chi-Yen could see now that he wore the robes of a monk of Seven Dragons—that in the shadows beside his head sat a box much like the one that had opened for her so long ago, although it appeared to be coated in dense moss from its exposure to this jungle land.

—*Rise.*

But the monk did not react.

"Rise," Chi-Yen said.

The man did. He looked at the dragon. He could not take his eyes away, studying it with intensity, as if at any moment he might blink and it would be gone.

"Earth," he said at last, his voice full of wonder. He turned to Chi-Yen. "Liu Kun?"

"Dead."

"With honor?"

"Very much."

"I am glad. He was a good man, when he was a good man."

Chi-Yen had not had time to mourn, had not yet processed the truth of her loss, but now she felt the first tears forming in her eyes.

—Be brave. Be strong. Our time will come.

"Be brave," Chi-Yen said. "Be strong. Our time will come."

She turned to see that the dragon had withdrawn its head from the hut, and so she followed.

—There is more.

In the clearing she remounted and once again the dragon dove into the earth. Again they traveled for hours, again she slept, and again they rose to a strange and alien land.

It was morning now and they stood atop a low hill overlooking cultivated fields and forests. Green grass was everywhere, with pastures segmented by stacked stone walls and low hedges. Sheep dotted the fields. In the middle distance stood a small village centered around a church with a tall gray steeple. Country lanes, bridleways, and footpaths met, merged, and parted again, headed for distant farms and estates. A wide river meandered through a gentle valley on its way to the sea.

"Where are we?" Chi-Yen asked.

The dragon pointed to a field at the base of the hill, to a ring of a dozen wooden wagons circled around a cook fire. They were shaped like the Conestogas of the American West, but in place of the stretched canvas covers these used wood planking for angled sides and curved roofs. They were elaborately detailed and painted in patterns of bright gold or red or green or blue. This was transport built not just for a journey, but for a life—permanent horse-drawn dwellings on wheels with doors, windows, and even chimneys.

Voices rose up from the caravan, shouts and laughter in a language unlike any she knew. Men and women walked from wagon to wagon, wagon to horse, tending to their business. A tinker hammered repairs to a pot. Musicians plucked strange stringed instruments and sang lively—and quite obscene, judging by the laughter—songs. Off to one side, a group of men sat playing cards at a table, piles of coins and treasure shifting owners with each hand.

"Is that—"

—*Yes.*

"Should we—"

—*No.*

Among the gold and jewelry and rusty knives up for ante was a box, pale blue in color and so intricately carved that it looked as if it would break with a touch or float away on a breeze.

—*Be strong. Our time will come.*

Once more they traveled through the earth. This time they journeyed for so long that Chi-Yen slept, woke, slept, and woke again. When they emerged there was no telling night from day. The world was almost black with only lighter gray highlights shifting the ground. She sat on the dragon's back, letting her eyes adjust, and it took a moment to realize that they were under water, somewhere in the depths of the ocean.

She felt the push and pull of tides moving her side to side, brushing her hair, floating her dress. She could even taste the salt on her lips. But the dragon's magic protected her from the cold and the pressure and even somehow allowed her to breathe. It could not protect her, though, from the gradual understanding that those gray highlights were the brine-encrusted timbers of a ship, smashed and scattered and half buried in the changing sands. Worse, here were the bones of men, untold fathoms deep, their stories at their end. And somewhere among it all, Chi-Yen did not need to be told, a dragon's egg in a box, unprotected, awaiting the day—

—*Our time will come.*

Their next stop was a high, snow-covered mountain pass, where she spent an hour in a stone hut with a dragon monk and his apprentice. They were a jolly pair, and delighted by company other than the llama that shared their quarters. They served hot tea and roasted a guinea pig and asked a hundred excited questions about the dragon whose snout could barely fit through their door.

They listened as Chi-Yen told what little she knew of their comrades—of the wrecked ship, of the blue box in the hands of gypsies, of the lonely guardian sick with malaria, of the death of Liu Kun. She warned them of Malvenue's Company.

At last the monk and his young apprentice put on a pair of thick, oversized gloves that covered their arms past the elbows, reached deep into the glowing, wood-fired oven, and together pulled out a box of their own. Ashes fell away to reveal a simple black cube, glossy and slick and without decoration, shimmering with heat.

"Be strong," Chi-Yen said. "Our time will come."

On the next leg she dreamed of dragons. There were seven in the sky, six of them in formation around the seventh like the leaves of a pinwheel, spinning and spinning faster and faster. The earth below was a wasteland of charred trees and rivers heavy with silt. A fog of ash choked the land for miles, and beneath heavy gray clouds the only colors in all the world came from the conference in the sky: brown and blues and gold, red, and green in a great rainbow swirl. And there were people, thousands of people on their knees, pleading and praying, awaiting the decision that would determine their fates.

Fate is an illusion, the dragon had told her. *You put one foot in front of another and you forge your own destiny.*

They emerged from the cover of earth into the hall of a great temple. Facing them in the room's central position of honor was a large gilded statue of the Buddha, with hundreds more smaller statues arranged on both sides. There were altars full of candles and brass bowls of smoking incense. Tall columns draped in red and gold silk supported ancient wooden ceiling beams, from which hung tapestries in more red, gold, and blue, some with abstract designs, others with pictures of dragons, others with phoenix birds or elephants or lions. Parallel rows of wooden benches spanned the room between columns, the benches covered with bright pillows and blankets.

—There.

Chi-Yen saw it. Placed casually among the tributes, among the statues and candlesticks and dharma wheels, was a box of familiar dimensions embossed and gilded in gold.

"There!" a voice shouted. "There!"

A mad rush of footsteps filled the room as men fanned out along the walls to make room for more who continued to spill through the doorway. There were a dozen at first, then twenty and fifty and they kept coming—men in crimson and gold robes, their heads shaven, shouting in both Chinese and other languages Chi-Yen did not know.

"Dragon! Dragon! Our time has come!" And in an instant there were ropes and nets arcing through the air from all directions. Chi-Yen ducked as a stiff cord grazed her cheek and fell down upon her shoulder. She pushed it aside. She had been in the temple hall for less than ten seconds. She had not even had the chance to dismount, which turned out to be fortunate, for now the dragon rose up, dove, and they were gone again.

And so five down, one to go.

They had been around the world—through it, rather—multiple times, and she had seen so many things in a blur of days. But the dragon had been right: For every hint of an answer, she needed a thousand more.

What was she supposed to do with these fragments of knowledge? She would have asked, but her companion was not talkative and she had used her one promised question. The rules of dragon etiquette were a mystery, but it seemed wise to remain silent.

At last they reached their final destination. It was unlike anything they had seen so far—just a vast expanse of white for as far as the eye could see. Snow and ice covered the landscape, featureless except for frozen, wind-carved dunes. The sun hung low above the horizon, fixed in an eternal twilight. There was no life here, not a bird in the sky, just an intimidating silence.

Chi-Yen dropped from the dragon's back. The crust of snow beneath her feet cracked but held her weight, although the cold shot through her boots and numbed her feet. This was no place for a calico dress. She thought of the ladies stockings she had cast aside back in the lair, of the camisoles and corsets, the bustles, caps, and aprons, the gloves and vests and capes, all of which might have served some practical use in this place. Combined, they might have doubled her survival time—which she did not expect to be more than a few minutes.

She pushed off toward a nearby mound of snow, the only possible hiding place. She stuck her hands into it and dug. The cold burned. Her fingers turned red then purple. But she dug and swept and within twenty seconds she had cleared a window into a block of solid ice.

The face that stared back at her was a horror, a grimace of contorted pain and rage, frozen with eyes wide open. Chi-

Yen jumped back, startled, her first instinct being to avoid the sword thrust. But the sword was locked in the ice as well, as powerless as the frozen man who held it.

She recognized the robes. Another monk of the seven dragons. He had died protecting his egg—not from some specific attacker, but from any who might one day approach. She could not imagine the willpower it must have taken to hold his pose all the way to the moment of death, to allow himself to be frozen as this eternally fierce protector.

"His time has come," she said.

—His time will come again.

The egg box at the monk's feet was almost impossible to discern within the ice. It was not that it was hidden or muddied by crystalline flaws—it was that the box seemed to be made of ice itself, or at least glass. She could see outlines of the box and see through it at the same time. The egg inside was pearl-like in color, but translucent. And the dragon within the egg, tiny, embryonic, coiled around itself—it moved. She could have sworn it moved. Chi-Yen was freezing to death and all she wanted to do was stare at this glassy lizard. The frozen monk was not so hard to understand after all.

A warm breath of air brushed over her and broke the trance. Her dragon lifted her onto its back and pulled her once more into the embrace of the earth. They traveled for many more hours but she did not sleep. Her mind would not let her. There were seven dragons and they needed her—for what she did not know.

"What happens now?" she asked.

—Now we rescue your friend.

And they rose into the Nevada desert, into a hail of gunfire and the thunder of horses' hooves all around.

Chapter Sixteen

Cold Beans and Rice

Sin-Feng remembered the last time he had been locked away in a jail cell—a time long before he had resigned himself to the ubiquity of injustice. He had been a child then and he had wept like one, confused and terrified. Older now, more experienced and facing much greater tragedies, he simply sat cross-legged on the wooden sleeping bench and waited for an opportunity.

Chi-Yen was gone, he did not know where, and Liu Kun was dead. Evidence of that crime—a light spatter of blood from the first or second shot, dried to brown—stained the simple vest that Sin-Feng wore in place of a shirt.

He closed his eyes and listened to the people passing by on the street outside, to their footsteps and voices, to the clip-clop of their horses' hooves and the rolling crunch of wagon wheels. He heard muffled fragments of conversation: A shipment of timber was due from California; There was a push to lay ten miles of railroad track in a single day; A man hoped to buy a new hat. Across the road a construction foreman yelled commands at his crew, his words lost in a din of hammering and sawing and colliding boards.

Sin-Feng needed Chi-Yen. He wanted Chi-Yen. He tried to filter out the nearby noises, listened for faraway shouts, for the calls of owl or meadowlark or coyote that they had once used to signal one another across distant desert—but nothing.

In spite of Malvenue's instructions, Sin-Feng's jailers had treated him well enough. There had been no beatings. A young boy came three times each day with large servings of beans and rice.

He had no visitors, but Chinese workers from the railroad stopped by during their time off to sneak a peek through the front door, hoping for a glimpse of the one who had gone native. Sin-Feng knew he was quite a sight. His skin had turned dark from years half-naked under the bare sun. His hair had grown out and grown long and unkempt, like a wild man's. He had made his own moccasins and buckskin trousers with leather tanned from his kills. His confiscated knife, bow, and arrows were displayed beside the sheriff's desk.

"There he is," the men whispered, "the great warrior Tam Sin-Feng."

It was rumored that he had battled with Indians against U.S. Army cavalry; that he had robbed the Pony Express coach three times; that he had killed a grizzly bear in a fair fight. He neither denied nor confirmed. The men of the railroad were no weaklings themselves, but Sin-Feng—even underfed as he was—projected a disciplined strength that none would dare challenge.

"Have you seen my friend Leung Chi-Yen?" he called out.

The men lowered their eyes, fearful of the prisoner.

"Where is the body of my master, Liu Kun?"

They looked to one another, doubtful, questioning without words.

"Who will help me kill the evil Basil Malvenue?"

And with that the men turned and fled, terrified of being incriminated by mere proximity to such a question.

It was no matter. The Englishman would come to him. And when that happened, Sin-Feng would snap the man's neck without hesitation.

The only question was what would happen to Chi-Yen in the meantime? Dear Chi-Yen. Sin-Feng knew that Malvenue would go to her first—she was the key to the dragon, after all. And he knew she would die to protect it. Sin-Feng did not like to think about that, but he comforted himself with the knowledge that she might just as easily kill Malvenue instead. But still … he did not want Chi-Yen to die. He would do anything to prevent that.

On the afternoon of his second day in the cell, the jail doors opened and the young serving boy entered with lunch. He carried two bowls of rice and beans, the wet beans poured over the mound of rice. The boy slid one of the bowls into the cell along with a spoon instead of chopsticks. Sin-Feng would not complain.

"Louis, that is your name, is it not?"

The boy nodded.

"Is the other bowl for my friend?"

Louis looked away without replying, but Sin-Feng had his answer. He tried to listen when the boy left, to follow the sound of his footsteps. But the boy weighed too little and there was too much noise outside the jail—sawing and drilling and digging and the repetitive earth-shaking pounding of heavy posts being driven into the ground.

"What are they building over there?" Sin-Feng asked the guard.

"That ain't your business."

And so of course it was.

During those brief moments when the jail's front door was opened wide, Sin-Feng studied the work across the street. He could see a two-level storehouse of some sort, already a completed building, but now a new shell was rising up around it. Sin-Feng at first assumed the work was related to the railroad—maybe something for loading and unloading passing trains. But from the sound of things, the railroad line lay quite a distance removed. And the new framework was rising up all around the building and even across its roof, not just on the side that faced the track.

"Is that where they are holding my friend Chi-Yen?" Sin-Feng asked.

"Wouldn't you like to know."

"She has done nothing wrong."

"Tell it to the judge in California. You all are fugitives from justice. There's a bounty on your heads."

His guard was no professional lawman, no former soldier, no gunslinger gone good. At most the man was cousin to the sheriff, or a brother-in-law—someone had given him this job as a favor. He wasn't a strong man or a weak man or even a short man with something to prove. He was just an average, poorly trained man likely to shoot his own foot with that pistol strapped to his waist.

I dare you to step near this cell, Sin-Feng thought.

"Basil Malvenue murdered my master," he said.

"Ain't how I heard it."

"There were two dozen witnesses."

"Chinese lie for Chinese. You people can't be trusted."

For the rest of that day Sin-Feng listened as the workers clambered through the rising scaffolding. In the late afternoon he heard an oxcart arriving and then a heavy load of timber being dumped into the street. He heard the stretch and scrape of rope and pulley and the bump of beams being lifted into place. He heard a crowd gathering outside. A shift from the railroad had let off, and the relieved Chinese laborers moved from the tracks to the building, drawn both by curiosity and the possibility of earning an extra dollar. Some went straight from eight hours on the rails to another eight hours drilling bolt holes in the beams and hoisting hinges and heavy metal springs and endless coils of rope. Others just stood and watched, entertaining themselves with wild speculation.

"It is a factory for building new train cars."

"It is a tower for processing cattle."

"It is a gallows for hanging one hundred men at a time."

In his mind Sin-Feng gave faces to these speakers, picturing them as men from his past, men from the gold fields in California or from the ocean voyage aboard the *Round World* or even from old Canton itself. He lined up Chin Hao Li, Ho Gee Hee, Deng Tsan-Tai, imagining them as hardened, hard-working men with missing fingers and faces scarred from ill-timed tunnel blasts. Chu Siew Choh, perhaps, already lay dead in the ground, struck down by the burden of having been a rich man for a single day. That could not have been easy to bear.

The shadows grew long and the sun set and the work outside continued unabated. Sin-Feng slept fitfully that night, disturbed both by his own dreams and by the reality of the racket and the bright artificial light piercing the gaps in the jail's facade. There was a new guard now who—as soon as the other left—locked the front door from the inside, laid down upon a blanket, and began to snore.

Sin-Feng felt powerless. He was capable of so much on the other side of those bars, but so little behind them. He was haunted by thoughts of Chi-Yen. She was all that kept him from giving up. Brave, strong Chi-Yen. What would she do in his place? The last time they had been imprisoned together, she had played their cellmates against one another to cause a riot. That would never work here, where he was the sole occupant. Was there another way?

When he woke in the morning, the day guard was back on duty. The boy Louis had come and gone. A fresh bowl of rice and beans had grown cold. He lay on his bunk, trying to ignore the sounds of the world outside.

The activity across the street had not slowed, but when the jail's front door next opened, Sin-Feng was still surprised by the progress that had been made overnight. He had only a few seconds of a clear view as his guard stepped outside for a look of his own, but he was stunned by what he saw. All that timber that had been delivered the day before had been attached one by one to the scaffolding so that the beams stuck out now at regular intervals perpendicular to the building's sides, like pins from a pincushion or the spines of a sea urchin. A tangle of ropes and nets draped from the cut ends, each connected to others in an intricate spiderweb of knots and nooses.

Sin-Feng recognized it instantly. He had seen drawings of similar structures on scrolls and musty tapestries deep within the library at Seven Dragons temple—scrolls he should never have seen at that age if not for the neglect and absence of his master.

"A trap," he said aloud to the empty room. "He builds a trap to capture a dragon!"

He knew Malvenue's plan now—the snapping footholds, the camouflaged cages, the anchored snares, the bait. And as quickly as he knew all of that, he knew what he had to do. He would set a trap of his own.

Sin-Feng ate his cold beans and rice. He would need the energy later. His lunch, too, he devoured. It had only been a few days now of regular meals, but he felt his strength increasing. When his dinner arrived, however, he set the bowl and the spoon aside. He waited until about an hour before nightfall. Then, one at a time and in no particular hurry, he began using his spoon as a catapult to launch cold beans past his cell bars. It took a few shots to refine his aim, the beans sticking unnoticed against the far wall. The fourth, though, hit the guard hard in the center of his forehead.

"What the hell?" The man was confused at first, not sure what had struck him or where it had come from. A bug, perhaps.

Sin-Feng said nothing. He waited for the man to return to his seat, then hit him again.

"You! Give me that bowl."

The guard stood. Sin-Feng adjusted his aim then launched a bean at the man's cheek. It left a brown smear beside his mustache.

"I'm warning you, boy."

The guard glowered at the prisoner. Sin-Feng stared back, expressionless, saying nothing. He set the bowl aside. The guard relaxed and returned to his desk, and then Sin-Feng pelted him in the eye with another bean.

"Goddammit!" The man rose to his feet and charged the cell. "I'll ram that damned spoon up your ass."

This went on for twenty minutes, the guard growing angrier and redder in the face with each shot. He had nowhere to hide within the small jail, no way of blocking Sin-Feng's aim. Sin-Feng, meanwhile, remained calm, never acknowledging the guard's questions or commands, which only infuriated the man more. Soon, though, the beans were gone and nothing was left but rice, and then there was not even that. Sin-Feng dropped the empty bowl onto the floor.

The guard laughed. "Who's the smart one now?" he asked.

And then Sin-Feng dipped the spoon into his chamber pot. It was a foul, lidless thing, half full and stained around its rim from the last several days of his fibrous, protein-rich diet. He launched the wet spoonful and it scattered in midair, the spray of shit staining the guard's shirt, the stench filling the room.

As Sin-Feng had hoped he would, the guard snapped. He grabbed the cell keys and a truncheon from the wall, unlocked the cell door, and swung it open.

That was all Sin-Feng needed. Liu Kun had trained him well. In an instant the man was whimpering on the ground, his arm twisted unnaturally back and Sin-Feng's knee against his spine. Sin-Feng threw the man's truncheon out of the cell, took his pistol from his holster, and held it to his head.

"One word," he said. "One word and I shoot."

He waited for the night shift guard to arrive, then he tied the two of them together, muzzled them to keep their shouts down, and locked them inside the cell. If he were lucky his escape would not be discovered until morning. He took his own knife but left the bow and arrows behind—they would attract too much attention—and slipped out into the dark.

He stuck to the shadows near the buildings until he came upon a clothesline stretched out from a window. He stole a pair of lightweight cotton trousers and a loose cotton shirt, both died indigo—the uniform of just about every Chinese worker in the west. With a bit more searching he was able to steal a pair of knee-high leather boots—he put them on, tucking the legs of the trousers into them—and a conical straw hat.

His disguise complete, he returned to scout the dragon trap, viewing it from all four sides. Men were still oiling hinges and testing trigger mechanisms, but the project was mostly completed. Did the Chinese workers even know what they were building? They could not. Who would believe it? And anyway, whether this odd feat of engineering would work, whether it could contain a creature of such magic, Sin-Feng could not say. But it was powerful enough to snap in half any man who made a wrong move trying to sabotage the system.

He watched all through the night without sleep, looking for an opportunity, but the workers continued to crowd the building until morning, when Basil Malvenue finally arrived. The Englishman was accompanied by four bodyguards and the boy Louis, who pushed a wheeled metal cart filled with burning coals. The guards were white men, a head higher and half again as broad as any Chinese. The boy was grim-faced while Malvenue admired the web he had spun, clearly enjoying the best day of his life.

Malvenue paid and then dismissed the entire work force, then ordered his guards and Louis into the building.

After a few minutes, when all was clear, Sin-Feng moved closer. He listened at the door and checked the covered windows. There were the four guards he knew of and there would be more at Chi-Yen's room, wherever that was. He thought he might be able to take them one at a time, but if he came across a group there would be trouble. He expected trouble.

When he heard the first scream he could wait no longer. It was a pained, ear-piercing cry of agony. Sin-Feng threw open the door and rushed inside, straight into a hallway crowded with all four guards. His adrenaline and years of drills with Liu Kun took over as he laid out two of the men without a thought.

"Chi-Yen!" he shouted. "Chi-Yen!"

But his words were drowned by what felt like an earthquake and sounded like a freight train as the building shook and slammed, the tons of loosely fitted wood and metal of the outer scaffolding colliding and bending and bouncing back to shape.

There was a stairway to his right and Sin-Feng made a move for it, but one of the guards hit him hard in the side, knocking him into the wall. He stumbled and the other guard hit him from the front, pushing him back toward the door, reversing his momentum. He landed on his back on the wood plank sidewalk outside, looking up at the structure that had seemed so solid a few minutes earlier. It now swayed wildly, still recovering from some great impact.

The first of the two men followed up with a kick to Sin-Feng's side and then the second reared back for one of his own. But then they both stopped as their jaws went slack and their faces twisted with terror. They turned and ran back into the building.

The dragon stood in the street behind Sin-Feng, eyeing the puzzle of traps. The beast was so much larger than it had been before—and angrier. There was a great commotion in the nearby streets. A crowd of people rushed toward them, many with weapons in their hands.

"He has Leung Chi-Yen," Sin-Feng said. "Inside. Upstairs."

The dragon nodded to him, just a quick acknowledgment, then began to walk around the building, slowly at first, studying. It picked up its pace, moving from a trot to a run. It circled seven times, Sin-Feng counted, before the speed became so great that it seemed the dragon might catch its own tail. Its feet left the ground and it was flying low, still circling, and then the earth began to rise up beneath it—dirt and sand and pebble, rock, and stone hurtling through the air in a great tornado, blasting the storehouse and the scaffolding with an intense spray of particles great and small. The wood began to weather and splinter, eaten away by the storm as if it had been sitting exposed to hard wind for decades.

The mob approaching on the street fell back from the rush of scattering debris, unable to keep their eyes open against the hail of earth and wood.

Sin-Feng grasped blindly for the doorway and made his way inside the building—a building that he knew was not long for this earth.

"Chi-Yen!" he shouted.

The guards were gone—both the ones he had taken down

and the ones who had driven him out. They had probably fled through the back door. With any luck they had been eaten.

Sin-Feng moved for the stairs. Halfway up he heard screams—Chi-Yen's and Malvenue's as well—and again the building shook with the force of cannon fire. A board gave out beneath his feet and he fell through to his waist, wrenching a knee.

As he hung there, wedged between two steps, there came a thundering crash just to the far side of the wall—and then the wall was no more. Sin-Feng clung for a moment to the fragile remains of the stairway, the wind again stinging his face, a blur of dragon scale and teeth and swirling earth his only view.

And then it all gave way.

He crashed into a world that was black and still and quiet—cozy, even. He lay in a warm pocket of air, almost comfortable, with at least four clear inches before his face, listening to the muffled crunch and tear of the world imploding above. Within his small space he could blink, could turn his head side to side, could wiggle his fingers and toes, but that was all. There would be no pushing back, no resisting what held him here.

It had been minutes at most. He had not lost consciousness during the building's collapse. He was not even certain that things had finished falling. And yet, strangely enough, a voice called his name.

"Tam Sin-Feng! Tam Sin-Feng!"

Chi-Yen?

"Are you here? Are you hurt?"

No, not Chi-Yen. But someone familiar.

"Here," he called back. "Here, I am here."

As soon as he said the words, he wondered if he had made a mistake. Could it be searchers come to return him to jail? But even if so, he had no choice. He was stuck and he could smell smoke. Somewhere in the rubble, a fire was burning.

A board above was removed and a shaft of light penetrated to the ground beside Sin-Feng's head. At the same moment he became aware of other rescuers sifting the mess. An anguished voice not too far away cried out "No, no!" and then, "Damn that Louis. I'll tan his hide," and "Sampson, Litchfield, get me out of here."

And then it was Louis himself, the serving boy, sticking his head into the hole, looking right and left, surveying the problem. "Very soon, Tam Sin-Feng" the boy said, and then he disappeared again.

"Damn you all!" came the other voice again—Malvenue, it had to be. "Get me out of here now. She's getting away."

She's getting away. That was the news Sin-Feng had hoped for. He heard the boards overhead being dragged off one by one, but he relaxed—there was no need to rush. He had done what he could; the dragon had done the rest. Chi-Yen was safe. That was all that mattered.

Then there came a loud crash near his feet and a pivot of debris above as a gap opened up overhead.

"Hurry now!"

A hand reached down for his and he pulled himself through a hole that was both opening and closing at the same time. He scrambled out, steadied by the boy Louis as the splintered pile shifted and snagged and at last set him free.

"We go. Quick. No time."

Sin-Feng looked back at the ruin from which he had emerged. He saw several men—he recognized two as Malvenue's guards—struggling to remove a heavy wooden beam wedged into the rubble just twenty feet away. Curses rose up at them from the ground. They looked across at Sin-Feng, scowling, ready to charge after him but unable to leave their posts.

Louis and Sin-Feng walked toward the southern side of town, toward the shanties and tents of the Chinese workers. Sin-Feng's right knee, twisted in the fall, sent a stab of pain into his leg with each step.

The streets were abuzz with excitement over the appearance of the dragon. They heard snippets of conversation all around. Everyone claimed to have seen it, whites and Chinese alike. People spoke excitedly of the girl who had ridden the wingless serpent into the sky. But Sin-Feng soon noticed a sharp, curious divide in opinions. To the Chinese, Leung Chi-Yen was a hero, a myth or legend come to life—a dragon rider bringing good fortune to a world much in need of it. To the white citizens, however, the girl was an assassin, an outlaw on a demonic beast who had led an unprovoked attack on their peaceful settlement. Already they were organizing hunting parties, with men readying their saddles and ropes and guns.

Sin-Feng knew he would never be safe in town, not after his escape from jail, not with Malvenue swearing vengeance. He asked Louis to take him to a stable, where in all the confusion he was able to steal a saddled horse, packed and loaded for a hunt. The boy begged to come along, but Sin-Feng knew that would be a death sentence for them both.

"I thank you for your help," he said. "It will be remembered."

He spurred the horse out of town, heading south into the plain east of the mountains.

It had been what? Four or five days since he last saw Chi-Yen. Another passed, and another. He knew he had to turn for the mountains—that was where he would find her—but in the distance always were gangs of other horsemen with the same idea.

He camped in an arroyo for several days and nights, resting his knee. He appreciated the horse, which made it easy to carry extra gear and travel great distances, but he would have traded it for his old bow and arrow. He felt more comfortable as a silent hunter, traveling on his belly through the brush.

He pushed on, making most of his progress in the early morning and evening, laying low during the day. Once he spotted a column of soldiers, infantrymen from Fort Ruby, headed north in the east—a patrol for Indian troubles in an area where Indians had mostly been eliminated.

By the end of a week he had put seventy-five cautious miles between himself and the town of Humboldt Wells. It was not a huge distance, but he felt more secure now making a turn toward the mountains. He followed a game trail that wound through rabbitbrush and greasewood and trampled saltgrass, watching the Ruby range grow as he closed the gap. Storm clouds boiled up from the far side, dissipating as they rose above the jagged peaks, their momentum not yet able to carry them into the eastern rain shadow.

It was mesmerizing, hour after hour, to watch the changing sky, to listen to the repetitive beat of his horse's hooves and the sound of distant thunder. He lost track of the day and dropped his guard. It was an unforgivable lapse.

A group of twenty men on horseback had recognized him before he knew they were there. He led his horse towards them, unaware, as they halted their own mounts and waited. When he saw them at last he was no more than two hundred yards from their line.

He could tell at a glance that they were men born to the saddle. Cowboys, they called themselves, their horses lean and strong and nimble, the men's gloved hands expert with a rope, their rifles and sidearms a simple matter of security in an unsettled land.

The Englishman Basil Malvenue rode among them.

"Tam Sin-Feng," he called out. "We never had the chance to talk."

And we never will, thought Sin-Feng. He pulled his reins

hard left and spurred his horse. It reared up and turned and ran hard, but it would not be hard enough. Sin-Feng knew it. It felt as if his horse's feet were stuck in the sand, moving in slow motion, while the posse behind rode them down. He heard a volley of warning shots. He hunkered low in his saddle and knew he was dead—not yet, but soon. Very soon.

There was a pain in his right shoulder. He could not spare a hand to reach back and confirm the blood, but he knew it was there, a dark spot spreading across his shirt. He eased up on his horse just to stay in the saddle. He scanned the landscape, looking for an advantage, anything—a river, a tree, a canyon. But the land was barren, just slowly rising foothills that he had no energy to climb. What he really needed was—well, he had no idea.

But he was happy to settle for what came next, which was a monstrous dragon rising up out of the earth beside his horse. Upon its back sat the most beautiful woman in the world.

Chapter Seventeen

Last Stand

As with so much of her life up to this point, Chi-Yen had no control over what was happening. She was only along for the ride. But what a ride it was! The dragon bucked and weaved, rising up into the air and then diving back into the earth like a dolphin breaching and chasing the wake of a ship.

The cowboys were in a panic. Their horses reared and whinnied and shook their heads. They tried turning left and then right, corralled by this giant snake that was everywhere at once.

A brave few men swung their lassoes, trying in vain to noose the dragon's tail or legs or neck, but one by one they were thrown and hit the ground hard. Clouds of dust and dirt smacked the air. Horses bolted and ran free, leaving the men scattered like dry leaves. Some moaned with dislocated shoulders or busted knees, or they gasped with the wind knocked out of them.

And still the dragon continued its weaving dance. Chi-Yen began to recognize a pattern, as if the beast were embroidering a backstitch loop around the fallen cowboys. She imagined an invisible thread trailing out behind, catching itself and pulling taut, piece by piece gathering up the land beneath them.

She spotted Sin-Feng in the center of the chaos, rising to his knees and then standing unsteadily, the first to fall and now the first to recover.

What was happening here? How had he come to be surrounded by all these armed men—two times ten at least—and Basil Malvenue, there he was!

"Hold fire. Nobody shoots but me," the Englishman said. But the cowboys he paid now paid him no mind. His money had no more meaning here, all purchased loyalties having vanished at the critical moment he needed them most. His men fired wildly, shot after shot banging out and echoing back from distant cliff sides in a jumbled, hollow crack-crack-crack.

The dragon continued its undulating flight through air and earth, defying the laws of nature, ignoring the weapons of simple men. It did not flinch or alter course or change its pace as the bullets flew by. Chi-Yen ducked from the spray of gunfire, clinging closer to the dragon's back, but she could not—and would not even if she could—command it to flee to safety.

Safety was not her wish. Sin-Feng was hurt.

As they circled behind him she saw the stain of blood on the back of his right shoulder. He stumbled through the scene, passing within steps of the men who had tried to kill him, but who now aimed their barrels at the great monster, ignoring all else.

"Stop the boy!" Malvenue demanded. "Stop the boy and we can stop the beast."

But they continued to fire and fire and fire at the fast-moving dragon until their hammers came down on empty chambers, then they dropped their useless guns at their sides.

"Sin-Feng! Sin-Feng!" Chi-Yen cried out.

Sin-Feng had fallen again to his knees and was about to drop to his hands as well. His face turned pale as he fought to retain consciousness.

"Dragon, help him!"

The dragon stopped all else and bounded to Sin-Feng's side. There was a moment of still silence as the unarmed cowboys gazed in wonder. Some were standing now, some still sprawled upon the ground. All cowered, resigning themselves to a gruesome death at the jaws and claws of this immortal terror.

The dragon, however, did not attack them. It attacked the boy. It went for his wounded shoulder, first ripping open the back of his shirt with its teeth, then biting and suckling at the wound like some ravenous bloodthirsty vampire.

The men watched, horrified and fascinated, waiting for the killing blow—but it never came. Instead, the dragon pulled back, paused, and spat a misshapen lead ball to the ground.

Chi-Yen, meanwhile, had dismounted and knelt beside Sin-Feng, holding his face in her hands, looking into his unfocused, half-conscious eyes. She turned to the stunned men all around her, her anger rising as she sought out Basil Malvenue.

"You!" she said. "Look what you've done." She rose up to face him, as fearless as the dragon itself. "You lie, you steal, and you kill. And for what? Because you want control over a creature that's here to help us all."

As she spoke, the dragon lowered its great head again toward Sin-Feng, nuzzling the boy, comforting him. The cowboys watched in wonder, speechless, their jaws hanging wide.

"All you care about is gold," Chi-Yen continued. "Gold and power. And you'll destroy anything or anyone to get it."

"You ignorant whelp," Malvenue said. "You have no idea.

You have no idea what this beast can do, what it's capable of. In the wrong hands—"

"The wrong hands? You speak of wrong hands as if you have more than one. There is no hand more wrong in all the world than yours." If she had been closer—and she considered taking a step forward—she might have slapped him.

Malvenue scowled. He gripped the butt of his holstered revolver. "You are no longer the sweet, naive girl you once were," he said. "That's a pity. It would have been so much more fun to kill you then rather than now."

He raised his gun and aimed it at her chest. She stood strong and fearless, never flinching.

"I've seen the other eggs," she said. "Every one of them. Your friends will never find them, not in this lifetime and not in any other."

If this news came as a surprise to the man, he hid it well. "A pity," he said. And then he fired his gun.

The dragon screamed a high-pitched, hissing scream, louder than any sound Chi-Yen had heard in her life. With both hands she covered her ears. The cowboys did the same. Malvenue, having only one hand, dropped his weapon to cover one ear and turned his head.

The dragon's eyes were red with blood and fury as it slithered a loop around both Chi-Yen and Sin-Feng, hoisting them onto its back. They rode a wave that moved through its entire body like a whip, starting with the head and then raising the tail fast and high into the air. The tail slammed back to the ground. The earth shook all around—shaking even the dragon itself.

Chi-Yen held her seat with one hand, the other helping to keep Sin-Feng's arms secure around her waist. She saw ripples spreading outward across the dry, pale soil below, like rings of wavelets when a stone hits a pond. But this was earth, not water, and that frightened her. Everything was happening too fast.

"Sin-Feng! Are you well?"

The boy began to reply, but at that moment the dragon rose again and slammed its tail once more. Malvenue and the standing cowboys fell to their knees.

"Hold tight," she warned, just as the beast rose up for a third and final time.

When the dragon's tail hit the ground again, the shock of the blow shattered the earth. They all felt it. The bedrock beneath them collapsed, granite fragmenting to dust. What had been solid became liquid. The cowboys flailed their arms and legs but found no hold, nothing they could grip to remain upright. They fell, splashing downward. Even the dragon dropped for an instant, Chi-Yen and Sin-Feng bouncing hard against its back.

Within the circle that the dragon had earlier flown, the land turned itself over, becoming a great quicksand trap for man, beast, and bush alike. The fallen cowboys called out for help, stuck now up to their waists—some even buried to their necks—in heavy silt. Those with able hands or arms struggled to dig themselves free, but each movement only pulled them deeper into the pit.

The dragon did not look back. It walked away from the ravaged field, its great feet making sucking sounds with each step until it reached firm ground. Its body rocked side to side as it crossed the difficult terrain, no longer with the smooth gliding motion to which Chi-Yen had become accustomed. As it gained speed she heard its heavy breath, then felt the heat of each angry exhalation as they accelerated through it.

Something was not right. First it was the click and scrape of talons upon the ground. Then she looked back and saw the beast's own tracks and the curving S-shaped trough where it dragged its tail through dune and brush. They would be easy to track. And the ride was rough. Each step jarred, more like bareback on a horse than a magical dragon.

"How badly are you hurt?" Sin-Feng asked.

She was glad to hear his voice, glad that he had recovered enough to speak. But she had not even had the time to consider herself. Malvenue had shot straight at her chest at close range. She should be dead, but she had felt no pain. Even now there was nothing—not a scrape, not a tear. Had the gun misfired?

"I am unharmed," she said. She was sure the gun had not misfired.

They moved at a rapid pace. Their enemy was far from view. The steep mountainsides loomed close ahead, putting them in shadow as they climbed the rising foothills. The rain that had been threatening for days began to make its first light landfall. They came within sight of a steep cliff face fronted by a small stretch of unstable talus. Without slowing, the dragon leaped into the air and dove straight for the solid granite wall.

Chi-Yen felt Sin-Feng's good arm tighten around her waist. She heard him let out a gasp. Having grown accustomed to this magical jump, however, she remained calm. She anticipated the still quiet of the earth, the safety of its embrace, and she looked forward to turning back to Sin-Feng, to telling him he had nothing to fear.

But she was wrong.

The force of the impact threw her from the dragon's back hard into the mountainside. Sin-Feng landed partly next to her, partly on top of her, sandwiching her against the granite face. An avalanche of small rock and sand rained down upon them, dislodged by the collision and by the noise of the dragon itself as it howled in agony, even louder than before.

Chi-Yen and Sin-Feng bounced and rolled with the mountain's cast off debris, tumbling and sliding until they came to rest in a cradle of rubble. They lay there, battered, bruised, dirty, unable to move as pain coursed through their bodies.

Chi-Yen was certain her ribs had been fractured. She saw a blur of unfocused gray sky above. She smelled rain and tasted a drop or two, but the weight of a few sprinkles upon her chest was almost too much to bear.

The dragon roared again. Chi-Yen heard a rhythmic crashing as it slammed the mountain like a mad, wild animal unable to comprehend the bars of its cage.

"Chi-Yen," Sin-Feng said, "beautiful Chi-Yen." He was kneeling above her. He removed his shirt and pressed the cotton fabric to her forehead, damping it, turning it, compressing a spring of blood.

"Do not say that," she said.

"But it is true. You are beautiful. You are the most beautiful—"

"Stop. Please." She closed her eyes. She winced. "Help me up."

Sin-Feng lifted her to a seated position. Her entire body pulsed. It would hurt for weeks. But she could move. She was intact. She could see the dragon now, and she could see the method to its madness—although it was clear that madness still ruled.

The great beast slammed and clawed at the cliff side, cracking and tearing at the rock, hurling massive broken pieces aside one by one. They fell with booming thuds that could be heard for miles around, mistaken for thunder by a world ignorant of the dragons among us. Already a large hollow had been carved out. Unable to fly into the earth, it was using brute force to dig a tunnel.

"The dragon saved my life," she said, "and yours."

"I fear that last battle has cost it dearly."

"Liu Kun taught us that dragons could never be harmed by the weapons of men. What could have happened?"

"Men have changed and so have their tools." Sin-Feng leaned back a bit, as stiff as Chi-Yen and wincing with each movement of his right arm. "I fear this world is no longer a place for dragons."

They watched through the afternoon and into evening, never rising as light rains came and went and came again. At last the noises ceased and they stood, supporting one another. They approached the newborn cave.

The entrance was wide and tall—about twenty feet by twenty—but it narrowed once inside. The cave floor, which was too dark to see, sloped upward as they walked. The dragon's soft, labored breathing sounded close, but they were surprised to climb one hundred yards at least, deep into the mountain, before reaching it. Its eyes smoldered, the only source of light in the cavern, but they were enough to illuminate the walls with a dull glow, which in turn outlined the pathetic coil of the dragon's body.

"Will it recover?" Sin-Feng asked.

Who could know? Chi-Yen had no words. She climbed atop the dragon's back and lay there, her arms embracing what she could. She cried, noiselessly so that Sin-Feng would not hear, her warm tears tracking the grooves between the dragon's scales.

Soon enough, Sin-Feng did the same.

When she woke in the morning, Chi-Yen struggled to move. Every muscle ached. Every joint was stiff. She rolled onto her side and from there she pushed herself to a seated position. She felt hard, sharp gravel beneath her palms. She heard Sin-Feng stirring nearby.

"Where is the dragon?"

They groped their way downslope toward the cave entrance, worried about what they might find. But the beast sat just outside atop a pyramid of refuse from yesterday's dig. It gazed downslope into the desert.

A strange humming buzz from the rock pile put Chi-Yen instinctively on edge. She jumped back from a western rattlesnake at her feet, perfectly camouflaged for this barren slope, dusty brown with misshapen gray diamonds across its back.

As it slithered past, Chi-Yen saw hundreds more snakes coiled upon the scree beneath the dragon, weaving through the broken earth. Rattlers shook their tails—that was the buzz—but there were other, quieter creatures as well: whip snakes and racers and gophers and garters along with skinks and horned toads and a variety of lizards. They encircled the dragon, all facing toward it like congregants at a church, like worshippers paying respect to their lord.

Chi-Yen and Sin-Feng stepped cautiously away. A single bite from a rattlesnake could cost them a limb or worse. But when the dragon turned to look back at them, they felt foolish. This summit, for now, was a place of peace. And considering how many times the two had dined on snake meat over the last half dozen years, it was the snakes who showed the greatest bravery.

So they climbed cautiously, watching their feet to avoid stepping on the swarming reptiles. There were thousands of them among the rocks. Each step put their ankles within striking distance of at least one rattlesnake, often several, coiled and quivering, heads lunging back and forth and side to side, somehow checking the instinct to attack. When they reached the dragon, a gathering of king snakes—striped red, black, and white—slipped away to clear a space for them. They sat.

The sun was an hour into the sky to the east. Through the morning haze they spotted a rise of dust a dozen miles away.

"I saw infantry a few days ago," Sin-Feng said. "Soldiers from Fort Ruby. Maybe thirty men."

"They'll be digging out those cowboys."

"They'll be coming after us."

The dragon stared out into the distance with eyes that saw much more than any human could. Chi-Yen wished it would speak. She wished it would tell her what to do. In her mind she begged it, she pleaded.

—Dragon, tell me. Speak to me.

But there was no sign that it heard. She stood and stepped around to face it. She placed a hand on its snout and gave it a soft caress. It seemed to smile. A wound in its scalp showed where a bullet had pierced the center of its horned shield, leaving a deep, ragged hole crusted over with dried blood.

"Can I help?" she asked.

The dragon shook its head. She could not.

"Your magic?"

Gone.

She took a deep breath, looked back out to the valley, then back to the dragon again. "We should move. Higher into the mountains. If we keep running they can't catch us. You're still faster and bigger and stronger and smarter."

But even as she said the words, she knew it would never happen. The frontier was getting smaller every day, with fewer and fewer places to hide. Running would only delay the inevitable. The dragon had chosen this place to make its stand.

When she returned to sit beside Sin-Feng, she tried not to cry again.

"I've seen so much," she said. "I have so many things to tell you."

But she said nothing more. Sin-Feng put his good arm around her shoulder. She did not object.

They sat that way for hours, not speaking, the two of them and the injured dragon, just watching as the cloud of dust advanced toward them through the foothills. A column of marching men took shape within it, the sun lighting up their dark blue coats and brass buttons and the long barrels of their modified Springfield rifles.

There were one hundred soldiers stationed at Camp Ruby, and Chi-Yen counted at least half that number marching her way. A pair of scouts led the procession, with the rest a good distance back. The men were all on foot, but were accompanied by a team of mules carrying supplies. In the late afternoon the company stopped half a mile away to rest, to eat, and to take turns glassing the dragon with their scopes.

"Their guns are accurate to six hundred yards," Sin-Feng said. He knew the damage they had caused in recent years to his Indian friends. "They fire up to thirteen rounds per minute. I can't even lift my right arm."

"This is my fault," Chi-Yen said. "The bullet that struck the dragon was meant for me. I was supposed to protect it, not the other way around."

They watched the soldiers fan out below and move forward, picking their way through rock and shrub. They were six hundred yards out, five hundred, four, three. Their captain called a halt and each man took what cover he could.

"We had better move," Sin-Feng said. "Get behind the rocks, at least."

He stood with difficulty, then held out a hand for Chi-Yen. He helped her up. Below them, the soldiers readied their guns.

"Wait for my command," she heard their captain say.

The dragon rose up on its perch, giving the soldiers a full view of what they were in for. It let out a great roar and clawed at the sky with its forelegs. The soldiers pivoted their guns toward it, nervously testing their trigger fingers.

"The world is mad," Chi-Yen told Sin-Feng, "and I am the maddest of all." Then she shouted down the hill: "Stop!"

Before Sin-Feng could grab her, she was walking.

"Wait," she called out to the soldiers. "I am unarmed. We are all unarmed."

She raised her empty hands to the sky as she stumbled over the loose rock, struggling to keep her balance and her footing. She felt a stab in her ribs with each breath and each jarring step. The pains in her body were so great that she almost stopped to rest halfway there. But this was too important. There would be no stopping now.

A dozen rifles swung to her as she approached. The captain held up his hand and shouts went down the line again, again ordering the men to hold their fire.

Malvenue was there beside the captain. Chi-Yen was pleased to see his distressed state. He had not bathed since being buried alive and then pulled like a carrot from the earth. He had lost his hat, his horse, his gun, even a boot.

"That's her, Captain," he said. "The one they call Leung Chi-Yen. Just shoot her now and be done with it, that's my advice."

Malvenue was livid, apoplectic, dry spittle whitening the corners of his mouth. The captain sighed and rolled his eyes. Beside him, a few of his companions chuckled.

"Listen to me!" Malvenue shouted. "She's a sly one. Don't believe a word she says."

But the captain offered Chi-Yen a canteen of water and even a corner of bread. He introduced himself as Timothy Connelly.

"Is this a surrender?" he asked.

"A negotiation."

It was easier than any had expected. The captain and his men, many of them Civil War veterans now stationed at the worst post on the frontier, had little heart for a fight against a creature that had just buried two dozen men alive. Still, the law was the law and Chi-Yen and Sin-Feng were both wanted for trial in California. Then there was the matter of the destruction of property at Humboldt Wells.

"If we turn ourselves over to you, will you let the dragon go?"

Now that was a question. A dragon was something you don't see every day.

"Your English friend here tells me the serpent shits gold. Is that true?"

Chi-Yen assured the man it was not. Basil Malvenue was mad. You know how Englishmen are. He believed too many of the stories he had been told as a child. This was not that kind of dragon—not something that flies through the sky and grants wishes and guards princesses in towers. No, this dragon was nothing but an overgrown mountain lizard, rare but not unheard of, a threat to no one and of no great value.

"It would cost you more to feed it than you would ever earn from it in return. You are a brave soldier, not a circus keeper."

"And you are a wise young woman. It's a shame you're a criminal, and that I have a wife back in Ohio."

"You flatter me, Captain. My body is broken and scarred. I am nothing but a humble peasant."

The captain shook his head and smiled. "Now I know you're lying," he said.

And so they made the deal. Sin-Feng climbed down to join them. The dragon remained behind, free to depart although it did not. The soldiers relaxed a bit, both relieved and disappointed that the action had been called off. Malvenue looked to the dragon and fumed, plotted, planned—this was not over, this could not be over, it could not end like this after all his work.

And of course it could not, because when there is peace, men find a way. They find a way to break it. It's in their nature. It's how the world works, how the world moves forward. Out with the old, in with the new.

One soldier spotted a snake in the brush near his boot. It was just lying there, coiled, resting, waiting, but on instinct the man swung his rifle down and fired.

"Rattler," he said, but the word was lost in the echo of the shot, which put all the men on alert. They raised their own guns and in that instant, with the writhing death of the first snake, the rest swarmed. Loyal soldiers all, the snakes rose up from their hiding places within and behind enemy lines. They lunged and snapped.

One man screamed and fell on the left flank, then another on the right. Others hopped and danced and shot their guns at the ground, which had come alive with squirming ropes of scale and venom.

"No!" Chi-Yen yelled. "Stop!"

But there was no stopping anything. One of the soldiers turned his gun on her. Before he could fire, though, the dragon charged the line and ate the man's head with one snap of its jaws and a single gulp. It then began running circles around the men, giving cover to its lesser reptile brothers with a whirlwind of dust.

One by one more soldiers dropped, crying out in pain, ankles and calves on fire with poison. But others made their way to safer ground and opened fire, plugging the dragon with rapid volleys from their .50 caliber guns. Chi-Yen and Sin-Feng and Malvenue lay on the ground, helpless beneath the spray of gunshots.

There was chaotic screaming all around and shouted commands and the smell of black powder and snake. One pit viper stared Chi-Yen straight in the eyes before slithering over her arm to get at the soldiers. She tried to count. At least a dozen men had fallen, perhaps twenty or more. Twice as many snakes lay motionless just within her line of sight, dead by bullet or hatchet or boot. But if anyone seemed to be winning—if it could be called winning—it was her dragon.

The might of the United States military had one card yet to play, however, and the standing soldiers untied its ropes and pulled off its canvas cover. It was like a canon, but not. A cart with large wood-spoke wheels supported a gun with not a single large barrel, but a circular arrangement of six. Three men worked to load cartridges with ammunition, to slot a cartridge vertically into a space atop the gun, and then to rotate a hand crank.

"Wait, wait, wait, now!"

As the dragon passed in front of the gun, they fired. One man turned the crank and the barrels spun and forty shots blasted out in less than five seconds. The dragon staggered, stumbled, but kept circling. The men pulled the empty cartridge and dropped in another.

"Wait, wait, wait, now!"

Again they fired. This time Chi-Yen saw the side of the dragon open up at the site of impact. A spray of scale and meat and blood erupted from a gash three feet wide and a foot deep.

The dragon fell, stood up, and fell again. It tried to crawl. It raised its great head and looked about until it found her. It laid down its head again, still looking into her eyes, not pleading, not desperate, not angry, just watching.

And then it shut its lids for the last time.

It was over.

The injured soldiers continued to cry out in pain, but at the moment the dragon died, the snakes gave up their fight and dispersed back into the desert. Basil Malvenue began a steady stream of curses directed at no one in particular, but decrying the stupidity and treachery of Americans and Chinese alike. He wandered into the desert alone with his one shoe, one arm, and no hat, and no one cared to stop him.

Sin-Feng and Chi-Yen helped to dress the soldiers' wounds. None of the bites, it seemed, were critical. The snakes had for some reason held back on their venom, giving enough to incapacitate but not enough to endanger life or limb.

As neither had fought in the battle, and as Captain Connelly now had his hands full with logistics for the incapacitated half of his force, he pardoned Chi-Yen and Sin-Feng of any crimes they might have committed.

"Let lawmen who care sort that out," he said.

However, he did order the head of the dragon to be sawed from its body and transported back to Fort Ruby then on to Washington, D.C. It was both proof for the unbelievable report he would soon issue to his commanders, and payback for his own headless soldier.

They all spent the night camped in the field of battle. Sin-Feng and Chi-Yen were too shell shocked to even speak to one another, and neither was willing to discuss in front of the soldiers what had just happened. But in the morning, when at last they were alone and the soldiers were nothing but a trail of dust once again faint on the horizon, Chi-Yen turned to Sin-Feng.

"Give me your knife," she said.

He did. She took it to the dragon's headless corpse, already bloated, reeking, and fly-swarmed in the desert sun. She would not hesitate; life was too short, and there was still much to be done. She kneeled beside the dragon and stuck the knife deep into the vent between the rear legs near the base of the tail. She sliced upward toward the abdomen, making an incision about two feet long. Then she set the knife aside and reached both hands deep into the opening. She turned her head away, holding her breath against the smell and squinting her eyes against the flies that peppered her face.

"What are you doing?" Sin-Feng asked, horrified, as she inserted her arm past the elbow and felt around inside the carcass.

She did not answer, but a short moment later, with a great sucking sound, she pulled something from the dragon. She stood and turned back to Sin-Feng, her arms wet from fingertip to elbows with blood and slime, and she handed him a great, wet egg.

"Guard this with your life," she said.

Epilogue

Journey to the East

The transcontinental railroad was completed in May of 1869. The hardworking Chinese laborers who had flooded the great desert territories moved on—some to other rail lines, some to mine silver from Nevada's Comstock Lode, others back to California or home to China.

The connection by fast rail of the eastern and western halves of North America marked the end for the native Indian tribes as well, at least for life as they had known it for thousands of years. The land was no longer theirs alone, and increasingly not much theirs at all.

Leung Chi-Yen wrote to Tam Sin-Feng that she had witnessed the hammering of the golden spike that joined the two halves of the rail line at Promontory Point in Utah. She had not planned to be there. She had no interest in the symbolism. But she happened to be passing by on horseback. She saw the crowds and stopped to watch.

She was on the trail of the one-armed man, and she had had some luck. A certain class of lady in the parlor rooms of Regent Street in Salt Lake City had given relief to Malvenue in the aftermath of his recent trauma. They told their stories to Chi-Yen. She knew their sadness, after all; she had been born into their world. They could have been her sisters, her mother, the ones she long ago left behind.

He was headed for England, they said. He was off to be knighted for his service to the Queen. At least that was his claim. But Chi-Yen knew better. The man had fallen far, and he had farther still to fall.

Sin-Feng received three more letters. Chi-Yen was in Cheyenne, Wyoming; she was in Kansas City; she was in Chicago. The pages wafted the scent of French perfumes and he pictured the lace and bright silks and the soft feather beds of a life he would never know.

He had begged her to stay. He had begged her not to leave.

"Marry me," he said.

But duty came first. Nothing could get in the way of that.

"Our lives are not our own," she said.

Sin-Feng had the egg to protect. He had a new dragon temple to build. And Chi-Yen … her mission lay elsewhere.

He imagined her transformation in those distant foreign cities. She knew so much already, but with each stop she would be assimilating herself just a bit more into that world. She would learn their fashions and their customs, she would speak their languages in their accents. She would become a refined, elegant lady, moving with ease through barbarian society, her past entirely hidden behind those magical, hypnotic blue eyes.

They would never know. They would never suspect.

Before leaving him, she had taken Sin-Feng to the dragon's secret cave. She packed what little she needed for herself and left the rest to him. She kissed him once and never again.

"Please," he said.

But no.

It was a year to the day since he last saw her, and seven

months since her last letter, when his new apprentice Louis ran to him with news of a package from London, England. There was no return address and, when he opened it, no note inside—just a box inside a box. But it was a box that told him all she wanted him to know. It was made of stone, intricately carved, a cube nine inches to a side. He remembered the day he had last held it, the day the Englishman had pulled it from his hands.

The man was dead now, Sin-Feng knew. A stiletto to the heart, a poisoned cup of tea, a wire round the throat—it did not matter how.

Chi-Yen had given Basil Malvenue his unpleasant reunion. She had done what she had to do. There were seven dragon eggs in the world, and she would be there to protect them all.

Sin-Feng would never hear from her again.

And Chi-Yen never would live a normal life.

A Note from The Authors

The Long Way is a fantasy novel with a backdrop of real historical events. We did our best to capture the truth of times and places that remain a mystery to most. In our research we read many histories of events as well as first-hand reports from sailors, soldiers, traders, missionaries, miners, and settlers. We tried to look past the obvious cultural biases of these accounts to present what we hope is a balanced tale. Any factual errors belong to us alone.

The dragons, of course, are real—and they have many more stories to tell.

How can you help?

If you want to read more of this series, the best thing you can do is spread the word about *The Long Way*. Tell your friends. Post a review to Amazon. Post a review to Goodreads. Write about it on your blog. We love to hear what our readers have to say.

What's next?

We have a futuristic science fiction novel scheduled for release in the first half of 2014, followed by the sequel to *The Long Way* later that year. For the latest news, here's where you can find us:

Twitter
@michael_c_ray and @theresevannier

Facebook
http://www.facebook.com/MichaelCorbinRay
http://www.facebook.com/TheresеVannierAuthor

Web sites
http://www.michaelcorbinray.com
http://www.theresevannier.com

www.ingramcontent.com/pod-product-compliance
Lightning Source LLC
Chambersburg PA
CBHW030529310726
48979CB00010B/1854/J

* 9 7 8 1 9 4 0 7 7 6 0 5 7 *